CHEN ZHANG

The Duties - A Novel

Every man, as long as he does not violate the laws of justice, is left perfectly free to pursue his own interest his own way, and to bring both his industry and capital into competition with those of any other man, or order of men. The sovereign is completely discharged from a duty…; the duty of superintending the industry of private people, and of directing it towards the employments most suitable to the interests of the society.

ADAM SMITH, THE WEALTH OF NATIONS,
BOOK IV CHAPTER 9

Contents

Preface

About twelve years ago, I was at the time very much unamused by different kinds of entertainment online and started to dabble in creative writing as a way for self-expression and fun at my home in the U.S. Given the development of events at that time, I came to realize that there would be an inevitable conflict between the United States and China in their respective national trajectories. With a few jotted down plots and notes, I tried to weave some of my related experience into this background of international development. I wrote on and off but never finished it, intercepted by small and big life events. The later development in the international scene over approximately ten years of time increasingly reinforced my earlier understanding and prompted me to complete the piece, however it would turn out.

In between, vicissitudes of life affected my schedules and I often saw this attempt to complete my first novel getting futile just as a long-time friend that one would eventually lose touch with, however much you wish to keep the friendship. Covid, however, turned out to be a blessing in disguise and afforded a precious respite in my busy schedule that made completion of this work possible. In the beginning of 2022, I finally finished my first draft and later had it revised by two editors including the one-time New York Times bestselling author Ms. Nina Bruhns.

I suppose many readers might find it less exciting to read the historical chapters of the novel. I have been advised to take out the entire historical parts and make it more like a real thriller. After much thought, I had to give up that temptation because deep down I felt the urge to make historical connections, either to provoke thoughts or at least to tell old stories.

Looking at the entire book, I think it offers a perspective of viewing current events and the individuals living through them, the anguish and struggle of common people and the conspiracies of special interests that could collude internationally at the expense of common good during the globalization process. It may also serve to remind people with origins in developing countries of their colonial past and to ponder their national development thereafter.

I hope that the readers will have fun reading the novel. In fact, this is probably the only goal as I definitely enjoyed writing it with the help from those mentioned in my acknowledgment.

As I am writing this preface, I stay in a hotel room of one the tallest buildings in downtown Qingdao, China, where the historical parts of the novel mostly occurred. The city is now going through a sluggish economy, following a three-year country-wide lockdown due to Covid. Out of the French window of the hotel room, a dramatic display of neon light show is on with lights changing repeatedly to a mirage of patterned colors coordinated across all downtown buildings. Out in the far distance, the old town's smaller landmark buildings dim with their twinkling lights inside the foggy shroud over the city. With its old pains but new hopes, the city is ushering into the New Year of 2024.

Enjoy reading.

Chen Zhang, December 2023

Acknowledgement

Greatly indebted to the editorial reviews of Ms. Nina Bruhns, a New York Times Best Seller author and of Mr. James Abbate, senior editorial assistant with Kensington Publishing Corp.

Chapter 1 The Meeting On The Internet

ashington, D.C., present day

The drudgery of daily life in the early 21st century took up the bulk of newly-minted lawyer Mike Nolan's waking hours. Work was as bland as flour to bread, and leisure was a controlled escape. He lived a predictable life built on stability, and made choices based on what he believed was best at the time. But the perfect and comfortable lives he yearned for would eventually change, leaving him to question how he got there.

When Mike got back to his D.C. office after a business trip to China, he immediately began to prepare and organize the final legal brief for his client, Yan Chemical, the Chinese respondent represented by Williamson & Grey, where he was employed as an attorney. He needed to do it before the U.S. Department of Commerce issued the final antidumping duty order in their antidumping investigation against Chinese soda powder exporters, one of which was Yan Chemical.

Antidumping duties were placed on foreign exports to U.S. when the government considered that goods were being "dumped." In other words, they were priced lower than similar domestic products. The antidumping duties were designed to protect American manufacturers from unfair pricing by foreign exports. The duties were assessed on the US importers of these exported goods. Each foreign exporter could have its own antidumping duty rate. Thanks partly to Mike's hard work, Yan had gotten a zero antidumping duty rate while most Chinese exporters were hit with the U.S. trade barriers.

As Mike examined his computer files, notes, and legal papers, he came across the name Wang Ping. He came to a sudden halt and his heart sank a bit. He had met Wang Ping on this latest trip to China. He'd felt sorry for the man. Ping was the former accountant with Yan Chemical, and had been let go due to a falling out with management. He'd then gone to work for another soda powder exporter in China, only to lose that job too. Ping wanted his old job back and asked Mike to help him, somehow believing that Mike had quite some clout over Yan Chemical's management.

But Mike merely worked for the law firm that represented Yan Chemical in the U.S. He might have some influence, but he didn't have the power to help Ping in any way except to provide moral support and encouragement.

There had been another twist to Wang Ping's request. His tone and expression seemed to indicate as much of a favor as a threat when Ping said he knew Yan Chemical had used fraudulent accounting records in their antidumping investigation, and that Ping had been fired *after* the fallout with that company. Mike hadn't noticed anything fishy in Yan Chemical's submissions—law firms merely received accounting data provided by clients. But then, Ping could be just bluffing. He really just seemed to be a disgruntled employee…even if he was a nice guy. Mike simply wanted this annoyance to go away smoothly in the natural course of things, and not get out of hand. In particular, not out of *his* hand so it affected his own job. He still had a big student loan from law school that he had to pay off.

He grimaced and closed the file.

The TV was on in the background, and suddenly it caught his attention. The news was on, and anchor was talking about Taiwan and China.

"The U.S. President announced yesterday that the United States plans to proceed with arms sales to Taiwan to the tune of $4.5 billion. The promised sales include conventional defensive weapons manufactured by Swift Industries. The Chinese government is expected to react fiercely about the potential sales amid the already tense economic relationship between the U.S. and China, soured by Chinese exporters' dumping practices and the so-called trade protectionism claimed by the Chinese against the U.S."

Mike watched hoping for more, but that was all the clip said. He returned his attention to his computer when a *ding* sounded, and he saw that Wang Ping was inviting him to a video chat. He hesitated, but accepted out of curiosity.

Wang Ping's face appeared on the screen. He was wearing a headset, and from the background he appeared to be at home, his face lit only by his computer screen. The rest of the room was dark.

Mike said, "Hello Ping. How are you?"

There was no audible answer even though Ping's lips were moving.

"Ping, can you hear me?"

No answer again.

"Ping, since the sound doesn't seem to be working, let's just type."

Mike pointed down to the keyboard and started typing. Before he finished, Ping had typed a greeting.

Wang Ping: *Hi Mike.*

Mike smiled and answered.

Mike: *Hello Ping, how are you?*

Ping must have come prepared. His next message came fast and furious.

Wang Ping: *Thank you. I am fine, and I hope you are, too. I just wanted to tell you that Yan Chemical still did not resolve my issue. I am planning to write to the U.S. Department of Commerce and tell them about Yan Chemical's lies and fraud accounting practices. Everyone should know how dishonest that company is and how badly they treat loyal employees. They only want to get ahead by cheating and making up numbers. That is not right, Mike. They should be held responsible for what they have done and promised.*

Mike quickly typed back.

Mike: *No, Ping, I would give a second thought. That's not the right way to do business. As a lawyer, I need to tell you that when you accuse someone of something that is against the law, you must have some kind of evidence they did indeed commit the crime. It has to be about facts and not just an opinion. Do you have any evidence that Yan Chemical lied or committed fraud?*

Ping looked at Mike and nodded.

Wang Ping: *Yes.*

As Ping was typing, Mike saw a shadow of a figure stealthily approaching Ping from behind. The person wasn't behaving like a wife or a family member. More like…an intruder.

Mike frowned.

Mike: *Ping, are you home alone?*

Ping was still typing as the shadow came closer then stopped directly behind him. A man wearing a black ski mask looked into the computer camera. He focused on Mike, and they locked eyes. Ping didn't notice anything, but his fingers typing on the keyboard. The masked man lifted his arm to the right of Ping, holding an ice pick in his hand. The man looked from Mike to the ice pick and back to Mike, smiling broadly.

Forgetting to type, Mike yelled at Ping, "Get out of there, Ping! Look out!"

Ping must have noticed his panicked expression, but still couldn't hear him. He looked confused.

Wang Ping: *What are you saying, Mike?*

Mike quickly hit a few keys to record the unbelievable scene playing out on his laptop's screen.

The attacker jabbed the sharp pick into the side of Ping's neck. Ping's eyelids fluttered a thousand miles an hour, his mouth involuntarily swinging open as blood poured out across his bottom lip like a waterfall. One gloved hand pulled Ping's head back by his hair and the assailant stabbed him once more with the other. And again. Ping's eyes were no longer moving. The man let his limp body crumple to the floor.

The killer looked into the camera directly at Mike, sneering as he wiped Ping's blood off the ice pick with a scrap of paper from the desk. He tossed the paper onto the floor before neatly placing the murder weapon into a sheath on his belt. He then took out a cellphone, snapped a picture of Ping's screen, and gave Mike a penetrating stare. Then he winked, and calmly pushed the screen down to close Ping's laptop.

Mike sat there for a moment, completely numb and horrified. He turned off the recorder, got up, and stumbled to the window to open it for some fresh air. With shaking hands, he got out his cellphone and punched in 911. Then he jerkily erased the number, thought for a moment, and dialed another number instead. While it was still ringing, he again thought better of it and hung up. He shut the window, went over to grab a Coke from the fridge, then came back and sat uneasily in front of his computer.

Holy crap. I just witnessed a murder.

A brutal murder, obviously committed by an assassin who loved his grizzly job and clearly had a great deal of experience.

But why was Ping killed?

And who could Mike trust enough to tell?

He pulled out a yellow legal tablet and wrote the heading *Ping*. Below it he drew a line down the center of the page. On the left he jotted down things he knew that Ping had done which might have angered someone, and on the right he wrote down the people and the companies who might be angry enough about them to want him dead.

What Mike had seen was no practical joke. If it had happened in the United States, he would have to immediately report the murder to the police. If he waited too long they would naturally wonder why he didn't report it right away, and even that small doubt in their minds might make his life a bit inconvenient...or possibly very inconvenient. Not to mention that as a witness, he would somehow have to protect himself from ending up sharing the same fate as Ping.

Thankfully, this whole crazy thing had happened half a globe away in Beijing, one of the largest cities in the world, at a residence for which Mike had no address. For the moment, the vast distance made him less concerned about his own security. But he was baffled by the more perplexing issue of how to report it, and to whom. Why would the DCPD care about a murder in Beijing? Would a police officer at the local station even bother to take down information about a murder so far beyond their jurisdiction? It would be a joke for a D.C. cop to accept a report on a crime that occurred in neighboring Maryland, let alone Beijing. He could just imagine the blank stares of the local cops if he tried. No doubt there were no official guidelines on how to deal with such things.

Attempting to pull his thoughts together, he started to write something on the left side of the legal tablet, then crossed it out and angrily threw the tablet across the room. He realized he actually knew nothing about Wang Ping except that he had been fired and he couldn't get his job back at Yan Chemical. Tonight Ping had said he had proof that Yan Chemical was lying and had committed fraud in the antidumping case Mike's firm was involved in. But Mike had never seen any of that evidence, nor had he seen what Ping was trying to type during their video call after confirming he had proof...before being rudely interrupted by his untimely murder. Everything that Mike knew in connection to Wang Ping added up to a big fat zero.

If he reported to the police that Ping said he had evidence against a multibillion dollar international company, but had not said where or what that evidence was, Mike would be laughed out the door. No way could he bring anything to the authorities that wasn't even substantial enough to warrant an investigation.

After realizing all of this, he pushed out a sigh and took a calming sip of his Coke. He leaned back in his chair, closed his eyes, and hoped that when he opened them again this horrible nightmare would simply be a bad dream he could barely remember.

But it wasn't a dream. Eyes closed, he was swamped with the memory of a sinister masked killer, spurting blood, and the terrified last look on Ping's face as the ice pick sank deep into his neck. Mike's eyes jerked open and his mind raced with a hundred jumbled thoughts, each one trying to cling to something stable and safe and give him a feeling of security. Staring nervously at his computer screen, he came to a terrifying realization.

Just because Mike didn't know anything about Yan Chemical acting fraudulently, and that Ping had never told him what or where he'd hidden the evidence against them, didn't mean the people who'd hired the assassin were aware of that. They might very well believe that Mike also knew everything Wang Ping knew.

Which meant that Mike might be the next target for whoever had silenced Ping.

Shit. He might be in immediate and lethal danger!

He picked up his phone and thought about whom to call. He would have to call the police soon, just in case, but he needed to talk about the whole thing with someone else first and get some advice. If he'd had a lawyer, he would call that person. Of course, he saw the irony in his position. He was a lawyer and had friends and colleagues who were lawyers. He even worked at a law firm. But he did not have a personal lawyer he could turn to or trust implicitly.

His friend, Heather Hanson, was a lawyer, but he intuitively sensed that he couldn't, or rather, shouldn't involve her. She worked for the opposing law firm on the dumping case and would no doubt feel obligated to tell the lead attorney about Wang Ping and his evidence. That would not only put her in jeopardy, too, but could ruin the big win Mike had recently chalked up for Yan Chemical.

He thought about calling his old boss, Neil Kreschmar, who managed a nonprofit company. But even though Mike respected him, Neil didn't really have the expertise that Mike needed.

He looked at his watch. He was running out of time. Every moment he wasted not having a second person be aware of the whole incident would seem suspicious down the road. Without much thought he dialed the phone number of his current boss, Patrick Steiner.

Patrick answered, "Hello."

"Hello, this is Mike Nolan. I just witnessed a murder."

There was a pause on the other end. Then Patrick said in a low voice, "Damn, Mike. Tell me what happened."

Mike told him everything he could remember about the video call, giving him a description of the murder and the assailant.

"Have you called the police yet?" Patrick asked.

"No, I wanted to ask your advice first."

"Good. Very good. Did Wang Ping give you any details about the fraud that Yan Chemical allegedly perpetrated?"

"No. Nothing. That is, he was typing information on the video call because we couldn't get the audio to work. He was killed as he was typing, and the message never reached me. He never hit send."

"Okay. So his typed words could still be on his computer."

"Right," said Mike. "Which means they could be retrieved by anyone who has his password or his laptop. And I'll bet that that guy with the ice pick took the laptop with him."

"Let's talk at the office," Patrick said. "You may still need to inform the FBI or DCPD."

Mike hung up the phone. He gazed at the framed photo on his desk, a picture of his grandfather, Tim Nolan. Gramps was dressed in a black leather jacket and a brown WWII peaked cap, standing before a yellow tiger-printed fighter plane, his face wearing a humble smile and exuding calmness. Mike tried to channel Gramps as best he could.

He leaned back in his chair, deep in thought, wishing everything could be undone, starting from this morning going straight from the plane to Williamson & Grey. Could he have changed something that might have prevented the terrible event from happening? He tried to recall what had happened between his flight landing and now, but couldn't find anything worth second-guessing. He also thought about rolling time back a month, to before he went to China and hadn't yet met Wang Ping. Five months before that, he wouldn't even have known any of the people involved, including Wang Ping, Patrick Steiner, or Mei, the woman whom he'd spent so much time with in China. Not Williamson & Grey, Yan Chemical, or even Heather from his last class in international trade law at Georgetown University.

He let his memory rewind as far back as possible, wishing to erase all connections to Wang Ping and start fresh…

Chapter 2 Law School Was Finally Over

ashington, D.C., one year earlier

A dove swooped over Capitol Hill, flying low around the various federal buildings in Washington, D.C. It fluttered over the gargoyle on top of an edifice overlooking 24th Street Northwest before it slowly landed and settled. Its body was pure white, its head bobbing over the busy street, its eyes gazing upon the flowing traffic, pedestrians, and everything else. Seemingly unaffected by the noise and gusty chills that permeated the April air, it now and then danced with mincing steps to adjust its position, as if trying to gain a better view of the world below.

Mike Nolan was among the pedestrians on the downtown street, a Georgetown University law student in his early thirties walking hurriedly to work.

Mike had a tall, lean build, with broad shoulders that gave him a commanding presence. A defined nose and forehead gave him an air of intelligence and determination. His facial expressions were quite reserved, often appearing contemplative or focused. He had a habit of furrowing his brow when deep in thought, and his eyes held a hint of intensity. Despite his serious demeanor, there were moments when a small smile would flicker across his face, showing his appreciation for a well-made argument or a clever joke. Mike stood straight and confident, with a posture that exuded a sense of self-assuredness.

He moved with purpose and determination, and when he spoke his voice was clear and steady. He gave the impression of discipline and determination, someone who strove to make a positive impact in the world through his studies and future legal career.

But this last year of law school was killing him, to say the least. He was taking six classes in the jurist doctor program at Georgetown, had a full-time job with a nonprofit organization on 24th Street, and was starting to prepare for the bar exam in July. He felt that during any given day the only time his mind was not occupied by civil procedures, contracts, and other legal subjects was when he was entering and exiting elevators, classrooms, and conference rooms, and when he slept at night. Therefore, the only time he was consciously aware of his surroundings was when entering and exiting the buildings, not before or after, as if his mere existence was real solely during those moments. All other times were filled with contracts, jurisprudence, torts, security regulations, and the like. Law school was *prima facie* and *ipso facto* tortuous and expensive. Finishing classes and receiving decent grades wasn't easy, and he struggled to maintain a GPA of 3.32, falling just short of the B+—which was 3.33—that the big law firms claimed to need for recruiting purposes. But he really had tried his best. He did not want to end up finishing law school with a six-figure loan amortized over thirty years, and that was why he maintained an 80-hour job-and-study schedule. But it seemed however hard he tried, the debt was not going to end up any smaller.

Anyway, it was all relative. The worst-case scenario would be to have a student loan debt of $150,000 without any job offer after graduation, but hopefully not forever. Like all other students, except some real lucky ones who had already landed big firm offers by now, he had to maintain a cool face and a positive career outlook. He was already fortunate enough to go to law school in the first place.

The day job at the nonprofit paid all right. He had been doing their database marketing for fundraising for a while, and his job was to target the best possible donors for the organization. He zeroed in on specific zip codes in the United States, then mailed requests for donations to those residents most likely to contribute to the cause of the nonprofit, which was protecting wildlife resources. The nonprofit had a lot of past donors, and Mike conducted a specific statistical model through a sophisticated computer algorithm to find out who was likely to respond to the donation campaign and then order the direct mail to target whichever zip codes were of interest. Among his regular morning chores was to run standard as well as customized reports using the statistical software.

"Hey, Neil, I saved the next month's mailout file under the M drive. Their probability of making a donation is in the top ten percent, given the last run of the scoring algorithms."

"Great, Mike, good job! Are they sorted by zip code?"

"Yes, sir, every record."

"How many total addresses?"

"About 100,000."

"Nice. Please send the encrypted file to the marketing firm to do the mailing."

"Will do. I saw the mailer design with a giant panda on it. Cute." Mike paused for a moment. "Hey, Neil, I never got to ask... How much does the direct mail company charge us for 100,000 pieces, including design, printing, and postage?"

"Around $100,000—about one dollar per piece. They do everything, so it's not too bad. Why?" Neil suddenly started to cough very hard and couldn't stop.

"No reason. They did such a nice job, I just wondered if they were expensive."

Neil kept coughing.

"Neil, are you okay?"

"Yes, I am just allergic, I think." Neil finally stopped coughing.

"Hey, I heard a way to deal with that when I was in summer school in China last time. You buy some pears, peel them and cut them into pieces, boil them in water for a couple of minutes, then eat the pear and drink the soup."

"Really? I'll give it a try."

Mike zigzagged his way through the office and glanced at his watch. He had to hurry. It was 5:45 p.m., just an hour before his next class started, and he had to take the metro from Foggy Bottom to Union Station and walk the ten minutes to Georgetown University Law Center.

When he arrived, he strode up the steps of the law center, which was backdropped against the stillness and grandeur of the Capitol Hill dome immersed in the golden glow of sunset. One or two of the dome's windows reflected sunbeams of piercing light as he turned, squinting in that direction. However many times he saw the Hill, it always invoked a sense of awe. Today was no exception as he made his way to the final International Trade Regulations class of the semester.

* * * *

It looked like class was about to end when Professor Stuart started to summarize several international trade cases between China and the U.S., particularly those that were appealed to the World Trade Organization.

"As we discussed, under the Byrd Amendment proposed by Senator Byrd, antidumping duties assessed against dumped imports are then redistributed to our domestic manufacturers in order to correct the financial damage done by their foreign competition. The WTO ruled against the U.S. in its practice of antidumping duty redistribution. As a signatory to the WTO agreements, now the U.S. will have to comply with international law. Will the United States rescind the Byrd Amendment? If yes, when? If not, is that okay? Also, after the three years during which you took public and private international law classes, what do you think about international law?" Professor Stuart glanced around the room, then asked the whole class, "Specifically, what *is* international law? Does it exist? If yes, who is enforcing it?"

A young lady in the front row raised her hand. Georgetown surely had the largest student body among U.S. law schools, and even after three years, Mike couldn't recall most of the names of his peers. But his professor could.

Professor Stuart pointed to the girl and said, "Yes, Ms. Heather Hanson?"

"Well, I think on one hand, international law exists because there are international treaties, and then there is customary international law that regulates states' behavior and international organizations such as the international criminal court, the UN, and particularly the WTO with its panels and appellate body, in order to adjudicate cases brought by state members against other state members. States whose actions contravene these legal decisions must change their domestic law accordingly."

Professor Stuart followed up, "But what if a state does not change its domestic law or practices? Again, does the U.S. need to comply with the WTO rulings such as the Byrd Amendment?"

"So that is the argument for the nonexistence of international law," Heather responded. "There seems to be no real method of enforcement at the international level, and at best, the enforcement is carried out through domestic means or compromises of international politics. The U.S. should comply due to the Supremacy Clause of the U.S. Constitution, but I'm not sure if the U.S. will comply."

"Well done," praised Professor Stuart. "In fact, your answer is better than the question itself. If you do go on to practice international law,

I imagine that five years from now you may find that the concept of whether international law exists is an oversimplification of the reality of the situation." He paused, allowing his words to sink in before concluding, "Thank you for joining me for the final session of International Trade Regulations. I wish you all the best in your future legal careers."

The students erupted into applause and began to file out of the classroom.

Mike walked up to Heather and said, "Hey, that was a great law school answer."

"Law school answer?" Heather blinked, smiling. She stood with confidence, her poise and stature conveying a quiet intelligence. Her sparkling eyes and warm smile belied a strategic sophistication that was both highly smart and undeniably sexy.

"Yes. You know—on one hand, and on the other hand," Mike said, alluding to the usual way of arguing both for and against a single legal argument by incorporating the relevant legal theories and notions that professors usually looked for to give points in reviewing exams.

"I'll take it as a compliment. But I just spoke what was on my mind," she said with a charming smile.

Mike nodded. "Well, I meant it."

"You aren't saying that I have no principles?" She lifted and tipped her face while squinting at him with a raised eyebrow.

"Well, principles don't get you the points you need in the exams, right?"

She smiled. "By the way, I'm Heather Hanson."

"I'm Mike Nolan."

"How come we haven't met before?"

"Well, I used to sit up front, but I was a little late today." And was damn lucky not to have missed meeting Heather at the last minute.

He dredged his mind for a topic to continue their conversation. He couldn't ask about her job prospects, as it could be a sensitive topic. You could self-disclose but not probe.

"Have you signed up for Barbri?" she asked, sparing him.

Barbri was a national bar preparation course.

"Yes, of course."

"Which jurisdiction?"

"New York."

"Me, too."

He quickly wrote down his deets on a piece of scrap paper. "This is my email address, in case you need me to cover you in the Barbri class or something. Let me know."

She nodded and they exchanged phone numbers.

When they parted, he boarded the metro and was on his way to his apartment. Too bad now was the wrong time to meet an attractive girl, with principles or without. His priorities were to first pass the bar and then find a job in his chosen profession. A lawyer needed to make money by practicing law. The main principle of a lawyer was to survive as one. That was paramount. Everything else needed to take second place right now. Including romance.

Most law schools in the United States did not really prepare their students for bar exams. After a few courses with Barbri, Mike wondered why those materials were not covered in law school so he could have saved the Barbri tuition. But the system was obviously not designed that way. The only path was to take the LSAT, go to law school, take Barbri, pass the bar, and then find a job, in that order. For those aspiring to finish the entire process, what was left after that was pretty much a huge outstanding debt and a sheer drive to accumulate billable hours—if and when you were lucky enough to be hired.

In the coming weeks, Mike found himself sitting quite naturally next to Heather at some of the Barbri review classes.

"Oh, no, my Outlook crashed. I had all my notes for the last two days saved as an email. I hope I saved a backup copy." Heather was staring into her computer with dismay.

"Let me see." Mike leaned over. "There's an auto-recovery function for Outlook files in Windows." He hit a few keys and was able to get the file back.

"Thank you, Mike. You're a lifesaver."

"Not a problem. So what are you doing after taking the bar? Taking a break?"

"I'm going to work as an associate with Baker & Lynch."

"Awesome! Not taking a break, then." He smiled, but felt a tinge of envy. "What will you be doing there?"

"International trade litigation, starting in September. You?"

"No kidding. I'm interested in the same area."

"Oh, really? Do you speak any foreign language?"

"Yes, I speak Mandarin. I did language training in Beijing for one year."

"That's great! That helps a lot in this area. Any particular firm you're interested in?"

Having a few offers in this bad economy would really satisfy his vanity. Unfortunately he was still waiting. "Not sure. I'm weighing a couple of options." He blushed a little from his fib.

"Maybe we should have a couple of drinks after the bar exam," she suggested.

"Sure. I'd like that."

* * * *

Back in his apartment that same evening, Mike sat in front of his desk and glanced at his grandfather's picture that sat on the corner, as was his habit in times of reflection. Grandpa Nolan had been part of the Flying Tigers, American volunteer pilots flying tiger-striped fighter planes who fought against the Japanese in China during WWII. The tiger on Gramps's plane spread its jaws upward and looked ready to jump right out of the photo and attack.

For the last month, Mike had been sending out about two dozen résumés a week, querying every firm that practiced international trade law that he could find. But he'd had no positive response yet.

Discouraged, he glanced over at the TV, where the international news had started.

"The Chinese government must stop manipulating its currency to its advantage, and efforts to secure U.S. jobs and improve trade deficits must be taken to safeguard the fundamental interests of our great nation," the president was saying vehemently in a news clip. "We want China to succeed, but not through its unfair practices of maintaining artificial foreign exchange rates to undercut U.S. workers."

Whatever.

Mike turned off the TV and opened his email, where he found an email from a secretary at Williamson & Gray asking him to schedule an interview with the firm.

Excitement and relief surged through him. Williamson & Gray was one of the largest firms in town that practiced international trade law. Working there would be amazing!

* * * *

Occupying most of the buildings within the three-mile radius from K Street to 15th Street NW, and from the White House all the way to 17th Street and Capitol Hill, were lobbyists, government relations branches of Fortune 500 companies, nonprofit organizations, and law firms. They hustled and bustled, promoting the interests of clients from all over the world trying to reach the U.S. market, to avoid prosecution in security fraud or monopoly charges, to get a license to export to the

U.S., to get approval to acquire a U.S. company, and a thousand other things. Their efforts were granted, denied, appealed, and either upheld or overruled within a cobweb of bureaucracies and courtrooms where the destinies of transactions worth billions of dollars were decided.

Williamson & Gray's reception area looked as magnificent as a museum lobby. As Mike walked through it, he couldn't help but feel impressed by the sophisticated decor and the impeccable attention to detail. The marble floors gleamed, the receptionist greeted him with a lovely smile, and the art pieces on the walls were impressive. Everything was designed to make a visitor feel each and every piece of furniture was significantly more expensive than he could ever afford. Mike thought it would be tough for a client to negotiate legal fees here, and that was probably the intention.

He tried to get comfortable in a blue velvet couch and blend in with the environment, but he quickly got into his head, sifting through the questions he might be asked, and practicing appropriate answers that were smart but not too cute. He tried to relax, studying each piece of furniture around him, hoping, somehow, that would help him say the right things during the interview. The wait dragged on. Law firms tended to make everyone, their clients in particular, wait excessively long in the reception area. Half the time they might actually be busy, but other times they were only making themselves appear to be.

Finally, a man in his mid-fifties wearing a flashy suit and a tie emerged from the back. He was very tall and wore a pair of dark amber horn-rimmed glasses. Behind the lenses his eyes were sharp. His face was a bit sullen but he put up a plastic smile that made Mike feel compelled to smile back.

The man reached out his right hand. "My name is Patrick Steiner, partner of the international trade practice of Williamson & Gray."

"I'm Mike Nolan. Nice to meet you."

"Follow me, please."

Williamson & Gray's corridors were extremely long, with rows of cubicles in offices on both sides. Mike followed Patrick Steiner, zigzagging through a few secretarial areas before they entered a corner office with French doors on both sides and windows overlooking busy K Street below.

After they sat down, Mr. Steiner asked, "Why are you applying with us, Mr. Nolan?" His gaze shifted from Mike's résumé up to Mike. It penetrated Mike's nerves with quite a pressure, as if he already knew the answer and only asked to test Mike's honesty.

Mike had been asked this same question numerous times. Every time he wanted to say, "To pay rent and my student loans." But of course, you've got to be more sophisticated than that. They expected something special, unique and out of the ordinary, to prove your interest was genuine, sincere, and long term.

"Well… I've had an interest in international trade law since I was an undergrad. In law school, I took a couple of courses related to it. I've been keenly following the major developments since China joined the WTO. Right now there are a number of rulings by the WTO against the practices of the U.S. Department of Commerce, such as the Byrd Amendment, which seeks to return assessed antidumping duties to U.S. petitioners. But I guess it will take a few years before the U.S. complies with this ruling and corrects its domestic regulation." At Steiner's raised brow, Mike veered back on track. "I'm well-trained in statistics and versed in statistical packages used for antidumping calculations. I also speak Mandarin Chinese."

"Impressive. Where did you learn Chinese?" Patrick flipped the pages of his résumé.

"An exchange program for one year in Beijing as an undergraduate."

"How did you become interested in learning Chinese?"

"My grandfather was a member of the American Flying Tigers fighting in China during WWII."

"Wow. Legendary. Anyway, as you know, I lead the international trade practice team here, and we represented foreign clients who went before the U.S. Department of Commerce in antidumping proceedings, as well as some big U.S. multinationals in matters such as export controls and the like." Steiner took a breath. "Right now we represent Yan Chemical, the largest soda powder producer in China, and we really need someone to beef up our argument against the petitioner in this case. The domestic petitioner is Ohio Chemical, and their counsel is Baker & Lynch. We need to drive down the antidumping duty margin calculation for Yan Chemical."

"As I've learned," Mike said, taking the helm of the conversation, "all the antidumping duties for these foreign clients are separately calculated. If we can get a zero rate for Yan Chemical in the investigation, they will forever be out of an antidumping order for that product. Which means they will in fact enjoy a complete monopoly of the U.S. market. What is their antidumping duty rate as calculated by the Department of Commerce right now?"

"Right now, we are at 2.56% for Yan Chemical," answered Steiner.

"So we'd need an additional 0.6% reduction to get them a *de minimis* antidumping duty rate. I'm up to the challenge, sir. I can use my statistics knowledge and review all calculations to see if everything is correct."

"We think we've really exhausted all possibilities related to company-specific factors such as consumption and financial ratios, so you would have to think of something else."

"I can try my very best."

Steiner gazed at him for a long moment, then said, "Good. Then we look forward to having you join us after your bar exam. We like Georgetown graduates."

Elation shot through Mike. Except for one tiny fly in the ointment. "Who did you say the opposite law firm was?"

"Baker & Lynch."

Damn. Heather Hanson worked on the opposite side of his potential new job.

Leaving the offices after the interview, he felt a mix of excitement and apprehension. He was excited to potentially work for such a prestigious firm, but at the same time, he was apprehensive about the possibility of running up against Heather, and worried how their friendship might be affected. He knew he would need to be extra cautious and professional in his interactions with her, especially when it came to matters of confidentiality.

Somehow, he couldn't shake the feeling that their professional paths were destined to cross, and he wasn't sure what that meant for the future of his career...or their relationship.

But he was eager to see where this new job opportunity would take him, and he was determined to make the most of it, regardless of the challenges that lay ahead—professional or personal.

Chapter 3 The Argument

M ike passed the bar, and he got the offer from Williamson & Grey. It was one of those six-figure offers that many law school career placement officers didn't believe their graduates deserved. Mike could finally sigh with temporary relief, though the prospect of making monthly payments on a six-figure tuition loan still haunted him. He was eager to start with the law firm as soon as possible, so he handed in his resignation at the nonprofit immediately and gave his two weeks' notice. The transition period to a new job was always exciting, with entirely new responsibilities to take on and past burdens to put away. But this transition was special for Mike because the job at the non-profit had sustained him for the past three years, and he felt reluctant a little to leave it behind.

"So, is this your last day," said Neil at Mike's farewell party.

"Yes, I'm afraid so," replied Mike. "I'll really miss everybody."

"You'll be missed, too," Neil said, and with good humor added, "By the way, your recipe worked. I got some pears, stewed them, and drank the whole thing. Cured! Thank you."

"That's great." Mike smiled and felt he'd done something good for his boss.

"So, how did your forecasting model go with the donations last month?" Neil asked.

"It did very well. Everyone with more than a ninety-percent chance of making the donation got our letter, and more than half responded with a donation."

"What model did you use?" Neil asked.

"A combination of both a logistics model and chi-square auto detection," Mike explained. "I've heard it was the method used by a successful political campaign forecaster—a political science professor who correctly predicted the current president's election."

"Oh, Professor Bob Durr? He was actually a classmate of mine at the University of Chicago," replied Neil.

"Really? Do you have his contact info? I wish he could share his thoughts on the method."

"Sure." Neil pulled up his cell phone and texted Mike the contact information.

Leaving the nonprofit's offices after the party, Mike found himself following a stream of pedestrians going toward the nearest metro station and almost unconsciously headed for the law school, something he had been doing every weekday for the last three years at this same time of day.

Then he remembered that law school was over and he had gotten the great offer from Williamson & Gray. Finally, he would be a licensed and practicing lawyer, with a paycheck of close to a hundred fifty grand a year.

But as with most other jobs, he would need to prove himself during a probation period. Other than somehow convincing the boss that his role in the firm was absolutely indispensable, he had no choice.

Once he started his job at the law firm, Mike spent every minute of his day reviewing the files for the Yan Chemical case, and found that Steiner had been right about the antidumping margins for Yan Chemical. Unfortunately, there was nothing Mike could find to improve their consumption ratios. In fact, their consumption ratios were already pretty low, and in some situations even lower than the lower limits of the industry range quoted in public sources. But consumption ratios were just numbers in the company's accounting books, and anyway, there was nothing to be done about them. The only potential new argument could come from the values used as the cost basis for these calculations, which in this case were taken from Indian surrogate values, most of which had been established in prior antidumping proceedings by the U.S. Department of Commerce. His objective was to find a lower value so the company could have a valuable zero percent rate for the investigations. However, after days of work he could still not find much improvement.

One night after his third week, he went home to his one-bedroom apartment, depressed because all his hard work was going nowhere. Exhausted and hungry, he turned on the TV, opened the refrigerator, and grabbed the leftovers from yesterday's Chinese takeout. When he started to warm them up, a report on the TV news caught his attention.

It was an interview with Congressman Jim Ryan from Kansas. "Well," the congressman was saying, "the Chinese government has definitely manipulated their currency exchange rates by undervaluing the yuan, so Chinese goods have flooded the American market and therefore stolen U.S. manufacturing jobs."

The anchorman asked him, "But isn't the low cost of Chinese labor the ultimate reason for their booming exports? In other words, even if the foreign exchange rate is corrected, will labor costs in China still be low enough to cause a further trade deficit?"

The congressman responded, "These are great questions for an economist. But with the current exchange rate, Chinese exporting companies can still make a profit even when their selling prices in the U.S. are at the same level as the cost of similar production here in the United States. There is a fundamental flaw that favors the Chinese companies in the artificial exchange rate that defies market forces."

Mike jumped to his feet as he realized he'd forgotten that important factor in his research. The cost of labor! Why hadn't he thought about the surrogate values for labor?

The next day, he searched all of D.C. for a source for international labor statistics, and learned that the only copy available was at the office of the International Labor Organization, the ILO. He needed to quickly let Mr. Steiner know what he'd found.

Just as Mike was about to pick up the phone, his boss stopped by his office. "Any progress?" he asked. "The deadline is tomorrow."

"I was just about to call you, Mr. Steiner."

His boss waved his hand. "Please. Call me Patrick. I always think you're addressing my dad when you say Mr. Steiner."

Mike chuckled. "Okay, Patrick. Well, there might be something worth checking in the source data that the Department of Commerce used to calculate the labor rate in China. They based their calculation on numbers published by the ILO. If they somehow used the wrong data, then their result must be wrong. I'm going over there to get the publication right now."

"Good," said Patrick approvingly. "Sounds like you're on the right track."

Mike wrote his name on the visitors' log at the ILO reception desk. He was surprised when he spotted a familiar name on the line above his in the log. Heather Hanson from Baker & Lynch, and she'd left just an hour ago. Was she thinking about the same loophole and trying to find a way to preempt his argument? His heart stuttered, but he quickly calmed down and located the ILO's annual yearbook with the figures in question.

He soon realized that locating the Department of Commerce's error in using the data would require days of research. The yearbook contained hundreds of data points from two hundred or more countries. But the deadline for the argument submission was tomorrow.

He started to look through the yearbook…and noticed the edge of a

Post-it note between two pages. He opened to the pages.

On the Post-it was a note in familiar handwriting. *Data from France and Germany mistakenly collected by the Department of Commerce and should be from wage form instead.*

Thank you, Heather.

He leafed to the wage form page and located the data from France and Germany. Two data points were lower than those currently used in the Commerce Department's analysis. With lower source wage data, the estimated labor rate for China would also be lower. With a lowered labor rate, the cost of production would likewise go down, the price would be relatively raised, and therefore the company would be less likely to dump merchandise to the U.S. at a low price.

Bingo.

He verified everything in the documentation, and concluded that Heather's note was correct. It was exactly the argument he needed!

Was Heather actually helping him? To his knowledge, she wasn't even aware that he was working on this project. And why would she help? Was she perhaps trying to preempt any potential arguments his firm raised? That could be true. If so, she should have thought about the consequences of leaving such a note in the only public source of labor calculation available in town—and thus easily uncovered by the opposite side of the litigation.

He was very puzzled, and started getting a little paranoid. Maybe it was a trap, and she already had developed a robust counterargument, so the note was just a diversion tactic to delay him building a winning argument.

All these thoughts flitted through his mind, but the circumstances were too demanding to allow any hesitation. The deadline to submit comments before the preliminary determination was tomorrow, and this data was his last hope to win.

No choice. He had to use it.

Chapter 4 The Hearing

The Herbert Hoover Building of the U.S. Department of Commerce was located between the Department of Treasury and the U.S. Customs building. Encircled by Pennsylvania Avenue, 15th Street, Constitutional Avenue, and 14th Street, the Commerce Building faced—on the east where its main entrance was—the Ronald Reagan International Trade Center. There, the offices of U.S. Customs were located, an agency that had existed before the United States Constitution was written. It was U.S. Customs that enforced all the antidumping duties to be assessed against imports coming from all over the world vying for a piece of the rich U.S. market in exchange for foreign trade dollars. The grand six-story building towered over Constitution Avenue on the south side, boasting fifteen Doric pillars that stretched from the third to the sixth floors of its façade, adding grandeur, austerity, and a touch of architectural and aesthetic charm for the tourists and passersby.

At 10:00 a.m. the next day, Mike arrived promptly at the entrance, his heart racing with anticipation. He was about to take part in a hearing before the Department of Commerce to determine their preliminary findings on the soda powder case. He couldn't help but think about the possibility of running into his friend, Heather, his rival on the opposite side. They would both try to sway the decision in their favor.

May the best lawyer win.

"Mike!"

He turned around and saw Heather waving to him. She was wearing a dark blue suit with shiny gold buttons, a skirt that fit her athletic body nicely, and a white silk scarf around her neck. She always looked great.

He decided to play it cool. "Hey, Heather! What a pleasant surprise. Which case are you on?"

Her high heels clicked against the glossy granite floors as she approached. "I'm on the team for Ohio Chemical against the Chinese soda powder manufacturers," she told him. "What about you?"

Mike acted surprised. "No kidding! You won't believe this, but…" He assessed her face, trying to detect the slightest trace of an expression that would betray prior knowledge of him working with her opposition. "What a coincidence—I'm actually working on the side of Yan Chemical."

She smiled with arched brows. "Oh, my God! Coincidence, indeed!" She glanced at her watch. "It's 10:30. Let's get inside and catch up later."

He hadn't detected any trace of a lie. She really did not seem to know that he was working on the same case.

Was it really Heather who'd left the note? Now he was baffled, and at the same time a little unsettled by the question—it had haunted him since finding the Post-it in the ILO yearbook.

The petitioner on Ohio Chemical's legal team from Baker & Lynch was vehement in advocating for the imposition of antidumping duties, listing the grievances experienced by the small U.S. soda powder maker in the Midwest they represented.

The U.S. attorneys hired by a number of Chinese manufacturers and exporter respondents then presented their counterarguments. The arguments were all over the place—economics, domestic subsidy issues, and everything else, including freight, distance to the harbor, surrogate values for the material inputs, and more.

Mike couldn't help but look at Heather on the other side of the table. Sitting next to Baker & Lynch's partner, she carried herself well, carefully making notes. When she raised her head and her eyes collided with his, she smiled slightly, tactfully avoiding any lingering looks. As the hearing progressed, he couldn't stop himself from stealing glances at her, watching as she made notes and listened intently to the proceedings. When their eyes met again, she offered him another small smile, sending a flutter of emotions through his chest.

The arguments raised by the other respondents and the counterarguments by Baker & Lynch took a long time. Finally, it was Mike's turn to introduce his argument.

He cleared his throat and began. "On behalf of Yan Chemical, we submit our argument regarding labor cost. We believe the Department of Commerce made an error in their labor cost calculation. Specifically, the data points for France and Germany were not taken from the correct reports. Using the correct data points, the Chinese labor surrogate value should be one cent less than originally calculated. This error would apply to all respondents, by the way."

Mike presented his case very calmly, taking only a fraction of the time used by the other lawyers. After he finished, he glanced at Heather once more. Again, he didn't notice anything unusual in her demeanor.

Her lead counsel, a partner of Baker & Lynch, unfolded his arms, put down the pen he'd been twiddling with during most of the hearing, and said slowly and calmly, "We welcome the Department of Commerce to review the calculations submitted by the respondent and decide the appropriate rate of labor for China."

Chapter 5 The Success

Standing before the crowd that had gathered in the Williamson & Gray's expansive hallway, Patrick Steiner held up a glass of champagne and cleared his throat to make a toast. "Due to our team efforts, and in particular those of Mike Nolan, our new associate in the international trade practice group, the U.S. Department of Commerce has issued a preliminary *de minimus* rate for our client, Yan Chemical. The result is only preliminary, of course. But we are all very proud of what you did at the critical last moment of this case. Congratulations, Mike! Keep up the good work. Way to go!"

Everyone applauded, and Mike smiled and nodded modestly. To be honest, he felt a little out of place. Only two months ago he had been a law school graduate with a six-figure student loan debt with a low-paying job. But thankfully, he appeared to be on his way to somewhere much better and more promising. Though this win had been a team effort, at least his job seemed secure now, and that nerve-racking probation period might finally be over.

You can't explain fortunes as much as misfortunes, someone had once said.

Patrick beckoned Mike over to a nicely dressed Chinese man in his mid-fifties. "Mike, I'd like you to meet Mr. Tang Jisheng, the CEO of Yan Chemical."

The man looked very young to be the CEO of such a big conglomerate.

"It's a pleasure to meet you," Mr. Tang said in fluent English, reaching out to shake hands. "We will continue to provide all the resources possible to defend ourselves in this antidumping case. We aim to be the number one soda powder seller in the U.S. market. We know you are a first-year lawyer, but we fully trust the decision Patrick made to bring you on board, and look forward to working with you for the remainder of the case."

"Mr. Tang," Patrick chimed in, "please rest assured that we will take care of Yan Chemical and not leave any stone unturned in this matter. Mike will be handling the verifications by the U.S. Department of Commerce, as well as the onsite visits in China by agency officers to inspect and verify your original accounting documents and the other reported information."

Exporters' attorneys usually attended these verifications, though Mike had not been expecting to be sent to China himself. But he really looked forward to the opportunity. It had been three years since his language training program in Peking University, and at odd moments he'd found himself missing China.

"I thank you for all your efforts." Mr. Tang smiled appreciatively.

Mike turned to Patrick after Mr. Tang left. "I can't believe he's so young."

"Well, it helps being the son of the vice chairman of the Chinese Military Commission."

After the reception, Mike gathered his things and was ready to go home. On his desk, he found an envelope addressed to him. Enclosed was a wire transfer receipt of $100,000 and a handwritten note from Patrick. *A bonus for all your efforts—didn't want to cause a ruckus in front of everybody. Thank you!*

Holy Toledo!

Mike was exhilarated. That would make a nice dent in his student loan. He quickly emailed Patrick an effusive thank you.

Still on a high, he wanted to share his good fortune with someone. He thought about his mother, but didn't want to wake her up, as she was three hours behind on the West Coast so the sun was barely up. The next person he thought of was Heather, but he dismissed that idea right away. She would probably not appreciate hearing about his bonus for winning the case.

But at that same moment, his phone pinged with a text message from her.

Heather: Hey want to have dinner this evening?

He didn't hesitate, and answered right away.

Mike: Sure, how about Le Diplomate on 14th Street?

* * * *

Mike arrived a few minutes early. The restaurant was bustling with patrons, and the lively, warm atmosphere was contagious. He requested a seat at a table near the window so he could people watch as he waited for Heather to arrive. He ordered a cup of coffee, sat back in his seat, and listened to the sounds of forks clinking against plates and the murmur of conversations. As he sipped his coffee and looked around, he felt a mix of anticipation and uncertainty. On one hand, he was proud of his achievement and eager to celebrate it with Heather. On the other hand, he was confused about why she, who was working on the opposite side, had left a helpful note for him in the yearbook. As he waited, he pondered how to approach the topic. He wanted to find out the truth, but without asking directly. He wasn't sure how best to do that.

Without thinking, he'd set his coffee cup on top of the copy of the Department of Commerce's Preliminary Determination on the Chinese Imported Soda Powder case he was taking home from the office. The order read, As of the date of order, the antidumping duty deposit rate for Yan Chemical is lifted. His fingers rested against these few lines, the hands of his wristwatch moving toward the words. With every click, the long hand of the watch inched closer and closer to 8:00 p.m. on the dial. When it pointed directly to the word lifted, Heather came in through the door and waved to him. He tore his gaze from the paper and returned her wave. She was wearing her attractive dark suit and light makeup. As always, she was a knockout.

"I guess we can only talk about public information," she said right off the bat after taking her seat. "Or anything other than the case, of course."

"Sure, I understand."

"Congratulations to you!" She sounded sincere.

He was tempted to ask outright if she had helped him with the argument, but held his tongue. What would it mean if she really had helped him? No. It would only make sense that she didn't mean to help, that leaving the note had been a careless mistake.

"Are you going to the site verifications in China?" she asked, looking curious.

"Yes, Patrick just told me I'll be going."

She smiled. "I may also go to Beijing to see another client around the same time. Maybe I'll see you in Beijing."

"That would be amazing."

Enjoying the conversation, he moved his coffee cup aside and leaned toward her so he could get a closer look at the beautiful woman before him. She had nice manners and carried herself well. She was fun to talk to. Occasionally she interrupted him to add a few quips to lighten up the conversation, while at other times she nodded affectionately, gazing into his eyes with tenderness. Weaving a hand around a lock of her thick blond hair, she presented the best picture of female charm that he had ever experienced.

As they continued their lively chat over dinner and talked about law school life versus working as a lawyer, he decided not to bring up the Post-it note at all. He just wanted to relax and enjoy the evening. After all, perhaps Heather had simply been doing her own research, and there was no deeper meaning behind her accidentally leaving the note. He was grateful to be in her company and was content to simply bask in the warmth of the moment.

Chapter 6 Song Mei's Fifth Job

Shenzhen Special Economic Zone, China, present day

As Mike and Heather chatted in the restaurant, in China the time was 8:30 a.m. the next morning, and it was the start to a beautiful sunny day. Yan Chemical's huge production floor was running at full capacity, producing cartons and cartons of soda powder in packages of different sizes to be loaded into shipping containers and trucked to the major Chinese ports and the many ocean vessels bound across the Pacific Ocean heading for the U.S.

Twelve hundred miles to the south, in the office complex of a candle factory located in the Shenzhen Special Economic Zone, China, a young woman called Song Mei awaited her turn in a long line. She was of medium build, with beautiful, delicate features and smooth, silky hair that cascaded down her back in soft waves. Her eyes were almond shaped, in a warm brown that radiated kindness and compassion. She wore a simple blouse and a long skirt, both in neutral tones, but the way she carried herself made her stand out in the crowded lobby. As she awaited her turn at the reception desk, she held her head high, a hint of a smile on her lips, her posture straight, exuding confidence in the face of adversity.

Today was the end of her employment with the candle company, a victim of U.S. antidumping duties. Despite the uncertainty of her future, Song Mei stood tall, a testament to her inner strength and resilience.

When it was her turn, she was handed an envelope from across the reception desk and told, "A total of 5000 yuan, your last payment for August."

Song Mei sadly fixed her gaze on the envelope in her hands.

Her friend Wang Lin was behind her in line. "Song Mei, count it to see if it is right," she whispered.

Mei did not open the envelope, but instead went straight back to her former desk to gather up her things. "No need to count. This is the fourth job I've lost to the antidumping duties. The Americans need to eat, too, I guess."

"Don't worry," Lin said. "I'm sure there are better things for you to do. I hear other factories are hiring."

Mei turned to her. "Which factory?"

"The solar panel factory down the street," Lin said. "Let's have a drink after I fetch my things."

"Okay."

Lin and Mei buried their sorrows in beer bottles and started to get more than a little drunk.

"So forget about that solar factory job you mentioned," Mei said. "I have friends from my hometown in Hunan working there, and they said the advertisement is fake, just for the investors."

Lin's shoulders slumped. "Darn."

"They are affected by the U.S. antidumping duties, too, and they've already started to lay people off."

"So unfair," Lin grumbled.

Mei nodded. "I'm tired of these uncertain jobs. I want to do something different."

"You should," Lin encouraged. "You have a strong accounting background, and you speak good English. You will have no problem finding another job."

"I've had enough of accounting," said Mei. "Maybe I should open a massage parlor? Ha!"

Lin giggled. "You are so pretty. In five years, you will be the madam of the house!"

They both laughed.

"You are a bad, bad girl!" Mei teased.

"I try," Lin said with a grin.

"You're lucky," Mei said after another sip of beer. "You have a home here in ShenZhen and don't have to pay rent. I have to pay rent and also send money to my father in Hunan."

"Why?"

Mei frowned. "Good question."

Last month she had sent her father 100,000 yuan so he would have enough for a down payment to buy his own apartment in Hunan Province, the hinterland. She didn't understand why she had to give her father the money to buy an apartment, the first apartment owned by anyone in the family. They had never had much money. When she was five, her mother had run away with another man. She'd heard this when she was eight years old, and only after crying every day, yearning for her mom. Her drunken father had cruelly told her that her mother would never come back.

Still, he had put her through high school and then college. The money she sent was her way to repay him. But after working for ten years in the most expensive industrial hub in south China, she still didn't have a place of her own. Her accountant job had paid a meager salary, and real estate prices were in the millions, effectively smashing her dream to own a home in this crazy town. And real estate prices were only climbing higher every day. The most she could expect from her father was that one day maybe he would smoke and drink less. Each and every time she heard a buzzing notice from her cell phone, she prayed it wasn't her father begging for more money.

Lin was lucky she didn't have to worry about drunken fathers and apartment rents.

"Life really is unfair," Lin complained. "If only I could have half of your looks."

"You are envious of *me*?" Mei feigned surprise. She was often the center of attention with the men they knew, but Lin was also pretty. "You're the one with a rich boyfriend."

"Oh, as if your boyfriend isn't loaded."

Mei went silent. "We broke up," she finally admitted.

"No kidding. You've been together for three years. Why the breakup?"

"We just realized we have little in common."

After talking some more, Mei said goodbye to Lin and returned to her apartment. She leaned against the balcony rail, looking out over the giant city full of neon lights twinkling against the backdrop of a vast expanse of sky. Deep down in her soul was a fleeting feeling of emptiness. Glimpsing a pack of cigarettes left there a few days earlier by Lin, she lit a cigarette and took a deep inhale. She slowly exhaled the smoke. She had never smoked before, but today she needed something to help with her mood. Suddenly, the city's skyline appeared blurred behind a sheen of tears.

Ever since she was little, she had been considered an attractive girl, tall with broad shoulders and a slim figure. Too bad she'd been born into a broken family with a drunken father living way out in the sticks. She had tried so hard in high school, then had gone away to college in this growing export hub in the south so she could carve out a better life for herself. But the harder she tried, the more distant the target seemed. She had always been very careful with the men she dated. Her last boyfriend had lasted three years, and the whole time she'd thought she was on her way to start a family. He had been doing well financially, but he hadn't been faithful. Some people were just not able to be monogamous, no matter how well they were treated.

She had also worked very hard at all her jobs. In one company she had been tasked with enforcing the intellectual property rights policy against the company using pirated software. She couldn't understand why she had been badly criticized for doing too good a job by the company owner, who had been the one who assigned the task in the first place. So after that she'd had to simply pretend to enforce the policy, and was actually expected to encourage the employees to use pirated software. She understood it when the owner said they couldn't afford the expensive legitimate software, but it wasn't right to be criticized. She couldn't do her job and not do it at the same time.

Why had she been born at this time of great opportunities but also great challenges? For her, it had been mostly the latter.

* * * *

Two nights later, Wang Lin stood in line surrounded by a dozen other girls, but she was impossible to miss. Her natural beauty caught the eye of a man with a cigarette who was lounging on a corner couch in the dimly lit room.

He kept his gaze fixed on her, his eyes roaming over her body twice, lingering on her chest. "Number fifteen," he finally muttered, lowering his head and turning away to tap the ash from his cigarette.

Ten minutes later, the man and Lin lay side by side on a king-sized bed. Her heart raced as his hand moved closer, reaching for her waist. She instinctively blocked him with her own hand.

"Is this your first time?" he asked.

She nodded, keeping her gaze on the tray ceiling and chandelier as she tried to tame her galloping thoughts. "Sorry, I can't do this," she said resolutely, starting to rise from the bed. "I'll ask my friend to pick me up."

"That's what you think," the man growled.

****

Mei received a message from Lin.

Wang Lin: Mei, I need your help. Come and pick me up at the nightclub near your home. I thought I would have some fun working here for a couple of nights, but I can't do it. I'm in Room 215.

Without hesitation, Mei rushed to the nightclub. When she arrived, she was stopped by an attendant at the entrance.

"Move aside! My sister is in Room 215 and I need to pick her up," Mei told him.

"I'm sorry, we can't let you in. You're not a guest," the attendant replied.

Mei's anger boiled over. "I'm not putting up with this nonsense! Holding someone against their will is illegal!" she yelled, pushing the attendant aside and rushing upstairs.

Quickly finding room 215, she pounded on the door. It opened to reveal a man in his fifties wearing pajamas, holding a towel to hide his face, afraid to real his identify to the intruder.

"Wang Lin! Wang Lin!" Mei called out, her voice echoing loudly in the hallway.

Lin emerged, tears streaming down her face, and threw her arms around Mei in a tight embrace.

"Are you okay? Are you hurt?" Mei asked, holding her tight.

"No...I'm fine," Lin replied, sniffing back her tears.

"Are you crazy?" Mei whispered, her voice laced with anger. She turned to the man. "Did you force my sister in any way?"

"No, I did not," the man replied calmly, still hiding his face.

"I'm telling you, if you forced her in any way, I'll make you pay," Mei warned, taking out her phone and snapping a picture of the man, who still tried to hide his face. With a firm grip on Lin's hand, Mei led her out of the nightclub and away from danger.

As they walked back to Mei's home, Lin said, "Mei, please don't blame me. I thought it was just a job and I could have fun. But it's not the same. When it really came down to it, I lost my mind. Thank you for fetching me."

"Don't put yourself down like that. You did the right thing in the end. But it's late. You should spend the night at my place. You'll be fine after a good sleep."

"Thank you, Mei. I would be in deep trouble tonight if it weren't for you."

"Don't mention it," Mei said as they went up to her apartment. "Let's both get some rest now. I have an interview tomorrow morning."

* * * *

Mei arrived promptly for her interview, eager to demonstrate her skills and qualifications.

The male human resources manager greeted her politely. "Ms. Song, we are a company with a long history in chemical manufacturing dating back over a century. Needless to say, we have a lot of applicants for the position."

"I am very good at cost accounting for manufacturing processes," Mei said proudly.

Just then, his desk phone rang. He picked it up, looking apologetic. "Sorry, Song Mei, I need to take this call."

As he spoke on the phone, Mei used the time to mentally prepare a closing statement about why she should be picked for the job. But her thoughts were interrupted when the HR manager's demeanor changed as he spoke on the phone and he became more focused. When he hung up, he turned back to her with a smile. "Song Mei, you are hereby officially offered the position. You will start next week with a starting monthly salary of 18,000 yuan."

Her heart leapt with joy and relief. "I really appreciate the opportunity to work for your company," she said gratefully.

But the HR manager just smiled absently, looking preoccupied as he said goodbye.

Mei couldn't shake the feeling that the phone call had something to do with her, but she didn't dare ask. Besides, what could it possibly be?

She left the office feeling elated she had won the position and excited to start her new job at the company.

Chapter 7 The China Trip

omewhere over the Pacific Ocean, several weeks later
Overlooking the great expanse of clouds through the airplane window, Mike pondered the result of the antidumping case. Yan Chemical had been the only Chinese exporter given a zero percent in the preliminary results, while all the other respondents had been assessed what was called the China-wide entity rate of 150 percent. If that remained the same in the final results of the investigation, Yan Chemical would be eliminated from the antidumping order and would effectively monopolize the U.S. market. The company had promised Williamson & Gray a 100 percent bonus in attorney's fees if that happened. They knew their financial stake in the outcome. It was a really big deal for Yan Chemical—the entire U.S. market. The amount of money they would make as a result was huge.

Mike stretched his legs, but having a business class seat did not make him any more comfortable. It was a twelve-hour flight to Beijing. Still peering through the window, he stared out into the darkness on the other side of the thick, transparent acrylic. All of a sudden, his heart was touched by something that was hard to describe. In an instant, his whole young life flashed through his mind. As he watched the parade of images of his life's big events, he wondered how he had gotten to where he was at that moment.

How had his life gone by so fast?

He tried to savor each technicolor image that sprang to his mind, watching intently the inner movie of himself growing up. He saw his two loving parents, and himself playing with his furry black-and-white cat. He played baseball and soccer and went to theme parks. He read all the books he wanted to read, on any topic, because his parents had encouraged him in all his interests. He remembered screaming and crying when the doctor stitched his split-open eyebrow after he was hit by a baseball bat at the age of five. It hadn't really been his fault. No one had ever explained how baseball was played, so he had just walked up behind the batter with the intention of asking him if he could play. He remembered that pain, as well as when his lower front tooth was broken the same way. He laughed to himself as he watched that scene roll by. Apparently, not everyone learned life's lessons the first time around. He hadn't played very much baseball after that. Yet all things considered, he'd had a wonderful childhood.

In junior high, one of his most exciting experiences was skydiving tandem with his beloved grandfather. Harnessed together, they'd jumped out of an airplane 15,000 feet above the ground. The moment of anticipation before stepping up to the open hatch was the scariest thing ever…right up until the jump. After that, freefalling through the weightless void was the most enjoyable thing in the world. He thought of that moment before the leap, trying to relive it. The scariest thing in the world became nothing when you faced it squarely.

Elementary school, junior high, and high school fast-forwarded quickly through his mind's lens. He'd had fun and made a lot of friends, but those experiences also flew by at lightspeed. Only the big events and emotional moments imprinted their images on his mind's playback. All the rest of his life just flitted through his brain like seagulls flying out over the ocean toward the horizon, all but unrecognizable. Including all those years of hard work in college and law school.

Had it really been worth it?

Ultimately, he answered the question with a very solid *Yes*. He had known it would be difficult and involved, but he'd had no doubt he would finish law school, pass the bar, and get a paying job as a lawyer. However, he hadn't predicted he would be working for such a prestigious law firm just days after he'd passed the bar. He was very thankful, and lucky to have gotten the opportunity. And to have won his first case so quickly because of an argument he had come up with on his own.

On his own.

Those three little words brought him back to reality. Had he, in fact, come up with the argument all on his own? Well, yes and no. He did come up with the idea for the argument, but it had been Heather—probably—who'd left the Post-it note pointing him in the proper direction to put together that argument.

He leaned back in the uncomfortable airline seat and reminded himself that law school was over. He had been tired...no, *exhausted* from all the schoolwork. And was more than grateful that the struggle was finally over—the exams, the time pressure, the sleepless nights, and endless study forever gone. All those years, driven by the thought of getting ahead and being successful, had been totally draining.

Mike slowly fell into a well-earned sleep.

* * * *

Beijing, China, present day

In the first decade of the twenty-first century, China had taken on a new outlook every few years and become a breeding ground for the nouveau riche. Between the soaring skyscrapers and the ancient palaces and pagodas, this new atmosphere was shrouded in an uncontrollable restlessness, voraciousness, and desire for material gains. It permeated the banquet halls of hotels, restaurants, and clubs, where favors and briberies were promised, schemes and stratagems crafted, and money and sex exchanged. The manual laborers still made meager incomes in workshops, factories, warehouses, and farms—even less than the ninety-eight cents per hour that Mike had calculated. The working classes then put their earnings into government banks that in turn lent the money to real estate developers, who sucked even more money from the working people who were forced to use their entire life savings just to pay for a place for their children to live.

On the first night Mike was in Beijing, he found himself in a posh hotel nightclub at the invitation of Mr. Tang Jisheng from Yan Chemical, whom he had met in D.C. A man and a woman singer were on stage performing traditional *Suzhou Pingtan*, while playing Chinese pipas, or four-stringed lutes, and telling the legend of general Hanxin from the ancient Han Dynasty.

The first pipa player sang:

Hurriedly chase, quickly ride;
Man is in a trance, mind is lost;
Can no longer see general's track or shadow;
Met a bystander and I ask the way.
Have you seen a general with a sword on his back,
Riding a horse with black bristle?

The second pipa player lilted:

Yes, yes;
He has gone for at least forty miles from here.

The first pipa player rejoined,
What, forty miles already...?
At hearing this, he is so worried that his soul is not at rest,
And now with a few stars and a bright moon up in the sky it is deep into the night...

Across the table from Mike, Mr. Tang sat next to a pretty young woman. He said slowly in English, "It is nice to see you back here in Beijing. This is Song Mei, our only accountant who can speak English. Do you like the music they're playing? It is very much Southern Chinese style."

"I like it very much. It sounds like the legendary story of Hanxin."

"Ah, you know it! Yes, Hanxin left Liu Bang, the first emperor of the Han Dynasty who was still fighting for his throne, after finding that he was not being considered for important positions. Xiaohe, an advisor of Liu Bang, in full belief that Hanxin was a great military talent, chased after Hanxin for many miles to bring him back to work for Liu Bang. Xiaohe recommended Hanxin to be the commanding general of the Han Dynasty."

"But later Xiaohe conspired to kill Hanxin after gaining enough power to threaten the rule of the Han Dynasty," Mike concluded with a smile.

"You are very good! How long did you study Chinese?"

"For one year, in Beijing."

Tang said, "Excellent. You know, we are depending on you for this antidumping verification, Mr. Nolan. I hope you will try your best."

"Of course I will."

"I heard that your grandfather served with the American Flying Tigers."

"Yes, during World War II."

"Also quite legendary. Now, may I ask you, Mr. Nolan..." Mr. Tang pushed his beer bottle to one side. "If you don't mind?"

"Please go on."

"What do you feel is the real difference between the United States and China right now?"

Mike wondered at the question. "It seems obvious that the differences are manifold."

Mr. Tang smiled mysteriously. "If you think about it, I don't believe there is much difference at all." He sipped his beer and continued, "No difference in the political system. You elect your government to be run by different political parties, and we also change the leadership within our government through various successions. There are different sections within the Communist Party as well. Both countries need to take care of the interests of the majority, meaning those who win according to the rules of voting. We find it very efficient with a one-party system. America wastes too much time debating issues."

Feeling it was a sensitive area, Mike hedged his words. "I guess the key difference is who decides whether the majority of the people's interests are taken care of—the people themselves, or their represen-tatives."

Mr. Tang lifted a shoulder. "Well, if they don't serve the people's interests, the representatives will step down in America. And also in China, if the performance of their representation is evaluated objectively."

Mike paused a bit, weighing how appropriate his remarks should be in order to keep a good client relationship. "How can the evaluation be done objectively if both the evaluators and the representatives are the same group of people?"

"They are not necessarily the same group of people as long as gov-ernments with different hierarchies have an efficient accountability system."

Mike wasn't sure he agreed, but he wasn't about to say that. "Thank you for your candor, Mr. Tang. I'm wondering why the emperors in earlier dynasties didn't do the same thing?"

"It is the last stop of accountability. If you don't do the right thing, you will be gone. Every Chinese dynasty in history was overthrown by revolution."

Mike hiked his brows. "Isn't voting a little better, so people can decide their fate in a more civilized manner and avoid social upheaval, or even war?"

Mr. Tang flicked a hand. "Either way, the result is going to be imposed by one group of people over another group. Our system works for us as long as we take care of the weak, less fortunate, and lazy, and also let the rich prosper."

Mike nodded. "That should be the ideal every society strives for."

"China was a very poor country back in the days of the dynasties," said Tang, "and it is still not rich. With a large population living in dire poverty back then, the Communist Party was able to enlist enough support from the people by giving them the promise of an egalitarian society. Communism is a very powerful ideology to win a revolution. But for development, complete state ownership has proven to be a failure. To sustain the results of the revolution, we need to evolve and adopt a measure of capitalism. That is what we have done. Individuals can now own companies and hire people in China. So really, what is the substantive difference between U.S. and China?"

"Well, there is one *big* similarity," Mike said dryly, hoping their differences could be reconciled with humor. "The rich and powerful remain so."

"I guess that is true. But, there is another similarity. China is not the only party benefiting from trade with U.S. I have not seen any studies on it, but I am sure China has supported the expansion of U.S. tech-based economic by containing its inflationary pressure. Just imagine if all Chinese imports were levied antidumping duties of twenty percent." Mr. Tang wasn't laughing. He glanced briefly at his Rolex. "Well, it's getting late, and I must leave to attend to an important matter. Ms. Song will stay and keep you company." He then said goodbye, got up, and left.

Mike took the opportunity to look squarely at Ms. Song. She was dressed in a dark velvet suit and white blouse. Two shining earrings lit up her cheeks, and her straight nose carried an air of amicable aristocracy, her eyes ready to offer a blanket of empathy and understanding.

"So you are a lawyer?" Song Mei asked in English, with a charming smile.

"Yes," Mike replied.

"Very interesting. Is an attorney's job really busy?"

"Yes, it can be…and usually is," he said. "How long have you worked for Yan Chemical?"

"I transferred here to Beijing three months ago. I had been working for an affiliated company down in ShenZhen."

"Do you like accounting?" Mike asked, smiling back.

She shrugged. "It's my job. I'm the junior accountant, in charge of cost accounting."

"Where in China are you originally from?" he asked in Chinese.

"Hunan Province. My father lives in the countryside." She glanced briefly up at the stage performers, hesitated, then turned back and said, "May I ask, where are you originally from in the U.S.?"

"My family is from the state of Washington, but I wanted to study politics and law, so I went to D.C. for law school."

"The United States is such a large country, at least on the map. Just like China." She gazed over at him, her eyes sparkling as much as her earrings, and rested her chin in a hand.

"It is. Also with oceans on both sides," Mike said, taking in the pretty lady before him.

"How are Chinese people doing in America?" she asked.

He chuckled. "Just like any other people, working and raising their families."

"Your Chinese is excellent," she complimented.

"Your English is not bad either."

He made sure to keep eye contact so she felt comfortable and secure. They talked about several subjects before turning to Chinese history and culture.

"You know the story of Hanxin. You must be familiar with Chinese history," she remarked.

He nodded. "Yes, I took a Chinese history class in the exchange program."

"Don't you think Chinese history is extremely…long?"

"It is, and very rich, filled with remarkable stories and characters."

"What impressed you the most?" she asked, tilting her head in curiosity.

"Well, I think Chinese history tends to favor characters with values of loyalty, wisdom, valor, heroism, forbearance, and sacrifice for the greater good. For instance, admirable people such as Zhu Geliang in the old times, and Sun Yat Sen in more recent years."

"Well said! You must know the novel *The Three Kingdoms* by Luo Guanzhong, about Hanxin." She smiled as she took a small sip of wine and put down her glass. They both glanced over at the two pipa players, who were bringing the performance to a close. "He once bore the humiliation of crawling under a bully's crotch so he could one day become a powerful general."

"But didn't he also treat the bully humanely after rising to the top?"

"Yes, there are many such stories of heroism and humanism in ancient China."

As the two pipa players continued, Mike took a long look at Miss Song. He could tell by the clothes she wore and how she carried herself that she had good taste and a great deal of self-respect. There was no trace of fake feminine wiles. Her lithe body's graceful movements belied a strong sense of feeling in control, with an added measure of dignity.

As they drank their wine they stole glances at each other, but he didn't know what she was thinking or how she might be judging him. She didn't let her facial expressions betray her emotions any more than he did. Mike had learned to do that in law school—and by watching *The Godfather* with his dad. *Never let anyone know what you are thinking.* That was a cardinal rule for a lawyer, as well as anyone on the other side of the law. He wondered if Miss Song had learned to keep her emotions hidden as a form of survival. She was just an employee, after all, not a boss.

"Hanxin was assassinated in a plot set up by the same man who helped him," she said in an abrupt change of overtone.

"Yes. Rise because of Xiaohe, fall because of Xiaohe, as the old Chinese saying goes," Mike remarked.

"I was a *Three Kingdoms* fan when I was little," she said, swirling her wine. "I listened to the story over the radio. Zhu Geliang was such a smart person, and he only had one wife. So loyal! But on the other hand—" She did not finish her thought.

"On the other hand, what?" Mike asked.

"I don't know if you read *The Three Kingdoms* carefully. After I grew up, I often thought about the episode where Zhu Geliang helped his master, Liu Bei, take over Jingzhou by borrowing the property from a friend, promising to return it to him. But he never did. Was that an outright lie and deception by Zhu Geliang? How could an honest person do something like that? I don't know..."

Mike was very impressed by Miss Song. He could see in her eyes that she was highly intelligent and sophisticated by any standard. Her eyes were the only part of her face that gave away who she really was inside, yearning for truth, and maybe more. He sensed that she'd had to make some difficult decisions in her life, and that she had a strong sense of righteousness. He felt she would ultimately take the paths that would enable her to make the right decisions in life. Then, in a single glance, he thought he saw a slight tinge of melancholy in her gaze.

He shook himself mentally, stopped analyzing, and moved on.

"Well, it's interesting you think that way," he told her. "As the old Chinese saying goes: Those who steal a hook are punished by death, and those who steal the country become emperors."

"I'm surprised I could talk this much about *The Three Kingdoms* with an American." Her expression gave way to a slight curiosity. "But why can the country be stolen? There must be something deeply wrong if a whole country can be robbed. A hook, one can steal and be punished for. But a country should *never* be stolen," she stated earnestly.

He thought Miss Song was a very principled young lady who somehow carried a lovely naivety.

He glanced around. "The performance is finished. Looks like they're closing the club."

"Maybe we can talk a bit more in the hotel lounge?" she ventured.

"That would be nice."

They moved to the lounge and he signaled for the waitress. "Let's have another drink," he offered, and ordered something for them stronger than wine, since the boss was long gone.

"What's our plan for tomorrow?" she asked when he passed her the drink from the waitress.

He took a sip of his cocktail, then said, "Well, I'll visit the factory and the accounting department. I heard the U.S. Department of Commerce officials will be there, right?"

"They will be there for sure. I mean, what about afterward?"

"Afterward, maybe visit the factory shop floors?"

"Sounds good."

He smiled at her sincerely. "Thank you for keeping me company, Miss Song."

She nodded sweetly and said, "Please, call me Mei."

They went on to talk of other things, especially discussing their favorite books and movies, As the night started to set in, he walked her to outside the hotel entrance. They stood on the busy street-corner, the sounds of car horns and chatter from the vendors creating a symphony in the background. He couldn't help feeling a strong connection with her, despite their having just met.

He held out his hand, smiling warmly. "It was a pleasure meeting you, Mei. I really enjoyed our conversation."

She smiled back, her eyes lighting up. "Same here, Mike. I never expected to meet someone who shares so many of my interests."

Mike looked at his watch. "Well, it's getting late. I should get going."

"Yes, me too. I have an early morning tomorrow." Did he detect a hint of disappointment in her voice?

He stepped closer and gave her a hug. It felt comforting, like a favorite blanket. "Take care going home. I hope we can do this again soon."

She hugged him back, lingering for several seconds in his arms. "I'd like that. See you soon, Mike."

With one last smile, they parted ways.

Mike felt a real sense of excitement for the future and their newfound friendship.

* * * *

Mike took the hotel elevator upstairs to his room, went to the refrigerator, and took out an apple juice. He walked to the balcony that overlooked the vast space shrouded with foggy mists amid the skyscrapers, listening to the clanking sounds of construction echoing through the Beijing night. He'd truly had a good time tonight.

He thought again how impressed he'd been with Mei's words. *How can a country be ever stolen?*

What a remarkable question!

He got ready for bed, climbed in, and leaned back against the headboard, going through what they'd just discussed. Hmm. Maybe a democratic country like the U.S. was the easiest kind to steal. Who could tell?

It also occurred to him to wonder why Mr. Tang had left the club early, leaving Mike alone with Song Mei?

A trill from the hotel telephone jerked him out of his thoughts. He picked it up. "Hello?"

"Is this Mr. Mike Nolan?" asked a male voice with a heavy Chinese accent.

"Sorry, who is this?" he asked, surprised.

"My name is Wang Ping. You don't know me."

"Okay. What can I do for you, Mr. Wang?"

"I have some very important things to tell you that may affect your business in China."

Mike digested that for a moment. "Who are you, exactly?"

"I am the senior accountant for Sanwen Chemical Works. We are also participating in the antidumping duties investigation of the U.S. Department of Commerce. Can we meet 8:00 a.m. tomorrow morning in the park across from your hotel?"

Mike felt instinctively this might turn out to be a really bad idea. But he was curious what the man had to say. "Okay," he agreed, and hung up the phone.

Instantly, he regretted saying yes. The call had made him uneasy. He'd never heard of this person, Wang Ping. Sanwen Chemical was a competitor of Yan Chemical, another respondent in this antidumping case. Why had their head accountant called him? Sanwen Chemical should have its own counsel. More to the point, why would Yan Chemical's lawyer want to have anything to do with Sanwen? Mike had gotten Yan Chemical a zero antidumping rate. What could Wang possibly have to say that would interest him? And why eight o'clock in the morning, before his first meeting at Yan?

Mike had more questions than answers. With the case in the last stages of completion, there really shouldn't be any more issues.

What if the call was actually Yan Chemical luring him into a trap? No. He immediately put that out of his mind. What would be the purpose?

Nevertheless, before getting into bed he walked around the room checking for hidden bugging devices. Then he searched for small holes in the walls where a tiny camera lens could watch him without being obvious. He had seen enough movies and heard enough stories in law school to know that anything was possible. People and corporations would literally do whatever was necessary to survive. He thought about it for a moment, and reluctantly added himself to the hypothetical list of things that would need to be cleaned up if push came to shove for Yan Chemical.

He walked around the suite a second time, scrutinizing every surface, rubbing his hand along each and every square inch of the walls, doors, and furniture to see if there could be any hidden cameras or listening devices. He searched the two blooming plants and the TV, along with every kitchenette appliance, cabinet, and drawer. He even looked inside the oven. Once he felt he had been sufficiently thorough in searching for what were surely only imaginary devices and cameras, he climbed into bed and slowly dozed off, drifting into oblivion as the Beijing night grew darker...

Chapter 8 The China Trip Continued

Early the next morning, Mike hurriedly ate the complimentary continental breakfast in the hotel dining room, checked his cellphone, and walked across the road to the park. There he met Wang Ping. It was not hard to know who he was because, although there were other people in the park, mainly older folks doing Tai chi, the man he pegged as Wang was standing alone by a small yet architecturally rich fountain whose multiple waterspouts were shooting water up five feet into the air. Also, the man was waving at him.

Mike waved back, then walked directly over and stopped in front of him. "Are you Wang Ping?"

The man was in his fifties, not very tall, and he wore a frown. "Yes. I am."

There were lines of exhaustion etched deeply on the older man's face. He had graying hair and a rumpled suit that spoke of long hours at the office. Despite his tired appearance, there was a fierce determination in his eyes, as if he were constantly worrying about something.

Mike introduced himself and offered his hand for a handshake.

Wang Ping responded with a firm grip and a nod, though his eyes never left Mike's.

"Nice to meet you," Mike said with an uncertain smile.

Wang Ping nodded, but his expression remained serious. "Likewise," he said, his voice deep and a little rough. "As I mentioned, I'm an accountant, and I've been working hard to provide for my family."

Mike could sense the concern in Wang Ping's words. He was clearly dedicated to his family, but the burden of supporting them seemed to weigh heavily on him.

"That's a noble thing," Mike said, trying to ease the tension.

Wang Ping shrugged, his eyes shifting briefly to the ground. "It's just what needs to be done," he said wearily. "I'm tired, but I can't stop worrying about my family's livelihood. It's a constant battle, but I'll keep fighting it."

Mike nodded in understanding, feeling a sense of admiration for the hardworking accountant.

Wang Ping said agitatedly, "I have to make this short because I may have been followed. I got your name from the U.S. Department of Commerce verification document, so I know you represent Yan Chemical. I worked for Yan for over twenty years, until I was let go. I started to work for Sanwen Chemical only six months ago. The reason I was fired from Yan Chemical was because I was not willing to inflate the revenue numbers in the financial statements of the company as Mr. Tang told me to. Yan is a publicly traded company listed on the Shanghai Stock Exchange. Posting fraudulent financials is basically stealing money from the investors. I could not do it. Mr. Tang said the company would buy my early retirement so I would not be involved anymore."

Mike frowned. "If that's true..."

"It is. And not only that, the numbers Yan reported in the antidumping questionnaires to the DOC were also fraudulent. I have all the evidence. Long story short, after I left, they never fulfilled the promised payment for my early retirement. Now that the antidumping duties have been assessed, after the preliminary determination Sanwen Chemical got one hundred fifty percent. But they lost a lot of orders, and many of Sanwen's containers held at the Los Angeles port cannot enter U.S. Customs. As a result, they plan to let thirty percent of the employees go. Including me. Because of what Mr. Tang did, I am without a job and have no financial plan to fall back on. I have two daughters to raise, and they'll both be going to college in the U.S."

"I'm really sorry," was all Mike could say. He knew that unemployment was not pleasant anywhere in the world. But as Yan Chemical's lawyer he had a strict fiduciary duty to the company, so he didn't know what he could do with this admittedly troubling information. "Is there anything I can do for you?" he asked instead.

"I cannot afford to retire at this age. I have a family and a mortgage. Because of Yan Chemical's pending zero percent assessment, they will be much better off than Sanwen and all the other companies, monopolizing the U.S. market. So yesterday I talked to Yan Chemical again. They know very well they owe me the retirement package, but they rejected my request all the same."

"What request?" asked Mike.

Wang rubbed his chin. "I want the money they promised me. I know they listen to you and are depending on you to nail down the win in their dumping case. Please, do me a favor and put in a word for me so they fulfill their promise." He swayed slightly in the silence. "I'm sorry this is awkward, being that we just met for the first time."

Mike sympathized with what Wang was going through, but didn't really know how he could help. "I truly hope everything works out for you. But as Yan's attorney, I don't have any say in their internal matters. And even though you and your company aren't on the opposite side, there is a conflict of interest between Sanwen and Yan Chemical that makes my involvement in your request inappropriate."

"But you're wrong," Wang told him. "It's actually very important to your case, because— How to put it? I have been instructed by Sanwen's management to dig into any accounting fraud by Yan Chemical in the antidumping investigation so they can expose it. Sanwen is determined not to let Yan Chemical drive them out of business."

"What do you mean, dig into fraud?" asked Mike, his mind spinning.

"Back before I was fired, I was the one who reviewed Yan Chemical's submissions to the U.S. Department of Commerce, and they significantly under-reported its usage of certain inputs. If they continue to refuse to pay me as promised, I will report their fraud to the DOC."

Mike puffed out a long breath. "Is that what you told Yan Chemical yesterday?"

Wang answered, "Of course not. I would never threaten them outright. I just want what I'm owed."

"I still don't see how I can help…"

"They will listen to your advice. And you have a vested interest in finalizing that zero percent determination for them."

"So you want me to go to Yan Chemical and tell them if they don't buy your retirement, you will tell the U.S. authorities about their alleged fraud?"

"I wouldn't put it exactly that way." Wang Ping slowed down. "I think you are a good man, otherwise I wouldn't have brought this up to you. Just please see what you can do for me. Here's my email address," Wang said, offering him a slip of paper. "Keep in touch. I'll try to contact you online."

With that, Wang Ping hurried away, glancing nervously at the people around as he passed.

Though he felt for the man, Mike wondered what he could do for him. Putting the email address in his wallet, he hurried to the office of Yan Chemical and waited there for the U.S. Department of Commerce officials who would start the accounting verification process. He couldn't help but wonder if they'd run into anything suspicious…

As it turned out, the verification of Yan's accounting records proceeded smoothly, and all the numbers checked out fine. The

DOC officers had no issues other than wanting to see Yan Chemical's operations in Qingdao, an eastern seaport city.

Mr. Tang decided that Song Mei and Mike should go together to the Qingdao subsidiary the next day, accompanying the DOC officer's visit. Mike had learned that the company's Qingdao factory was the biggest operation within Yan Chemical, and that the company actually had its origins in Qingdao. Mike was looking forward to seeing it. And he was secretly glad he would be with Mei without Mr. Tang's presence, so he could ask her advice about his unexpected encounter with Wang Ping.

After finishing the day's work, he walked back to his hotel room. He unbuttoned his shirt and leaned against the balcony, looking out over the vast fog and haze outside, the result of prolonged pollution caused by thousands of manufacturers in the Beijing area. Back inside, he turned on the TV and sipped a mouthful of water.

The TV anchor announced in Chinese, "The Chinese authorities are meeting with their American counterparts in consultations over twenty or so Chinese export products subject to antidumping and countervailing duties levied by the United States as a result of their unfair protectionist practices."

The room phone rang. Mike had already received a few questionable calls, but again he couldn't help being curious, and answered. "Hello?"

"Hi, is this Mike?" A female voice in English.

"Yes. Who is this?"

"It's Heather. I think I mentioned I'd be here in Beijing on business. I was hoping we'd run into each other. Do you want to grab a drink?"

"Hi, Heather!" He could barely contain his excitement. "Sure, I'd love that. How did you find out where I'm staying?"

"It's listed on the verification report."

"Oh, right. Where should we meet?"

"You are not concerned about client confidentiality?" She laughed.

He grinned. "Nope. No way we're discussing any client information."

* * * *

Mike walked with Heather along Wangfujing Street, which was packed with busy food and snack peddlers, whose delicacies they enjoyed several of as they strolled along.

"Isn't this great?" Mike took a bite of his sugar-coated hawthorn berry.

"Yes. I can't believe how busy it still is, even this late in the evening."

"China is a far cry from what it was twenty years ago."

"Do you think it will ever be a rival to the United States?"

"Pretty sure the United States thinks so."

They picked out a restaurant with delicious scents wafting over the outdoor dining area and sat down at a table, where they ordered dinner and sodas.

"Did you ever expect practicing international trade law would be like this?" asked Heather, gesturing around them with her frosted glass. "I'm so excited about all the travel."

"To be honest, sometimes I don't think I've actually started practicing law, at least in the strict sense," he admitted.

"Oh, really?"

It had all felt so random, falling into this amazing career. And ironically, most of his success had been because of Heather.

Or had it…?

"Can I ask you a question?" May as well find out for sure.

She grinned. "Can't promise I'll answer."

"Why did you tip me about that surrogate value error for the labor argument?"

She leaned back in her chair and regarded him. "We said we wouldn't talk about business. But I guess that's all public information by now."

He nodded. "Did you leave a Post-it note for me in the yearbook at the ILS library?"

She narrowed her eyes a little. "I did leave the Post-it. But it wasn't meant for you. I was just following instructions to leave the note in the book."

"Instructions from who?" he asked, puzzled.

"One of the Baker & Lynch partners."

Which made no sense to him. "Did you not feel your firm's response to my argument was…weak?"

"Not really. I wrote the initial draft and the partner revised it." She pursed her lips. "Still, now that you mention it, there were a few arguments on our side that I felt were pretty good, but were stricken."

"That didn't seem odd to you?"

"What are you trying to say?" she asked.

"Well, I just thought maybe your firm didn't try hard enough on the labor argument."

"I don't know. Maybe." Heather seemed momentarily baffled, too, but apparently didn't want to talk about it. "Which airline did you fly?"

"United." He decided to play along. "Speaking of travel, ever study any quantum mechanics?"

She hiked a brow. "I may have. Why?"

"There's a fascinating theory that says an electron can be transferred instantaneously over thousands of miles. They say someday people will be able to travel like that."

She laughed. "Right. Like Star Trek."

"One moment you are sitting in your office in D.C. and the next you are on Wangfujing Street in downtown Beijing."

She nodded. "And hopefully the man who just arrived in Beijing is the same man as he was in D.C., not some jumbled up version."

"Hopefully." Mike made a face. "Apparently two electrons can communicate with each other over a huge distance, so it really doesn't matter how long they are apart."

She tipped her head with an impish smile. "Huh. Sounds kind of like…love," she said jokingly. She sipped her Coke. "I recall that all electrons travel at the speed of light around the nucleus. And since everything is at the speed of light, the electrons can appear both here and there at the same time."

"Time stops at the speed of light, according to Einstein," Mike said.

"So I guess the travel thing makes sense."

He nodded. "He said every occurrence, movement, and event is all just probability, and that there are no certainties."

"Does that mean I only *probably* exist?" she asked, and nibbled at the remains of her dinner.

Mike have her a cheeky grin. "As electrons, maybe. But out here in the human world, there is definitely certainty." He gestured with his chopsticks. "For example, politics and rules determine the destinies of individuals and nations alike."

"Certainty?" She pondered for a moment. "Okay, I'll give you that. Because as time progresses, the probabilities always reduce down to just one. But"—she held up a finger—"no one knows what happens next *until* it happens."

Intrigued, he said, "Granted. But you still know the probabilities before they happen, right?"

"I guess you could estimate them mathematically," she offered.

He was vaguely surprised she knew so much about the subject, and asked suspiciously, "By the way, what's your undergraduate degree?"

"Mathematics." She winked. "Princeton."

"Well, hell." He took a gulp of soda. "In that case, back to love," he insisted. "We know it's the kind of transient feeling most vulnerable to manipulation by the opposite sex, right? But I guess that's not true love."

"Transient? Well, that's certainly not true love. But I suppose *perceived* true love can end up that way. I think it's important to distinguish between love and addiction. Both people benefit from love, spiritually and materially. But only one person benefits from addiction," she said calmly.

"That's…deep. And disturbingly enlightening." Mike realized there was way more depth to Heather than he had first believed. She wasn't just a brilliant lawyer, she was just…brilliant. "I'm definitely not going to ask you whether God exists or not."

She pointed her chopstick at him. "God only exists when you act on your own."

"You sound like someone who went to Princeton," he drawled. "Though I say God must exist if there was nothing before the Big Bang."

She gave a neutral hum. "The universe has been expanding ever since. But who knows what happened before? What if the universe was *shrinking*? Maybe everything had been reduced into one concrete mass, the largest black hole ever. Then *bang*! The Big Bang. And the trend reversed from shrinking to expanding."

Mike chuckled. "We sound like two geeks from *The Big Bang Theory*,"

Heather snickered. "Ha ha."

A comfortable silence fell over them for several minutes.

"Do you think China is as materialistic as America?" she asked at length.

"I suppose people are the same everywhere." He let out a breath. "To be honest, I don't really want China to become America, even though it seems to be catching up."

"You don't like America?"

"America is a great country with great problems," he said after a short pause.

"Like materialism."

"Amongst other things."

"Right. Greed is good. Isn't that what we've all been taught?" she said. "In practice, if not in theory. Capitalism at its best."

"Not if greed is beyond reason or conscience. That can never be best."

"Can you name anyone in the world who does not want fame, money, sex, and/or status?"

"I'd have to think about that one. But if all of us are selfish, money-hungry, status-seeking robots, what can be special about any human relationship?" he asked.

"Good question."

"Well," he said with a sigh. "I'd like to think there's more to America—and being human—than greed."

* * * *

The next morning, Mike and Mei boarded the bullet train from Beijing to Qingdao. The train could reach a speed of two hundred kilometers, or approximately one hundred twenty-five miles, per hour. Inside the train was very clean and well-organized. Mike and Mei were in business class, separated from the other cars by a sliding glass door, and sitting in futuristic leather seats that were ergonomically adjustable-360-degrees and extremely comfortable.

"The train is very impressive," Mike remarked. "There aren't very many railway networks in the U.S."

"China has the largest high-speed train network in the world, equal to the total length of track in all other countries combined," Mei told him.

"How long until Qingdao?" The same distance as from D.C. to Charlotte, North Carolina, which he happened to know took nearly nine hours on Amtrak.

"Just three and a half hours."

"No kidding." Mike whistled. "Quick."

When they arrived in Qingdao, Mike and Mei checked into a four-star hotel near the Yan Chemical factory. They went to tour the various operations that afternoon. One of the local managers picked them up in a Mercedes sedan and drove them to the industrial development zones where the Yan Chemical plants were located.

Compared with the low, smoggy sky in Beijing, the air was much better here in Qingdao. The Mercedes took them along the seaside where the boulevard meandered through hilly terrain, with seawater on the right and European-style villas on the left. Viewed from a distance, the old town looked very much like it could be in Europe.

"This city reminds me of Germany," remarked Mike.

"I've been here twice and I really like it," said Mei. "But you're not far off. This was a German colony back in the beginning of the last century."

"Oh, yeah." He recalled that Qingdao had been a frequent topic in his contemporary Chinese history class.

"How many factories are there in Qingdao?" he asked.

"Thousands," Mei said. "It used to be a big center for textile and light industrial products. Yan Chemical has kept some of those operations here, and has also invested in toy manufacturing."

"The air is certainly better than in Beijing," he said gratefully. "The smog there is as thick as pea soup. Too many factories and too much pollution."

"It's been like this everywhere in China for years now, and it's not very healthy."

"What factory are we seeing first?" he asked Mei.

"The toy factory. It's over there."

She pointed to the right, and the driver turned into a giant parking lot filled with hundreds of cars and even more bicycles. They drove to the entrance of the factory, where a man in a suit and tie came out to meet them.

Mei spoke Chinese to the man, introducing Mike to him. They shook hands and walked inside. Apparently Mei knew the managers here, as they all greeted her respectfully and nodded politely to Mike. They walked through the eight-hundred-foot-long plant, where Mike saw hundreds of workers sitting at their workstations, all very focused on assembling small plastic toys of different colors and sizes. He noticed that the fastest moving things were the workers' fingers as they delicately and quite deftly managed to make something out of what seemed like almost nothing, just small, unidentifiable shapes of colored plastic. Once the objects were completed they were gently put in a specific bin, and their true identity was revealed. There were many kinds of toys—robots, birds with wings, cars and trucks with movable wheels and doors that open and close, and tiny airplanes with retractable wings.

All of a sudden, Mike had a totally different perspective on small toys. It wasn't until today that he could associate these plastic gadgets with so many people making a living. Even though you saw the assembled items in American homes every day, it created an entirely different feeling when one knew that behind each single item there was organized production involving masses of people.

As they walked down the long, narrow aisle, Mike studied the workers. They didn't seem happy. One or two of them looked up and smiled at him and his chaperones, but he thought they might be new in the factory because no one else was putting on a happy face. He realized that this factory was similar to ones in the town where he grew up. Not a lot of smiling—they were also no-nonsense affairs. The attitude was essentially: Let's just get the job done and go home. If the Chinese workers in this factory were making less than the dollar per hour he'd calculated after correcting the DOC error, then their lives couldn't possibly be too comfortable. Perhaps they were working hard and fast so they could go to a second job, which would make their lives only a little bit easier. It seemed somewhat paradoxical to him.

"Where do the workers come from?" he asked.

"Most of them come from cities in hinterland areas, so they're away from their homes and living in factory dormitories."

Mike's mood was sinking and he fell into a troubled silence, until Mei suggested going to dinner at a seaside restaurant. The driver turned on the radio in the car. It was a popular song by Bruce Hornsby.

Standing in line marking time,
Waiting for the welfare dime,
'Cause they can't buy a job;
The man in the silk suit hurries by
As he catches the poor old lady's eyes;
Just for fun he says, "Get a job."

Mike got lost in the melody and lyrics. Obviously, people struggled to make a living everywhere. Except for the very few lucky ones in the world, everyone had to work hard to survive. He had been in the same position only six months ago with his huge student loan.

Mei must have noticed his change in mood and guessed the reason. "These workers were lucky to have jobs in such a big company," she said. "The labor system in China is not significantly different from the U.S., but here employment contracts last one to three years for the workers."

"That should help," he offered as the song continued.

That's just the way it is;
Some things will never change.

Mei asked, "Do American companies frequently bring antidumping cases against foreign exporters?"

Mike nodded. "Yes, against many exporters all over the world—

Europe, South America, and of course China. In the U.S., certain industries are dying, while others, such as technology and financial services, are very well developed and make a lot of money. Those industries push the cost of living higher and higher, so it no longer makes economic sense to engage in manufacturing due to labor costs."

"Interesting."

"Don't know if it's a good thing, though—a country without its own manufacturing industry. What if China stops supplying the U.S.?"

That's just the way it is;

That's just the way it is, it is, it is, it is...

The Mercedes sped along the shady coastal road, and they soon arrived at a lovely seaside restaurant. The ocean outside the window was calm, lapping against the reefs with the soothing sounds of the waves. The setting sun had started to tint the western sky blood-red.

After they were seated by a waitress, Mei said, "Mike, I know the food here. Will you allow me to order? Do you like seafood?"

"No argument here. I like seafood. What kind of food do they serve?"

"Here in Qingdao, it's usually Shandong cuisine or Lu Cai."

"What's distinctive about it?"

"It's based on the original tastes of the ingredients. How to say it… They try not to interfere with ingredients by adding too much spice, sweetness, or other strong flavors. It also includes all different sorts of ingredients so as to offer a balanced diet."

"I like that. Sounds very healthy."

Mei told the waitress, "We'd like to order crispy fragrant chicken, green onion sea cucumbers, tofu vegetable, and braised mushrooms."

Mike's mouth was already watering. It was as though Mei could read his mind when it came to ordering food. "Won't that be too much to eat?" he asked.

"Never mind that. Mr. Tang picks up the tab," she said with a smile.

"Speaking of Tang… What do you think of your boss?"

Her expression stayed neutral. "He's okay. I don't report to him directly. He just assigned me to this project because I speak English and know accounting. He offered me the job, so of course I'm grateful."

Mike had been wanting to ask Mei about the man he'd met yesterday morning, and now seemed to be a good time to bring it up.

"Mei… I have a question. Have you ever heard of Wang Ping? He was another accountant at Yan Chemical."

She looked puzzled. "He was still in the company when I first started. But after a few weeks, they said he resigned. How do you know him?"

He waved a hand. "I don't, really. I just met him briefly yesterday." Wang's name hadn't caused any ripples in her expression, so he figured that was all she knew about the man, and decided to drop it.

She pointed out through the large windows. "Look at that sunset! What lovely colors."

The sun had turned into a shimmering red-orange ball against the crimson sky. In the blink of an eye, it sank below the horizon. They both gazed at the glowing orb until it had completely disappeared.

"So beautiful," he said, and glanced back to her. She seemed lost in the moment. "Penny for your thoughts?" he said softly.

"It's like life, isn't it?" Mei sighed at the fading sunset. "Sometimes I get sentimental watching the sun go down. When I was growing up in Hunan Province, I often watched it with my grandmother."

"Were you close?" he asked.

"Yes, till I was five. What about you? Were you close to any of your grandparents?"

"Oh, yeah, for sure. My grandfather was really special. He once took me skydiving." It was Mike's very favorite childhood memory.

Mei's eyes went wide as saucers. "Skydiving? As in jumping out of an airplane?"

"Yes! It was great. You should try it!"

He laughed at her expression, then looked back at the sky outside.

It was getting darker with each passing minute, and a full moon was slowly rising. As night fell, the ocean stretched out in an endless expanse, a tranquil and mesmerizing scene made all the more breathtaking by the soft glow of the moon. Its silvery light was captured in the gentle ripples of the sea, creating a glittering pathway that led the way to the horizon. The air was filled with the sound of the gentle lapping of waves against the shore, a calming lullaby that soothed the soul.

The buildings of the nearby city sparkled with life, their lights twinkling in the darkness like stars in the night sky. The colors of the city came alive, reflecting off the ocean in a spectrum of hues that danced in the gentle breeze. The tall skyscrapers reached toward the sky, their neon lights casting a cheerful glow over the city and its residents. The streets were alive with activity as people moved about, the hum of their chatter and laughter adding to the vibrant atmosphere.

The contours of the mountains rising behind the shore remained steadfast and unchanging, an enduring presence in the landscape. They towered above the surrounding terrain, their slopes etched with lines carved over millennia by the forces of nature.

The mountains around Qingdao were a symbol of resilience, a testament to the unwavering power of the natural world, their unchanging form a source of comfort and familiarity to the people who lived in their shadow. The mountains were more than just a physical feature of the landscape, they were a part of the local memories, woven into the stories and legends of the people who called the area home.

The mountains did not change. But the people who lived below them did. As so did the society that ruled them, and the industries the people built...or tried to. Those were more like a river that flowed through time, ebbing and flowing, ever changing, stretching back a hundred years and more, connecting the past to the present in a tenuous thread of lives lived…

Chapter 9 Mr. Tong's Dream

Qingdao, China, Spring, 1918

The sun was still that sun, the moon was still that moon, and the mountains were still those mountains, in the same seaport city of Qingdao in northern China where Mike and Mei were having dinner. But the time was almost exactly one hundred years ago: early 1918.

The Qing Dynasty had been overthrown seven years before. The northern Beiyang government was now in control of China, and Dr. Sun Yat-sen had returned to southern China from exile in an effort to unite the country. In 1897, the Germans had occupied Qingdao and taken it as a concession from the Qing Dynasty. During their reign over Qingdao between 1987 and 1914, before being taken over by the Japanese, the Germans built almost the entire city, including the Governor's Mansion, the Sailing Club, the Catholic church, the entire seaside area dotted with Gothic-style hotels and elaborate mansions, everything. They also installed public utilities, including electric streetlamps in 1899. The city had then been taken by the Japanese from the Germans in 1914 during the initial phase of World War I, which was still going on. China had joined World War I on the side of the Allies in 1917 and sent laborers to Europe to aid the Allies. Qingdao was the only World War I Asian war site between Germany and Japan.

During the Japanese occupation of Qingdao, the streets were bustling with people from all walks of life. The city was located on the coast, facing the ocean and backed by a mountain range. The atmosphere was one of uncertainty and tension as the Chinese people struggled to adjust to the recent changes brought about by the occupation. The residents of Qingdao carried on with their daily lives, making the best of their circumstances.

The streets were lined with traditional Chinese architecture featuring tile-roofed buildings with carved wooden doors and intricate sculptures. During the day, the streets were filled with vendors selling their wares and haggling over prices in the busy marketplaces. Despite the occupation, the local culture remained strong, with people proudly wearing traditional clothing and participating in cultural festivals.

The ocean was a constant presence, dotted with fishing boats and cargo ships, its vast expanse stretching out before the city. At night, the moonlight shimmered on the water, casting a soft glow over the city. In the distance, the mountain range loomed, a reminder of the beauty and majesty of the land.

On an electric wire strung between streetlamps near Dengzhou Road perched a small, pure-white dove. Its head was in constant motion, swiveling this way and that as it surveyed its surroundings with intense curiosity. The dove's beak would occasionally move to pluck at its feathers, a nervous habit that spoke of its inner turmoil. The dove's sweet and melodious calls echoed through the air, filling the world with its gentle song. Its frequent *wooing* sounds were a reminder of its existence, a declaration of its presence in a world that often seemed big and overwhelming. As it sang, the dove's emotions were a mixture of yearning and uncertainty, a search for connection and a longing for a sense of belonging in a harsh and unforgiving world.

Down below on the street, a line of Japanese policeman patrol walked past the Shuang Shengwei Fabric Company.

In 1918, Mr. Tong Xiyao, General Manager of Shuang Shengwei, was only twenty-eight years old. He was full of youth and polite in his manners, exuding a confident and composed demeanor. Despite the stresses and demands of his position, he carried himself with a steady grace, never losing his composure or letting his emotions show. His eyes held a sharp, insightful gleam, suggesting a quick mind and unwavering intelligence. His facial features were well-defined, with sparkling eyes, a steady gaze, and high cheekbones that gave him a commanding presence. His firm jawline betrayed his determination and inner strength, suggesting that he was a person who could handle any situation with ease and come out on top. Yearning for success and opportunities for advancement, he was always full of business ideas, one after another, his mind quickly accessing products, prices, markets, and the cost of labor. The shrewdness of this young businessman was just as certain as the sun rising every morning.

Tonight Tong was working late at Shuang Shengwei, busy reviewing the fabric company's accounting records.

"Accountant Liu, which fabric had the most sales last month?" he asked, looking across the table at Accountant Liu. Tong's mind was spinning as quickly as possible to analyze what the numbers would mean for his business opportunities.

Whenever Tong talked with Accountant Liu, it was almost always about the numbers of the operations. Accountant Liu was in his early twenties and had only worked for him for a short while. Until today, Tong had not taken the time to look carefully at the smart young man. Liu wore glasses that perched on the bridge of his nose, which served to enhance the studious, diligent image he exuded as he carefully recorded and analyzed the company accounting records with precision and attention to detail.

Despite the late hour and the demanding nature of his work,

Accountant Liu's eyes never left Tong's. Liu's smile was always filled with a sense of pride and great respect. He was always attentive and ready to answer any question, however difficult, eager to prove his worth and earn Tong's trust. He was a loyal and dedicated employee, and his commitment to the company's success was unwavering.

Accountant Liu smiled helplessly as he answered, "Manager Tong, what else? The Japanese Red Lotus fabric had the most sales, as usual."

Tong nodded. "It has been like that for over a year already. What is their imported price?"

"We bought at nine silver dollars per piece and sold it at nine-point-four. Still lots of customers. Who wouldn't buy colorful fabrics for their wives and daughters?"

Tong wished one day that Accountant Liu would just think like him, but he knew that he was the boss for a reason. He always needed to think about things no one else would have time for. "Accountant Liu, let me ask you this. How much does it cost to produce the same piece of fabric undyed?"

"The Japanese piece is two feet one inch wide, six-foot-four inches long. To have it made in our hometown of Changyi and shipped back to Qingdao it costs a little bit over five silver dollars." Accountant Liu furrowed his eyebrows a bit.

"How much would it cost if we dyed it by hand?" Tong asked almost without even thinking.

"I don't think we could generate enough quantity or match the quality. We have tried many times." Accountant Liu sighed.

"So, four silver dollars per piece goes into the pockets of the Japanese." Tong quickly calculated the numbers on a piece of scratch paper on his desk. "Just because we don't have the dyeing machines. You know what? We should buy them."

"Do you think we can win this war?" Accountant Liu glanced at the newspaper on his desk.

"Which war?" Tong was momentarily baffled.

"The Great War, of course," Accountant Liu answered.

Tong waved a hand. "Oh, *that* war. It has been four years since the Germans were driven out by the Japanese, and the Japanese have occupied the city ever since. Why is China fighting a war in Europe? Well, if the Beiyang government wants to fight that far-off war, let them! I need to fight a war of business against the Japanese right here," Mr. Tong said decisively.

"How do we fight them?"

"Accountant Liu, what is the Japanese machine manufacturer's name? Do me a favor, contact the fabric dyeing machine producers in Japan and find out how much money we need to buy the equipment. Then find me a Japanese translator and I will go to Japan myself and arrange to import the machines."

"It is the Osaka Wakayama Stock Company," replied Accountant Liu, lowering his head and taking a second to think. "About thirty thousand silver dollars."

"That much? I need to talk to our investors." This would be no small deal. To date, there were no dyeing machine in the entire country of China. To add color to fabrics, Chinese workers had to apply dye by hand in the most rudimentary workshops using large dyeing vats. Dyeing machines would be able to generate high quality colored fabric with even application of colors.

You cannot trap the wolf without sacrificing the baby! Tong thought.

He quickly told Accountant Liu, "Let's do it, whether the investors agree or not." A four silver dollar profit was real and warranted no hesitation. Once he set his mind on a path, he would follow it with full force until he saw results.

* * * *

The Japan trip went very well. Tong was very pleased he had been able to by thirteen sets of fabric dyeing machines to bring home with him. While in Japan, he had also visited a couple of needle manufacturing factories. No needles were currently being made in China, which made him think that might be another good opportunity for profit. Maybe someday in the future he'd look into it. At the moment, he was only interested in setting up his fabric dying business.

Back home in Qingdao, he quickly selected a shop of over ten thousand square meters on Deng Zhou Road in East End and hired fifty workers, and opened the Shuang Shengwei Dyeing Company. It was the first Chinese-owned factory that used a dyeing machine in China. In addition, he hired Mr. Song Qingqi, who was a Japan-educated sales consultant.

Tong glanced up as Accountant Liu strode into his office. "Manager Tong, look! The fabric's color is not right." Accountant Liu held two pieces of cloth in his hand. "This is the Japanese Red Lotus. This is ours. Ours is more of a scarlet, and the Japanese is a bit more crimson in color. Their pattern looks happier and more stable."

"Ask Consultant Song to come to the office," Tong said with a frown.

Mr. Song hurried into the office. "Mr. Tong, I took a look at the fabrics. It seems that when the fabric was delivered, the seams were not even. We need to flatten the fabric before printing it so the seams are even and the cloth can take the dyes evenly."

Tong nodded. "Any other possible reasons for the difference, Mr. Song?"

"Yes. We need to adjust the pressure of the dyeing machine rollers themselves."

"Great. Let's go to the shop floor to have a look. We should do a test as soon as possible."

Tong hurried to the shop floor with Liu and Song and carefully examined the outputs. The dyeing machines were huge, like small submarines. As they studied the raw fabrics, Tong was distracted by an uproar that rose outside the workshop.

He opened the window and peered out.

Ranks of students with banners waving marched eastward to Jiaozhou Road shouting, "China has won the war! China has won the Great War!"

Tong shook his head and gave a bitter smile. *Won the war? Then why are the Japanese still here...?*

For the past several weeks Tong hadn't been able to eat or drink much, and he couldn't sleep much either. He'd spent most of his time in the workshop worrying. The investment he'd made for the machines had been far too much. Fifty thousand silver dollars. That amount could probably feed the entire population in his hometown in Changyi County for a whole year!

The original business model had actually been quite good. The company had purchased the dyed fabric made in Japan and then sold it locally and in northern China. But because they were now engaging in direct competition with their own suppliers, the Japanese no longer wanted to supply Shuang Shengwei with the Red Lotus brand fabric. With this much investment tied up in the dyeing business, Tong did not have enough capital to expand or even to sustain his original retail business. Time was pressing. There must be production, and soon.

"Manager Tong!" yelled Accountant Liu as he ran into Tong's office with others close behind. "Good news! Mr. Song helped figure it out! We simply added a bit of acid into the dye at a certain temperature, and now the color is right!"

Tong gave a cautious sigh of relief. Finally, after several months of efforts, Shuang Shengwei Dyeing Company would hopefully be able to produce dyed fabric as good as the Japanese products.

Tong could not hold back his excitement. He spoke quickly to Accountant Liu. "Try it three times and see if the color remains the same. If so, let's roll it out, and get the machines running day and night. Inform our sales team and tell them to order ads in the newspapers around town for the new products. Then contact the wholesale vendors in Jinan, Peking, and Tianjin. We're going to distribute all over northern China. But we'll need a name. A Chinese brand name that will let everyone know our products are made in China."

"Right! What name should we give it?" Accountant Liu asked enthusiastically.

Tong pursed his lips and thought for a moment. "I think it should be called MuLan Joins The Army. Everyone knows the old story of MuLan, who joined the army to fight the foreign invaders. Go hire the best designers in Qingdao to design the trademarks and register them right away. The Japanese Red Lotus retailed at nine-point-four silver dollars per piece. We will sell at eight-point-nine. Accountant Liu, the quality is the most important. We must outperform the quality of the Japanese Red Lotus!"

* * * *

A month later, Shuang Shengwei Dyeing Company's entire retail unit in Qingdao was geared up for the marketing of the Chinese-made MuLan Joins The Army fabrics. The retailers in other Northern Chinese cities were also ready.

When sales were finally launched, Tong was nervous. He closely monitored the factory to control the quality of the company's machine-dyed fabrics. After the first week of sales, he was anxious to hear the reports from the local retail units as well as those from wholesale vendors in other cities.

"Mr. Tong! Great news! Our roll-out promotion worked great and MuLan is selling very well! Customers are lining up at our retail stores, and it looks like last month's production will be sold in just two weeks!"

"What about the Japanese Red Lotus?" Tong asked anxiously.

"The Red Lotus did not move much. Our MuLan has the right color, the fabric is stable, and it costs fifty cents less per piece. Why would someone buy the more expensive Red Lotus?"

Tong beamed. "This is very good! Very good indeed!"

"Mr. Tong, look at our ads in the local newspaper." Liu held it up. "You see it is in color and really stands out!" He read the headline aloud. "MuLan Joins the Army debuts in Qingdao and northern China! Buy domestic products!"

"It looks great!" Tong smiled even wider. "If this continues, we should be able to recoup our investment in two and a half years." He took the newspaper from Liu and reviewed the ad, but couldn't help noticing the news headline that screamed above the fold.

Treaty of Versailles gives away all of Shandong Province to the Japanese!

The newspaper was dated May 4, 1919.

"Is the Bciyang government doing anything at all about this?" he asked, incredulous. "Will the Japanese be here in Qingdao for good?"

Accountant Liu sighed. "It is better not to talk about politics. It is more important to make money. We are out-competing the Japanese Red Lotus, and I think we are more patriotic than the government."

Once again, Tong heard an uproar down on the street. Angry, demonstrating students were flooding down Dengzhou Road waving flags and shouting, "Strive for sovereignty! Return Qingdao to China! Down with the Beiyang government!"

But despite the tumultuous political climate, the beauty of the summer days in Qingdao offered a moment of respite, a reminder that life went on even amidst the chaos. Qingdao was cooler in the summer of 1919 than in later years, partly because there were far fewer industries heating up the atmosphere. In those days, there were only forty registered companies in the entire seaside town. The sun was bright, but there was shade under the many trees, and with the sea breeze coming off the ocean, the temperature always felt cool and relaxing. The air was filled with the sounds of rustling leaves and the sweet scent of blooming flowers.

But 1919 was a summer of change and unrest. The cool air was thick with tension and the constant sounds of protest echoed through the streets. The students marched, their nationalist slogans ringing out like a call to arms. The Beiyang government was under enormous pressure, and the future of the seaside town of Qingdao was uncertain.

Amidst the turmoil, Tong and Accountant Liu remained focused on their work, keeping their eyes on their company's progress and making sure the business continued to thrive. Tong closely monitored the quality of the fabrics, and Accountant Liu worked tirelessly to keep the company's finances on track. Their factories were buzzing with activity, the machines humming as they produced the new Chinese-made MuLan fabrics. Optimism abounded.

* * * *

One day, Tong was strolling Shandong Road, the busiest road in Qingdao—which was later renamed after Dr. Sun Yat-sen. Tong wanted to see how fabric retailers were selling his MuLan Joins the Army. Though the Japanese military police might appear at certain times, the streets were clean and lined with shops, restaurants, cinemas, and post offices, and teeming with life. Tong started from the west end of Zhongshan Road and walked east, toward the sea. The rhythmic sounds of the sea came on waves of cool breeze, which made walking through the Japanese-occupied town even a bit comfortable. Most of his fellow pedestrians were wearing grayish clothes and the rickshaw pullers in the streets wore their distinctive hats. Occasionally, Japanese women wearing colorful kimonos walked by him with their parasols. He'd also noticed lately that more and more young ladies in town wore the traditional Chinese *cheongsam*. That day, to his satisfaction, he recognized immediately that they were all made from his MuLan fabrics. The vibrant hues of the Japanese kimonos contrasted sharply with the elegant Chinese *cheongsams*, making the young Chinese ladies even more alluring. Contrasted with the usual dull, everyday clothing, Mulan Joins the Army fabrics appeared especially elegant.

Tong started to smile. "We will all be able to afford colorful clothing soon, the Chinese and Japanese alike."

* * * *

Back at the office, Tong spoke with Accountant Liu. "I think we should add more pattern varieties to our line and push Red Lotus out of the market."

Liu gulped. "Mr. Tong, Red Lotus just telegrammed that they found out about our MuLan brand and threatened to stop supplying us with Red Lotus and raw fabrics."

"Let them do what they want. Just talk to the Shanghai supplier to secure different raw fabric suppliers."

"They said they would retaliate against us if we don't stop outcompeting Red Lotus."

Tong snorted. "What do you think they can do? They've already occupied Qingdao."

* * * *

Three weeks later, Accountant Liu walked quickly, yet calmly, into Tong's office with a sense of urgency, his eyebrows furrowed in concentration. He took a deep breath before speaking, his eyes fixed on Tong.

Tong understood immediately the news Liu was about to share was very important.

"Mr. Tong! Red Lotus recently lowered their prices by twenty percent, and ever since, our inventory has started to pile up."

Bad news indeed. "How much can we lower our price to break even?"

Accountant Liu did a quick calculation. "Fifteen percent."

"Let's do it then. Let's save our market share and forget about the profits for now. But see if the new Shanghai supplier could lower their prices as well."

Liu shook his head. "Already asked. The Shanghai supplier said they are at rock bottom."

Tong narrowed his eyes. "At the current price, the Japanese must be losing money. There is no way they can be making a profit."

A short time later, Red Lotus lowered its price by another twenty percent, and Shuang Shengwei's fabric inventory started to pile up even more significantly. Tong had no choice but to lower MuLan's prices to match, but every time he sold a piece of fabric, the company now lost money.

He needed to find a solution!

"Accountant Liu, normally machine-dyed fabric is a very profitable business, so we must keep our share of the market. Can we increase our pricing in some other products to make up for the losses in the machine-dyed fabric?"

"Mr. Tong, we tried, but the markets are price-sensitive. The Chinese people are still very poor and are pinching pennies for these products. It is hard to see a way." Accountant Liu chewed his tongue, ruminating deeply. "When I went to college at Yashita University, I learned that the Japanese government subsidizes key export products. For every dollar of certain exports shipped to China, the Japanese government pays twenty percent back to the Japanese exporter. We are not competing with the manufacturer of Red Lotus, we are competing with the Japanese government! How can we afford to do that?"

Tong grimaced. "Did the Beiyang government actually sign the Versailles Treaty?"

Accountant Liu shook his head. "No, they did not, but the Japanese are still not leaving Qingdao."

Tong wanted to pull his hair in frustration. "Without a strong government, what is the use of businessmen like us? Accountant Liu, we must continue selling MuLan for as long as we can keep it running."

Liu gave him a sympathetic look. "You have been at the factory day and night lately. What about your wife and two boys? You should go back home and be with them."

"Yes," Tong said, and set aside his papers. "You're right."

* * * *

The fabric competition continued head-on until 1922, when the Japanese withdrew from Qingdao as a result of the Washington Conference. The people in Qingdao took to the streets to celebrate the end of foreign occupation that had begun in 1897.

Unfortunately, Tong's fabric-dying company could no longer continue to operate. Not after losing such significant amounts of money competing against the Japanese exporters. Despondent, Tong walked around the workshop and fussed with the dyeing machines. He leaned on one and looked down, staring at the well-trodden floor, troubled as well by a conversation he'd had with his wife the night before.

Climbing into bed, as they settled beneath a rich cloth fabric, his wife had told him, "Fang Fang is just eight years old and he wants to join the army when he grows up." She glanced over at him worriedly. "I really don't understand that child. This is a difficult time for our country, but what parent wants to send their children to the battlefield? Can't you say something to him? Steer him in the right direction?"

"Yes, why not just be a simple businessman?" agreed Tong. "No stealing, no robbing, no killing. Just live a peaceful life. But then again, what is the future of businessmen in China? I worked hard for fifteen years and still couldn't compete against the Japanese fabric. We should let him do whatever he wants to do. Let him join the army or word for the government, as long as he likes it. When he grows up, he'll know what he really wants to do."

His wife only listened, frowning.

"Honestly," Tong went on, "I don't think this cloth-dyeing business will work any longer. The Japanese are backed by their government, so they can recoup their loss through subsidies. We can't. Overall, we have only made enough money to break even, merely earning back the price of the machines and the rent for the workshops. I want to close the company and sell the machines." He sat up in bed. "Last time I was in Japan, I visited some Japanese needle factories. I want to get into the needle business instead. If we can produce needles here in China, it would mean a lot to the Chinese people. And to our family."

As he drifted off to sleep, he felt a renewed sense of purpose. Maybe he could solve all his financial problems and also help bring about real change by opening a Chinese needle factory.

Chapter 10 Mr. Yin's Return to China

Qingdao, China, 1928

The ship's horn roared as it pulled into the Qingdao Harbor, China, and Yin Zhizhong craned his neck to watch his homeland approach. The landscape was shrouded in a huge cloud. Yin could barely make out the tiny specks moving around the docks or the faint silhouettes of buildings in the dense fog. He deeply inhaled a breath of the cold, wet air. Despite the mist on the sea, he keenly felt the joy of being back home and was ready to put his newly gained knowledge to good use. Though only in his late twenties, there was a maturity in his expression and demeanor that belied his youth, reflecting his many experiences in Japan and the lessons he had learned there. So many childhood memories and people's faces suddenly came alive in Yin's mind that his heartbeat sped with excitement and his eyes grew wet with tears.

It was very good to be home.

After finally finishing his degree at the Hiroshima Advanced Industrial School, he couldn't wait to get back. His graduation couldn't come soon enough. He had spent countless nights staying up doing the reading, working on projects, and preparing for presentations. He had been puzzled by equations and struggled to fit three-dimensional mechanics on a piece of paper. Not to mention that he'd done all of it in Japanese—a language he'd quickly gained fluency in during his first few months there. He was proud of the work he'd done and satisfied with the knowledge he'd gained. He also knew he'd made connections that would be valuable in his future career.

As Yin Zhizhong stepped off the ship he was greeted by his parents and relatives, their familiar looks and voices exuding homey feelings of warmth and admiration. Leaving the dock, he looked back at the crowd conversing in his native language and tried to imprint this image of returning home in his mind. As he pushed his way through the throng, he smiled to himself. Armed with a new degree and the latest industry knowledge, he knew it wouldn't be long before he made a name for himself in Qingdao and—who knew?—maybe in all of China.

The very next day, Yin visited his old friend, Mr. Tong.

"Welcome back, brother!" said Mr. Tong, looking exuberant. "I've been counting the days!" His eyes lit up as he walked toward Yin and reached out for a tight handshake.

"It's good to be home," Yin said, smiling. Even though they were in Mr. Tong's office, the sound of people doing business in the office below penetrated the walls, so Yin had to raise his voice. "I hear that Longyuan is the biggest textile wholesale company in Qingdao. Congratulations!"

Mr. Tong gestured to the office below. "We're going eight years strong. How did your education in needle manufacturing go? You know, there's a really high demand for needles in China right now. The Japanese left seven years ago." Tong seemed anxious to hear Yin's ideas and obviously still exalted over the end to the many years of foreign occupation. The engineer carried an air of assurance, a businessman who wanted to do something big.

Yin nodded. "So I have heard."

"Yes, the city has been our own for a while. You and I need to do something great together." Tong handed Yin a cup of tea.

"I believe that with what I have learned, I could bring something special to this country," Yin assured him as he accepted the tea. "What I need is your business acumen."

"And my money?"

They both laughed in an outburst of joy.

Tong walked over to his desk and pulled out some papers. "Well then, let's draw up a plan. We Chinese talk about the timing of the heaven, the convenience of the location, and the harmony of the people. I think right now we have all three!"

* * * *

Hiroshima, Japan

It was just one month later when Mr. Yin was once again back in Hiroshima, waiting in the Japanese customs office. This time he was there for business. He had successfully closed a deal on some needle manufacturing equipment and was waiting in the customs office for the export declaration to be approved by the Japanese customs. He looked out over the harbor through the window and watched the Japanese ships pass by, tacitly worrying about his plans for this equipment.

Out of the corner of his eye, he saw the office door behind the counter open. A customs officer trotted his way, looking at the documents he held in his hand and shaking his head. "You can't take this equipment out of the country," he said in a sullen and frigid voice. "Exporting this equipment is prohibited by the Japanese Empire. We'll have to hold onto it." Behind him on the wall hung a black and white portrait of Japanese Emperor Hirohito, his eyes staring out from behind his gold rimmed glasses at anyone looking that way.

"How c-can that be? The eq-quipment is merely for civilian use!" Yin stuttered in Japanese.

"It does not matter. It's considered strategic equipment and subject to Japanese export control laws." The officer handed the documents to Yin and returned to his office.

Yin was shocked. How could they do this? The equipment was integral to his and Mr. Tong's plans. But his disappointment only lasted a second. He remembered that his old classmate, Utada Taro, was working as the manager of the Hiroshima Needle Factory. If he could get him to agree, they could open a joint factory together, and with a Japanese person on their management team, they would be able to transport the equipment to their factory in China.

"You always had the most brilliant ideas in class," Mr. Utada said as Yin looked at him sincerely with an expression that conveyed this was Yin's last hope. "I've heard there's a very high demand for needles over in China. I can't think of anyone better than you to execute this plan with. As for the equipment, if there's a will, there's a way."

And sure enough, after some meetings with government officials, Yin was back en route to China, along with Mr. Utada and the needle manufacturing equipment.

* * * *

Qingdao

Yin was greatly enjoying the truck ride from the harbor docks to Tong's company. Mr. Utada, his new needle factory partner, was at his side and the Utada family furniture was on the back of the truck. Yin was gleeful at the prospect of surprising Mr. Tong with the good news.

"Welcome, Welcome, Mr. Utada!" Mr. Tong waved from the company's front entrance when Yin and Mr. Utada stepped out of the truck. Looking a bit baffled, Mr. Tong's eyes went straight to the bulky load on the back of the truck which was covered by grass-green colored canvas.

Mr. Utada bowed. "Mr. Tong, it is a pleasure to meet you." He gestured to his suitcases. "I have brought my entire family with me. May I unpack my things?"

Yin was impressed with Utada's nearly fluent Chinese.

Mr. Tong smiled but continued to look confused. "Really? Here in the factory?"

Yin stepped forward with a grin. "Brother Yin, let him, let him!"

With a few employees' help, a few of the large packages were laid out on the factory floor. Mr. Utada squatted down and opened one of them. He pulled out some clothes and set them aside. Then he tilted the box toward Mr. Tong.

Yin could hardly contain himself, trying not to spill the beans.

Tong gave a small gasp. "What is this?" Nestled within the clothes were shining metal parts. Mr. Tong still appeared at a loss.

"There are a lot more of these in the boxes up in the truck, Brother Tong," Yin said, unable to stay quiet anymore. "Since it is forbidden for Chinese citizens to buy and export Japanese manufacturing equipment to China, I signed on Mr. Utada as our business partner. He told Japanese customs officials he was moving here to Qingdao. And we brought the factory equipment over with his furniture and luggage."

Mr. Utada beamed. "We just have to put the equipment back together and then we can get to work."

At first Mr. Tong was shocked and speechless, but then he burst into laughter and slapped Yin's shoulder heartily. "You! I thought you were smuggling arms!"

Watching Mr. Tong and Utada shaking hands and laughing together happily, Yin felt overjoyed that he had won this first battle. But this was just the beginning. Now he was ready for the real hard work ahead.

Yeah, he was really looking forward to it.

Chapter 11 The Needles Made in China

In a little over a year, The ZhongJi Needle Factory, the very first needle factory ever in China, was up and running in Qingdao. Mr. Tong felt great! He loved hearing the chanting, clicking, whirring, and all the various sounds of metal meeting metal that was coming from their new modern equipment. The last time he had run a manufacturing business was exactly a decade earlier. His original thirteen cloth-dyeing machines had been resold to another businessman interested in doing what Tong had envisioned a decade ago. Tong had needed to do something new, something more advanced, and yes, with new technologies.

Wholesale cloth trading had been a great career and it had made him a lot of money, but it just did not feel as exciting as it once had. The trading business was really like a peddler's gig, simply passing merchandise from one to another. But manufacturing was the real deal, creating steel needles from scraps of metal! Even better, the machines did most of the work and machines never needed to stop for rest.

The factory launched smoothly and business was brisk in the beginning, but just two years later, in 1931, sales were slowly stagnating. There was something mysterious about the passage of time. Tong almost felt that time stopped when the machines were silent, which was happening more and more lately.

"What do you mean they don't want to buy our needles? I thought everybody needed needles!" Tong yelled at Accountant Liu. He couldn't understand why their business was starting to fail after just a few years.

"It's nothing to do with our quality, it's just that people can buy cheaper foreign products."

"How is that possible? We have the best machines, and there is no overseas transportation cost. Plus our pricing gives us little profit." Tong lowered his head and frowned as a thought came to him. "Is it because of the Japanese government subsidies?"

Mr. Yin threw up his hands. "What else? The damn Japanese subsidies are killing us!" he said. "It's not fair that they subsidize the needles to reduce their price so more people over here can buy them."

Tong let out a deep sigh of frustration. However hard he tried, he could not cast off the grim specter of the foreign dumping that had haunted him for the past decade. It had already turned one of his dreams into a nightmare and now it was happening all over again. First it was the dyed fabric, now the needles. He had the best machines and the needles were made right here in China. But he still could not compete against the damn subsidized foreign imports in the Chinese market!

Tong closed his eyes and counted to ten to calm his nerves, then slowly opened them and firmly said, "There must be *something* we can do to make our needles affordable."

Accountant Liu shuffled some documents on his desk. "Well, most of our costs come from the raw materials," he said after looking them over.

"Which we import from Japan," Mr. Yin said pointedly.

"And it takes a long time for the raw materials to get here," said Tong thoughtfully.

"I'll see what more I can do to keep costs down, but there isn't any way that I know of to get the raw materials domestically," said Liu somberly.

Tong still had work on his mind when he arrived home for dinner. He tuned out of the conversation his family was having around him and tried to come up with a solution. But it wasn't long before he suddenly felt his wife's hand on his arm.

"I said, did you hear that the Japanese invaded Manchuria?" His wife looked concerned.

"Wait. What?" Tong could not believe his ears.

"Tong Fang says he heard at school that the Japanese started fighting in northeast China."

Their son Tong Fang's cheeks were flushed with excitement. "They attacked Shenyang!" He sat erect in his chair, and even at twelve years old he was almost as tall as a grown man.

Tong focused on his son. "They really invaded China? Again?"

"Yes! I can't wait to grow up so I can fight the Japanese!" Tong Fang exclaimed.

"Settle down, Tong Fang," said Tong's wife. "Don't get ahead of yourself."

But Tong Fang's excitement didn't dim. "Teacher Ying says that one way we can fight the Japanese is by boycotting Japanese goods. To boycott means to—"

"Yes, we know what boycotting means," she interrupted.

"You say they are boycotting Japanese goods?" asked Tong, perking up. This could be the solution he'd been searching for. If Chinese shoppers were boycotting Japanese goods, then they would have no choice but to buy ZhongJi needles, since theirs was still the only needle factory in China.

"We should boycott all Japanese goods." Tong Fang turned to his mother. "Do we have any Japanese goods in our house?" He stood up from the table and looked around the kitchen as if the Japanese goods were going to fight him right then and there.

"Sit down, Tong Fang!" she urged. "Finish your dinner and then you can look. But remember, boycotting means to not buy, not to destroy. Don't be silly."

* * * *

In the next few weeks, Tong noticed that all around him attitudes among Chinese consumers were beginning to shift in his favor. Students were out on the streets every day demonstrating against the foreign invasion, demanding that citizens and businesses boycott Japanese goods.

As Tong expected, ZhongJi experienced a sudden and tremendous growth. Tong and Mr. Yin devised a big plan that would boost production. "Brother Yin," Tong said to Yin one day after work, "you've heard the calls to boycott Japanese goods, right?"

"Yes, the students are demonstrating a few blocks from my house. They're causing quite a commotion."

"Do you see how this will benefit our business?"

"I do. For now anyway. But how long do you think it will go on for?"

"True, the boycott may not be the solution forever. We need to fix the underlying problem while we still can."

The last time Tong and Yin were in Japan they had purchased some Japanese blueprints for needle manufacturing machines. Looking thoughtful, Yin brought them out of a drawer and unrolled the blueprints onto a table.

"You have an idea?" Tong asked, walking over to join him.

"Look at these machines," Yin said and pointed. "There's one machine for hammering the steel down, another machine for boring the eye of the needle, and yet another for cutting the needles to size."

Tong nodded. "Yes?"

"I believe we can combine these three separate machines into one large machine that completes all three processes more quickly, one after the other."

"That would certainly save a lot of time," said Tong with a nod. "And bring costs down. Do you really think it's possible to build such a machine?"

"Well, there's only one way to find out. But I think right now many of our investors are having second thoughts about ZhongJi because of our poor sales of late. Why don't you and I start a new company with this new technology?"

"Good idea. I like it! The GongYu Company in Tianjin has expressed an interest in working with us. Maybe we can start it together with them."

"Excellent," Yin said with a smile.

"We can name the company JiLu, referring to the two locations of the investors."

"Fantastic. You work on the business side, and I will concentrate on the technology."

After carefully consulting his plans, developing several prototypes, and suffering countless all-nighters, in 1931 Yin's invention was finally ready. It was even better than he and Tong had hoped for. The big machine was two hundred times more efficient than using three separate machines, and it even saved on raw materials. This greatly reduced the costs of the final products, which the customers boycotting Japanese goods appreciated.

So late that same year, Tong and Yin opened the JiLu Needle Factory, located at No. 8 Liyun Road, Qingdao. It was the first full-scale needle factory in China using advanced technologies.

In the meantime, protests against Japanese imperialism were growing, and calls to boycott Japanese goods were getting louder. In response, the industrialists and businessmen of Qingdao went on strike. Mr. Tong cut ties with Japanese merchants and refused to travel to Japan to trade, and many other companies followed suit. During these tense times, even though prices were still high, business at JiLu Needle Factory grew rapidly thanks to Chinese consumers seeking alternatives to Japanese goods. They finally had a chance at competing against the subsidized Japanese needles.

Things were looking good at their new company, and this was all achieved without any help from the Chinese government. When Tong registered the patent for their new machine, he won an award from the Ministry of Industry. His name along with the JiLu Needle Factory gained wider recognition. The annual output of the factory was 6,000 boxes of needles with 250,000 needles per box, grossing one and a half billion needles each year. The offices of the JiLu Needle Factory expanded to include locations in Jinan, Shanghai, Tianjin, Beijing, Chongqing, and Xi'an. They even exported needles to other countries in Southeast Asia. Needles were one of the few Chinese products that could be exported at that time. With its new reputation at home and abroad, JiLu Needle Factory set out to become an exemplary leader in Chinese industrial independence.

JiLu Needle Factory gained attention locally as well. The chairman of the province of Shandong, Han Fuqu, and the mayor of Qingdao, Shen Honglie, asked to visit the factory. Tong and Yin decided to throw a gala in their honor. They polished the machines, cleared as much space as they could, and brought in tables and decorations. At the very last minute, they were informed that Sun Wen, the son of Dr. Sun Yat-Sen, would also be coming to the party.

"Did you hear that Sun Wen will be attending our gala?" Yin asked Tong.

Tong's face lit up. "Really? That's very exciting!"

"I know! I hope it all goes well tonight," said Yin nervously.

"I'm sure it will. They already know our company is highly successful. We just have to keep them entertained."

Tong and Yin were socializing with the other guests when they were alerted that Chairman Han and Mayor Shen were arriving. They waited anxiously near the entrance to greet their guests of honor. In a few moments, Chairman Han, Mayor Shen, and Sun Wen appeared at the door. Tong and Yin rushed forward to greet them.

"Welcome!" said Yin.

"We are honored that you could join us tonight," said Tong.

Shen Honglie was an imposing figure as the mayor of Qingdao. He had a strong and sturdy build, and a rugged face that showed the marks of years spent in the political and military arena. His sharp, piercing eyes seemed to take in everything, and his stoic expression exuded an air of confidence and authority. His hair was cut very short, reminding people of his military background even though he was wearing traditional civilian clothing. Despite his many years in the military as a commander of a Chinese warship, he carried himself with the energy and poise of a civil official , and it was clear that he was a leader who commanded the respect of those around him. Whether he was making decisions for the city, representing Qingdao in negotiations, or simply greeting visitors, Shen was the epitome of a confident and capable mayor.

The men exchanged introductions and greetings, and then Tong and Yin took their guests on a tour of the factory. Yin showed them the machine he had invented, and described the manufacturing process to them, proudly explaining how they had increased productivity and kept costs low.

"I see that you and Mr. Yin are very intelligent and business-minded," said Mayor Shen to Tong afterward. "I'm so glad that your business is successful in spite of all that's going on."

"Well, we really began thriving when the boycott began," said Tong.

"I'm glad consumers have an option to buy Chinese-made needles. It was a huge accomplishment to establish the first needle factory in China," said Mayor Shen. "Many other businesses are struggling to find goods that aren't made in Japan."

Tong pursed his lips. "There should be an easier way to help businesses buy domestic goods."

"It is a real headache to find products sources that operate here in China. It would be much easier if there was a central place where businesses could go to buy Chinese-made things," mused Mayor Shen.

"It would indeed. The only commodity exchange right now is run by the Japanese. They demand high commissions and sometimes manipulate the market in favor of their own goods. We really need to establish our own Chinese commodity market."

Mayor Shen grinned. "Bright minds like yours make me hopeful for the future of this city. How about we bring this idea of yours to life?" He scanned the room, then clapped Tong's shoulder. "Come. You need to talk to the president of the Chamber of Commerce, Song Yuting."

* * * *

The next day, Tong met with Mr. Song and told him in detail about his plan. Mr. Song was also impressed with Tong's idea and agreed it would be a boon for businesses in Qingdao. They agreed they would arrange more meetings to bring the plan into fruition.

Tong also had plans about another, more modern weaving venture, a continuance of his dream in the manufacturing realm. Tong's old friend, Sun Huizhi, was working with him on it. Mr. Sun had bought one hundred and seven weaving machines in Japan and shipped them back to Qingdao. Because he used to do a lot of business there, he was able to export the machines without any problem from Japanese customs. The new weaving machines were automated to weave fabric with little supervision. They were some of the first automatic machines in China. Tong and Mr. Sun named their new company Wufu Weaving Factory.

"Well done, Brother Tong," said Mr. Sun on the day they opened the factory and started production. "I can see why everyone has such high respect for you."

"Well, I couldn't have done it without your help, Brother Sun." Tong smiled and turned to the machines. "Let's see how well they work."

The workers they'd hired pulled a few levers and pressed a few buttons. Within seconds the weaving machines came to life. The clack of metal on metal and the whir of yarn spools filled the factory.

Half an hour later, a worker came over to Tong and Mr. Sun carrying a piece of white fabric. "Here it is, boss."

The fabric was woven very tightly. Tong picked it up and felt the fabric between his fingers. It was as smooth as water. "Excellent quality."

"It was so fast, too," said Mr. Sun. "Imagine how much fabric we can make in a day."

"We'll be able to bring prices way down for our customers. This is very good for business."

Wufu Weaving Factory was the largest mechanized weaving factory in all of Qingdao. Tong was making a hefty profit from it since the low production cost kept the prices down and sales high. He was very pleased with the venture.

The earlier successful visit of the dignitaries to Qingdao Jilu Needle Factory had brought the attention of the factory's success to the citizens of Qingdao, and they were very proud of their city's leading role in manufacturing.

In the meantime, Tong and Mayor Shen continued to discuss plans for the Chinese commodity exchange. Mayor Shen secretly established an organizing committee so as not to attract the attention of the Japanese. The exchange opened in September, 1931, and it was wildly successful. Chinese businesses were booming and everyone was happy. Except, of course, the Japanese.

One day Yin rushed into Tong's office and cried, "It's terrible! The representatives at the commodity exchange were attacked."

Tong sprang up from his desk. "What? By whom?"

"I don't know." Yin huffed, out of breath from running to Tong with the bad news. "The victims reported it was some men in black."

"Do you think it's—"

"Absolutely. It must be."

Tong sighed. Just when things were starting to go right for his businesses, now there was another difficult hurdle blocking his way.

"These damn Japanese invaders can't stand that we're successful despite their unfair subsidies." Tong threw his hands in the air in disgust.

Yin scowled. "There has to be something we can do."

Tong sat back down wearily. "I'm sure we'll think of something."

It was later confirmed that the attackers were, in fact, Japanese-hired ronins who had concealed their identities with the black disguises. Tong took the attacks personally. He needed to come up with a safer place for the exchange.

After several secret meetings with colleagues, Tong decided to move the commodity exchange to Beijing Road, in the busy downtown area. Surely, the ronins wouldn't dare attack people in front of so many witnesses. The strategy turned out to be sound, and the ronin were never heard from again.

Tong and the commodity exchange committee decided to raise funds for a brand new building on Tianjin Road in Qingdao to house the exchange safely. With the money in place, they applied for government approval. The building was completed and put to use in 1933.

Tong felt great relief and happiness that everything, yes, everything was finally falling into place again.

Meanwhile, his son, Tong Fang, had grown up to be a young man. He had been studying aviation at the Central Aviation Academy in Hangzhou since 1934. While he missed Shandong and his parents, his studies at the Aviation Academy kept him busy. With this education, he was one step closer to achieving his dream of fighting the Japanese. Upon graduation, Tong Fang joined the Chinese Air Force in Hangzhou under the Nationalist government, and was posted to work at a large military air base.

At the same time, Tong seized an opportunity to import one hundred thirty sets of fabric dyeing machines from Japan, and started Liu Fu Fabric Dyeing Factory, the largest dyeing business in Qingdao. This was Tong's oldest dream. His working theory was that as long as the business was big enough, he could drive the costs down and out-compete Japanese products.

By 1937 when Tong was forty-eight years of age, he owned sig-nificant shares in the first needle factory in China, plus he owned the largest dyeing fabric factory in Qingdao, held an extensive fabric wholesale business, and was a founding member of the commodity exchange in Qingdao.

But deep down, he sometimes felt a fleeting moment of unease. In fact, in the last few years he had the growing feeling that all this success had only been loaned to him and could be taken away any time. The Japanese had occupied the whole of northeast China for several years. For a military truck to travel from the southernmost part of China the Japanese controlled, to Qingdao where Tong was, it only took a day or so. It would be so easy for the city that he loved and had transformed so much over the past few years to once again be occupied by the Japanese. It would always be painfully possible.

During the summer of 1937, Qingdao was unusually humid and

cloudy. Tong wondered if the depressing weather might be portentous of an unpredictable turnabout in the city's future.

* * * *

Tong's suspicions were unfortunately correct. On September 18, 1937, the Japanese invaded BeiPing, an offensive later known as the Marco Polo Bridge Incident, and then marched southward toward the capital of Shandong, Jinan.

As the new year dawned, unable to hide his worry, Tong tried to find a solution with Yin, or at least some solace. "What will this invasion mean for our business?" Tong wondered nervously.

"Every business in Qingdao is suffering right now, and I fear it's only going to get worse," Yin said shaking his head sadly. He looked… defeated.

Tong sensed that Yin was very troubled. "It's true. We must prepare for the worst." Searching Yin's expression, Tong braced himself for more bad news. "Do you have…a plan?"

"Yes," said Yin. "I want to sell JiLu. My wife and I are leaving next week."

Tong stared at him blankly. "You're going to…leave? For good?"

Yin waved a hand. "What other option is there?"

"We stay and fight to keep our businesses going! This is Qingdao. We belong here. Are you just going to turn your back on your city? Abandon our companies?"

"Listen, Brother Tong. What makes you think things will get any better? Or even stay the same? Do you think the Japanese will treat us well?" He scoffed. "That coward Han Fuju has run away with his forces. There's nothing left to protect us from the Japanese."

"We have a duty to protect our employees. We can't force them by closing down to either work for the Japanese or starve. We can't just abandon our workers. They rely on us so they can feed their families." Tong didn't know what else to say to keep Yin in Qingdao. The fact that Yin spoke fluent Japanese would be a huge help if the Japanese occupation dragged on.

"We have families to feed, too," Yin declared.

"We need to stay for them, too, if not for our businesses." Tong saw his words had failed to convince Yin.

"There are opportunities for business elsewhere, Brother Tong!" Yin roared, then took a moment to collect himself. "I say we burn everything down when we leave. That way there will be nothing left of this company for the Japanese to steal."

"Brother Yin!" Shocked, Tong felt stabbed in the heart by the word "burn." He stepped closer to his old friend. "I'm not leaving. I live here. This is still part of China." He took a deep breath. "What will happen if we leave? The people of our city will be forced to wear Japanese clothes and use Japanese needles. No! We must not abandon our customers or our workers."

"Brother Tong, I know this is upsetting, but think about it—"

"I have thought about it. I was born here, and whether it's the Chinese or the Germans or the Japanese in power, I will die here."

Tong felt his world start to crumble around him. He didn't know what else to do except to keep the businesses running. He was a businessman, and running his business was his only duty.

"Well," said Yin, "with that, Brother Tong, we will part ways for now. Since you aren't leaving, I won't sell my shares in JiLu. They can stay with the company." Yin held his arms out to Tong. "And now I must go." Tong wrapped his arms tightly around him for a final embrace goodbye.

Tong was shattered that his business partner was actually leaving. Yes, he realized how serious the situation was with the Japanese occupation, and he understood how risky it was to stay. But there was no choice. Not for him.

"Good luck with everything." Yin released him and held Tong's gaze. "I mean it. You must always protect yourself and your family first. The businesses only come second."

"We will meet again, brother," Tong assured him.

As Yin strode past him and out the door, Tong thought back over all their years of partnership. What would his future be like without his trusted business partner?

Yin didn't look back.

Tong watched sadly through the window as Yin crossed the street and ducked onto a rickshaw, and it gradually trotted to the end of the Dengzhou Road and disappeared from sight.

The bright afternoon sun shone through the window, casting a warm glow on his face. He gazed out, taking in the bustling city scene, trying to grasp the reality of what had just happened. People rushed along the busy street, vendors called out to customers, and carts creaked their way down the pitted road.

Tong felt a sudden knot in his chest at the thought of running the business without Mr. Yin. It all felt so…overwhelming. Despite the commotion all around him, Tong felt utterly alone, and desperately uncertain about the future.

Chapter 12 The Japanese Have Come

Qingdao, China, August 14, 1937

On August 13, 1937, Japan launched a massive attack against Shanghai, China. Miles away in the beautiful and tranquil seaside town of Qingdao, it was a summer no different from any other, except for the atmosphere of evil spirit shrouding the city. The sea wind was particularly strong, with gusts of warm air smacking dead bodies and gunpowder blown from the distant fighting.

Along with the hilly roads and stone villas left by the Germans in Qingdao was the former stately Governor's Hall, where the municipal government of the Republic of China was located. Perched on the roof on this day was a white dove. With its keen gaze it observed the people going in and out of the building, as if it was aware of the impending danger and was determined to keep the town safe. Despite the chaos and uncertainty surrounding it, the white dove held its position, ready to take flight at a moment's notice.

As Mayor Shen Honglie sat in his office ruminating over a local map of Qingdao, his brows were knitted together in deep concentration. Sitting opposite him was Public Security Bureau Chief Liao Anbang.

"Chief Liao, where do you think the Japanese will come from? From the land or the sea?"

"Mayor Shen, I think they will come from the sea." Chief Liao paused. "But I think most likely they will come from both the land and the sea."

Chief Liao's voice trembled a little but he ended his words forcefully.

Mayor Shen was surprised at Chief Liao's prediction, which was his own expectation as a graduate of the Japanese Naval Academy. "You are exactly right. Shanghai cannot be defended right now. How can Qingdao possibly be?"

"No way, especially if we are put on the defense." Liao sighed.

"How many Japanese factories are there in Qingdao? And how many Japanese?" Shen asked.

"There are over twenty major factories and about twenty thousand Japanese."

At this, Mayor Shen's mouth twisted into a sneer, his eyes narrowing with distaste.

* * * *

As a group of Japanese sailors walked down Dexian Road on that August day, a sense of unease filled the air. The road was home to the American Catholic Holy Work High School, a peaceful institution surrounded by lush greenery.

Suddenly, a figure appeared on the road ahead, causing the Japanese sailors to halt in their tracks. The figure was a sinister-looking Japanese ronin, but dressed in the uniform of a Chinese soldier. The sailors watched in horror as the ronin drew a gun from his holster and aimed it at them. With a deafening *crack* a shot was fired, and one of the sailors fell to the ground, a crimson stain spreading rapidly across his uniform. The other sailors scrambled for cover as the ronin made his escape, leaving behind the dead man.

The scene was chaotic as shocked people rushed to the side of the fallen man and the other sailors. Everyone struggled to make sense of what had just occurred. The image of the ronin in his Chinese uniform and the violence he had brought to this peaceful place would be forever burned into the memories of those who witnessed it.

"Mayor Shen," announced Chief Liao, "the Japanese military sent us an official communique threatening to invade and demanded we surrender the city. If we don't, they will invade right away. They have a fleet positioned south of Qingdao. They said—" He stopped abruptly.

"What did they say?"

"They said if we surrender, they will make you the chief commander of north China."

Shen frowned. "Tell them I am not in the office, that I have gone to Li Cun for a while. You will be entirely responsible for the defense of Qingdao. Launch a counterattack and execute the plan we discussed as soon as they invade. If they send another official notice, tell them that I will respond after I come back."

* * * *

Three days passed.

"Mayor Shen," called out Chief Liao. "The Japanese Navy has not launched an attack. Japanese Consul Nishihara Yanichi wants to see you."

"Let him come. I will meet with him here in my office."

Consul Nishihara Yanichi walked out his car and up the stairs of the old German Governor's mansion. Mayor Shen watched him from his window on the third floor.

When he arrived, Mayor Shen said in fluent Japanese, "Mr. Nishihara Yanichi, the Japanese fleet has violated Chinese territory. Why are you here?"

"Mayor Shen, with high respect, I only convey a message from the Japanese Empire. If you surrender, you would be made the highest commander of all civil affairs in northern China."

"Highest commander of all civil affairs," Mayor Shen repeated. "I do not know why you Japanese insist on imposing civil positions on me. I was admitted to the first position in the Japanese Naval Academy in 1905." He sneered. "Don't you know I have a background in the military?"

"Mayor Shen, of course, of course. It would be a pleasure for the Imperial Japanese Army to extend positions commensurate with your talent."

"Mr. Nishihara, please convey this message. I have no orders from my government to withdraw, and when I was a student in the Japanese Naval Academy no teacher taught me how to surrender. If you attack, I will do everything within my power to defend Qingdao. I mean everything." Mayor Shen looked into Nishihara's eyes through his horn-rimmed glasses with a sternness intended to cast chills down the other man's spine.

From August to December that year, the Japanese did not dare to attack Qingdao. On December 13, the Nanjing massacre occurred. At the same time, Provincial Governor Han Fuqu ordered his forces to withdraw southward and left Jinan, the capital of Shandong Province. The Japanese troops encircled Qingdao from both inland and the sea.

In mid-December, Mayor Shen ordered the preparation for the city's defense plan to be implemented, and started to evacuate the civil government to the south. On New Year's Eve, from his office window Mayor Shen took a final affectionate look at the seaside town he had administered for six years. He said calmly to Chief Liao, "I order the immediate bombing of all Japanese factories in Qingdao."

Mayor Shen then went down to his car and climbed in. As he drove away from the city, a long series of huge explosions occurred, shaking the land vehemently and quaking through the nearby sea. The rattling booms lasted for hours, echoing for miles in the industrial areas where the Japanese-owned factories were located. It was these factories the Japanese had feared would be destroyed, so they did not invade. Yet they were all lost anyway.

As his car sped away, Mayor Shen was filled with a mix of emotions. On one hand, he was proud of the bravery he had shown in ordering the bombing of the Japanese factories. On the other, he was burdened by the heavy responsibility of his decision. As the loud explosions echoed throughout the city, he couldn't help but feel a twinge of sadness at the destruction he had caused. But despite this, he remained resolute, knowing it was for the greater good of his people.

Across the city, Mr. Tong was jolted awake by the terrible sounds.

His wife sat up in bed and asked, "Have the Japanese invaded?"

Tong comforted his wife. "Not yet. It must be the Japanese spinning mills that were ordered destroyed by Mayor Shen."

As he got up and gazed out the window, he was struck by the fiery lights illuminating the night sky.

The explosions went on and on, as if to celebrate the new year in a very odd way. Tong looked out of the window again, where the sky reflected the bright lights of the resulting fires. "That is a lot of machines destroyed. The Japanese deserve it all."

As it approached midnight, the residents of Qingdao were filled with a sense of anticipation for the new year, but mixed with uncertainty and fear. Mostly fear. The memories still lingered in their minds of the Japanese invasion twenty years earlier when they had fought the Germans for control of the town. And now, as the people prepared to welcome the new year, the Japanese had returned to fight the Chinese, casting a shadow of unease over the town.

Tong could not sleep. As he gazed out at the night sky lit up by the blasts, he wondered what the future held for Qingdao. Would the Japanese seek revenge on the Chinese factories now that their own had been reduced to rubble? The thought filled him with dread as he braced himself for the uncertain days ahead. He also started to worry about his son, Tong Fang, who after graduating from the

Central Aviation Academy in Hangzhou, now served as a pilot in the Chinese Air Force.

Just a few days later, in January, 1938, Japanese warships entered the Qingdao Harbor, followed by Japanese troops marching in by land. After a sixteen-year respite, the Japanese had returned to the town they'd once taken by force from the Germans and given back to the Chinese.

This time there would be no giving it back.

* * * *

Chongqing, China, 1938

After their troops invaded Beiping (then Beijing) on July 7, 1937, the Japanese took over all of northern China. In the middle of 1938, they invaded Shanghai, after which their Air Force invaded Hangzhou.

Tong Fang sat at his desk in Chongqing, staring blankly at the paper before him. The news that had reached him was devastating. His hometown of Qingdao was lost to the Japanese. A wave of anger and frustration coursed through him as he thought of the loss and the very real possibility of his parents being in danger. Fang was filled with a burning desire for revenge, ready to take to the skies to face the enemy.

His hands tightened into fists, the veins bulging under his skin as he thought of the injustice that had been inflicted upon his home. A fierce determination was etched upon his face, reflecting the resolve in his heart to avenge the fallen and protect his loved ones. He could not shake his worry for his parents, their safety weighing heavily on his mind. He was ready for battle, his emotions a complex mix of rage, fear, and love for his hometown and family.

He stood up, the anger and frustration in his body coming alive and pulsing with a ferocious energy. He was determined to take on the enemy, to defend his home, and to bring justice to the wronged.

Ever since he heard that the Japanese had invaded Hangzhou, Tong Fang had been pleading with his commander to go into battle. He could hardly believe his ears when Commander Lu finally called his name. At last!

He was surprisingly calm as he suited up, clipped on his helmet, and climbed into the cockpit of his Hawk III, built by the American Curtiss Aeroplane and Motor Company. It was the best fighter plane in China at that time. He proudly taxied out, took off, and soared into the air, following the rest of the planes into battle.

His radio crackled to life, and the staticky voice of Commander Lu sounded in his cockpit. "Tong Fang, can you hear me?"

"I can hear you, Commander," said Fang. His heart was pounding in his ears with excitement.

"Good. Do you see the enemy fighter plane approaching on your left side?"

"Yes, Commander."

"I'm sending you and Airman Jia after it. He'll attack first from the left, then you'll come in on the right. Just as we practiced."

"Got it, Commander."

"Good. Airman Jia will go on my signal. Go get 'em."

After a few moments, Fang heard Commander Lu order Airman Jia to attack. Jia's plane soared through the air, and Fang banked to follow after. Suddenly, a flash shot out from the Japanese plane. Airman Jia's plane canted to one side, then start falling to earth in a slow spiral. Fang didn't have time to think about what Airman Jia must be feeling as he fell to his death. The Japanese plane was centered in the crosshairs of Fang's gun. He pulled the trigger.

A direct hit!

The Japanese plane exploded before him. He felt no emotion when he saw a dark, limp, mass eject from the cockpit and soar through the sky.

Commander Lu came on the radio and ordered him back to base.

"Aye, Commander."

Despite the loss of his friend, Fang felt only excitement. He was finally getting back at those bastards! Finally, he had started to fulfill his destiny.

Fang continued flying successful sortis for the next few months, gaining a lot of respect from his fellow airmen and his superiors. But his personal victories were not enough to fend off the Japanese troops. The Chinese troops retreated, and Fang moved to an air force unit in Chongqing, then the capital of China under Chiang Kai-shek.

* * * *

One day, Commander Lu called Tong Fang into his office.

"I have a new assignment for you. One that doesn't take place on a battlefield."

Fang was surprised, but ready for anything. "What do you need me to do, Commander?"

"Your father's in the fabric business, correct? I hear he makes some of the finest fabrics in the country."

Fang was proud that his father's importance was recognized by such a high-ranking officer. "Yes, that's right, Sir."

"General Chennault and our American friends need fabric blood chits printed to give his men so the local citizens can easily identify injured American pilots when they ask for help." Commander Lu pulled out a piece of cloth from his desk drawer and showed it to Fang. "Here's our prototype. We need them to look something like this."

The prototype blood chit showed a large flag of the Republic of China with a few words identifying the pilot as American and instructing civilians to help him, promising a reward if they did so.

"We need the ink to be waterproof and insoluble, so it won't wash away if the pilot lands in water. Does this sound like something your father can handle?"

Fang knew for certain that his father would be up to any task to help fight the Japanese. "Of course, Commander. I will write to him about it."

Commander Lu smiled and shook his hand. "Excellent. Oh, one thing about your letter, Tong Fang." He leaned in and lowered his voice. "We are very lucky to have our postal system still intact, but I still worry about the Japanese getting their hands on our letters."

"Of course, Commander," said Fang, understanding immediately.

"This is top secret information, and we don't want this getting into the wrong hands."

"I'll think of something," said Fang. "And take care of it right away, Commander."

* * * *

Qingdao, China, 1938

These days, Mr. Tong was busy figuring out the accounts for his companies and preparing to make some difficult decisions about the future of his businesses. More and more Japanese had started moving to Qingdao. He had heard in private discussions with other business owners that the Japanese were going around forcing local companies to sell to them. So, when a battalion of Japanese soldiers stormed into his factory with their rifles and bayonets and demanded to speak with him, he was not surprised.

Zhao Qi, the newly installed Japanese mayor of Qingdao, led the way, all the while interpreting for the Japanese.

One of the Japanese soldiers directed a loud statement at Tong, after which Mayor Zhao turned to him and said, "Mr. Tong, I am from Yie County, you are from Chang Yi County. We are both fellow citizens from Shandong. The Japanese now want to implement three ways to work with the local Chinese businesses they have selected. First through cooperation, second through joint venture, and third through sale. They like your needle factory and want to buy your business."

Tong smiled. "Brother Zhao— Oh, no, I mean Mayor Zhao. Didn't you go to Germany to study German? How come you've started to speak Japanese? Do you learn to speak the language of whoever is in power? Did the Japanese soldiers lead you here today, or did you lead them?"

"Hey, my dear brother Tong! Look at what time it is. Are you still in the mood for joking?" Mayor Zhao looked awkward and helpless. "They led me here, okay? Is that okay with you? I don't speak Japanese, but there is only so much to know about their policy. We all understand what's what, right? They don't understand Chinese for sure." Zhao Qi approached Tong. "Do you think I want to play this role? I have no other choice." He waved a hand. "I am not talking with you about this. But I will ask you a favor. Just work with me and you will make both our lives a lot easier."

"No, I will keep my business." Tong said coldly, turning his head aside. "In no way do I want to be a traitor and collaborate with the Japanese. I'd rather be smashed jade than a tile kept whole."

The Japanese soldiers took a step closer, their weapons clanging.

"Please, Brother Tong," said Mayor Zhao. "These soldiers don't understand what I am saying. Think about this. We Chinese have an old saying: A hero does not take a direct hit that he can avoid. Think. You sell the businesses, but you still manage them and everybody still has their rice bowls in hand and can feed their families. Where is the Chinese government now? Nationalist, Communist, or whoever it is, it doesn't matter. If people like you and me don't stand out and do a little bit to keep a balance between these bastards and our fellow Chinese, who will? It is our duty!"

"Mayor Zhao, give me another reason why I should." Tong said.

"Isn't one reason enough? These bastards can tear us into pieces. Listen, I don't like my position here. First it was the Germans, now the Japanese. I know I won't leave behind a great name when I'm gone. But the Japanese will go on robbing, and we Chinese have to live today! This is about more than you," Mayor Zhao said emphatically. "Think of your employees at least! They will be jobless when you are gone. The Japanese will simply take over your factory and ship three hundred Japanese ronins to run the factory." Mayor Zhao sighed. "When the war is over, I swear to God my only interest will be compiling a local history for Qingdao. Brother Tong, I will keep an entry for you as the first Chinese who imported Japanese machinery for machine dyeing in China, which you rightfully deserve. Is that good enough?"

A Japanese soldier shouted something at Mayor Zhao. The mayor looked at him in shock, then shouted something back. He turned to Tong. "Listen, we're running out of time. Negotiate with them. Let's not ask for trouble."

Tong turned to his friend. "Accountant Liu, how much profit margin are we making?"

"Twenty percent."

Tong turned back to Mayor Zhao. "How about we allow the Japanese to just use my three businesses, but get five percent of the profits?"

"I can try asking," said Mayor Zhao.

He said something to the Japanese. To Tong's surprise, they burst into laughter.

"They want more than five percent," said Mayor Zhao. He lowered his voice to a whisper, "Give them more."

Tong looked at Accountant Liu. "Ten percent?"

"Ten percent would still be fine for us," Liu agreed.

Mayor Zhao went back and forth with the Japanese for a while. Finally, he turned back to Tong. "They accept your proposal for the other two factories, but they still want to buy the needle factory."

"Why the needle factory?" Tong asked, though he knew damn well why. JiLu had the best technology of all needle factories. Mr. Yin had worked hard developing those machines.

"Because your machines are the best in the country, even better than Japanese technology. You know that, Mr. Tong."

Tong shook his head. "Unfortunately I cannot sell you JiLu because I am not the exclusive shareholder. The other major shareholder, Yin Zhizhong, went to southeast Asia for business. Tell them they can buy the other two factories I solely own. They can buy them at six times the earnings because those factories have the best weaving machines available. For JiLu, I can't sell them any shares because I don't have the authority without the agreement of the other shareholders. However, after the first ten percent profit is distributed among the existing shareholders, the Japanese can get ten percent profit."

After conversing with Mayor Zhao for several minutes, most of the Japanese soldiers finally left Tong's office, while the officers stayed behind to deal with the paperwork. Tong reluctantly signed away Liu Fu and his other retail business, and wrote up the profit share in Qingdao Jilu Needle Factory.

"One more thing," said Mayor Zhao. "They want you to be part of the Security Maintenance Committee."

Tong hiked his brows. "What does that committee do?"

"You would be representing the local businesses to the Japanese," Zhao said, not exactly answering the question.

"Why would I want to be on it?" Tong asked suspiciously.

"Well, the invaders can force you to, for one. It also pays handsomely."

"I can't accept any payment, and I don't want to join the committee.

But I can bring the concerns of Qingdao Fabric Business to them, I guess."

Mayor Zhao smiled. "I'll let them know." He started heading toward the remaining Japanese soldiers, then turned back and said, "You're doing the right thing, Mr. Tong. For now, at least. Thank you for keeping Qingdao safe. Remember, it's now illegal to do business in areas not controlled by the Japanese."

* * * *

One day, Tong received a letter from Tong Fang, but when he opened it up there was only a short message.

Father,

I really miss the dumplings Mother used to make for me. They were so delicious, especially when dipped in vinegar.

Tong was very confused. Did Fang really send a letter all this way just to say he missed his mother's dumplings? He saw that the paper was a little wrinkled, as though it had been wet. He thought of the vinegar Fang mentioned in his letter. As an expert in dyeing fabric, Tong knew that heat made acids change color. He held the paper up to the candle flame to see better.

He watched the writing appear before his eyes.

Dear Father,

I'm so glad you figured out how this invisible ink works! This letter contains an order directly from the military, so I wanted to make sure it wouldn't be seen by Japanese eyes.

We need some blood chits printed for our American allies in the Flying Tigers. Since you are a prominent figure in the fabric dyeing business, my

*commander requested your expertise to make these blood chits. Specific
instructions are enclosed.*

Hope all is well in Qingdao.

Your dear son,

Tong Fang

Tong glanced at the instructions. He knew exactly what had to be
done.

The following day, he notified three of his most trustworthy workers
about the plan. First, they needed to formulate an ink that was durable
enough to hold up to water. Then they needed to figure out a way to
hide the printing until it was shipped to Chongqing. They decided to
print the designs of the blood chit with an oil-based ink that could not
be washed away. Then they would dye the fabric with a vinegar-based
dye that would cover up the designs but could be removed with heat
at the Chongqing air base before distribution.

To make things even more difficult, this all had to be done while the
factory was in Japanese hands. Every day, Japanese soldiers patrolled
the factory keeping a close eye on the manufacturing process. Tong
decided to mark this project as fabric for retail stores, and thankfully
it flew under their radar. Tong wrote a letter back to Fang.

Dear Son,

I have received your letter. The vinegar trick was very smart!

*The order is being processed. We had to create some new inks to hide the
designs from the Japanese. They have seized the company and patrol the
factory every day.*

*I have enclosed instructions on how to reveal the designs on the blood
chits when they are delivered. Please share them with your commander.*

*Mother and I miss you very much. Remember this, son. Fighting the
enemy is your duty as a soldier. We are proud of you every day.*

Father

* * * *

Chongqing, China, 1938

In Chongqing, Tong Fang was called into Commander Lu's office after his English class.

"We've received the blood chits from your father, Tong Fang," said Commander Lu. "We've successfully processed them, and they're exactly what we need."

Tong Fang was proud of his father's work. "Very good, Commander. I'm glad I could be of help."

"We have another special assignment for you. We would like you to personally deliver the blood chits to General Chennault and his troops. After you deliver them, you will stay there and work with the Americans."

Tong Fang's chest swelled with pride. "Yes, Commander."

* * * *

Kunming, China, 1938

Before he knew it, Tong Fang was entering the barracks of Kunming and greeting the Flying Tigers, a battalion of around one hundred pilots and crewmen recruited from the American Navy, Marines, and Air Force. They were the best and brightest, so were paid three times more than ordinary U.S. soldiers.

The first man he met was tall with short black hair and smiling eyes. "Tim Nolan." He offered his hand. "I'm from Seattle."

"Tong Fang." Fang shook his hand. "I'm from Qingdao."

"Seattle?" a brown-haired man with tan skin said. "I'm also from Washington."

"Oh, really?" The two men shook hands. "It really is a small world."

"I'm Chuck," the second man said to Tim and Fang.

They exchanged greetings.

"So, what brings you here, Chuck?" Tim asked him.

"Well, I'm recently divorced. Made a lot of mistakes, so I'm trying to forget about things back home."

"You will soon, I'm sure," said Tim. "I was a retired army officer, but got recruited for this opportunity. What about you?"

Chuck smiled. "Chennault was my former commander. How about you, Tong Fang?"

"My father is in the fabric business in Qingdao. He printed your blood chits. I was sent here to deliver them, then to stay and work with you Americans."

"You must be so proud of your dad."

"I am," said Fang, beaming.

* * * *

Tong Fang and the rest of the Flying Tigers attended a meeting led by General Chennault. His cheekbones were so sharp they appeared sculpted. He looked very intimidating, and his gaze sent a chill down Fang's spine.

General Chennault surveyed everyone in the room and spoke firmly. "At ease, men. Today we welcome those who have traveled thousands of miles from Burma to Kunming to join the American Flying Tigers. Welcome."

The room burst into applause.

"I will give you this lecture now, and will repeat it whenever I have the chance. When engaging Japanese fighters in the air, do not let them get behind you. They are extremely skilled pilots and any regular maneuvers will not work on them. What you need to do is climb very quickly then do a slow nose dive to shoot. That way you are always behind or above them, and their aircraft is always within your sights. Remember this. Your lives depend on it!"

The men in the room nodded somberly.

A young man piped up, "Sir, how far do we pursue the Japanese fighters?"

"Great question. Don't pursue them too long. Just far enough to get them away from the battlefield." General Chennault glanced at Tong Fang. "Actually, now is a good time to talk about this. In the event that you are forced down and not able to return to base, you need to show a blood chit to the locals to identify yourself as a friendly. Tong Fang here was sent from Chongqing to work with us, and he brought us the blood chits. Tong Fang, could you please stand?"

Fang stood up and saluted all the men. He opened the bulky package and pulled out a blood chit to show the soldiers. "My name is Tong Fang, and I serve with the Chinese National Air Force in Chongqing. My father owns a fabric printing factory and made these for us, even though his business is under Japanese control. He asked me to thank you for helping the Chinese fight our common enemy."

The men clapped again.

Fang continued, "These blood chits are washable and will not lose their colors. We have two for each pilot. Your own code is woven onto the back of the fabric. If you are lost, find the local civilians and show them this code to identify yourself."

"What does it say in English?" asked Tim Nolan.

"Below the national flag of the Republic of China, the Chinese characters say, 'This foreigner has come to China to help in the war effort. Soldiers and civilians, one and all, have a duty to rescue and protect him.'"

As Fang passed out the blood chits, one by one the soldiers thanked him. Fang was so proud his father had done this. Not only was he supporting the efforts of the Chinese, but he was also saving American soldiers' lives.

Chapter 13 The Chinese Surveillance

eijing, China, present day
The phone rang in the office of the Tang Shengli, the vice chairman of the Chinese Military Commission, located in the Chinese naval headquarters at the Ministry of National Defense in Beijing.

Vice Chairman Tang picked up the phone. "Yes?"

"Vice Chairman Tang, this is Li Yan from the Jiuquan military satellite monitoring unit. Our military surveillance satellite has captured photos showing that American-built destroyers are currently en route to Taiwan, and they are carrying W-3 bombers onboard."

"Go on," Vice Chairman Tang prodded.

"Based on these actual images, we are certain these W-3 bombers and destroyers now being shipped to Taiwan are materially different from and greatly exceed the value that was publicly announced by the U.S. when the sale was made. We believe it is impossible for the equipment in the photos to be worth only $4.5 billion as they stated in their public declaration of value. We have asked our military attaché in Washington D.C. to try and confirm our suspicions."

Tang took a moment to digest this potentially alarming news. "How many units are shown on the photos?"

"So far, we've seen ten W-3 bombers and ten destroyers. That's enough strike power to equip an entire new navy's stealth attack capability."

Hearing that, Vice Chairman Tang frowned. "Please do not disclose this information to anyone else yet. Treat it as Level One confidentiality. Have the attaché confirm the data and send me his report as soon as possible."

Tang walked over to the military map on the wall and studied it, quickly assessing the situation. China's newest aircraft carrier was currently being dispatched to monitor the situation around Huangyan Island, a hotly disputed territory between China and the Philippines. These twenty new W-3 bombers and destroyers being shipped to Taiwan's navy would drastically increase their offensive ability, which would in turn significantly impact the military balance throughout the Taiwan Strait. China's People's Liberation Army Navy would never launch an attack on Taiwan, due to probable U.S. interference, but with these additional munitions, if Taiwan initiated an offensive against China, he questioned whether the PLAN forces along the southern coast could withstand the attack using their dated conventional weaponry.

Tang's heart sank at the thought, but he gradually calmed down as he gazed out the window at the tranquil scene of Beijing at night, a city filled with twinkling neon lights. "After all, what country willingly goes to war these days?" he murmured hopefully to his empty office. Other than Russia, of course, but they weren't involved.

He turned to stare at a red phone on the corner of his desk, which he had used only twice in the last ten years. The first time was when a U.S. surveillance airplane was forced to land on Hainan Island, the second time was when U.S. bombers bombed the Chinese embassy in Yugoslavia.

Three weeks later, he picked up the phone for the third time.

"Yes, Vice Chairman Tang?" said Chairman Fu, the Chinese president and chairman of the Chinese Central Military Commission.

"Chairman Fu, I want to report that our military satellite monitoring surveillance has detected a large number of destroyers currently en route to Taiwan. We believe the shipment is part of the arms sale to Taiwan recently announced by the U.S."

"I see. You mean the $4.5 billion worth of weaponry, right?"

"Yes, but we've calculated the actual value of this weaponry to be much greater than was announced."

Tang frowned. "How much more?"

"We believe ten times more."

Despite Tang being skeptical of all announcements by the U.S., he was still shocked. "Ten times more? What weaponry is involved?"

"Ten destroyers and ten W-3 bombers. Our military attaché in D.C. is investigating the discrepancy."

"If what you believe is true, combined with Taiwan's conventional weaponry, this new shipment from the U.S. will mean Taiwan's military capability will exceed that of our own South Sea Fleet. Is that correct?"

"Yes."

"I'm surprised because the U.S. has never before sold W-3 bombers to anyone. These bombers are not meant for defensive purposes but are designed as offensive weapons, are they not?"

"Yes. They have extremely high stealth capabilities and can fly from Taipei to Beijing in just two hours without any radar detection."

Tang chewed on that for a moment, then said, "To be honest, I am not too worried about Taiwan. But with our brewing conflict with Japan over Diaoyu Island, and our problems with the Philippines over Huangyan Island still escalating, I fear that a strengthened Taiwanese naval fleet and air force will mean China won't have the military dominance needed to deal with all our potential issues at the same time, if they all blow up at once. What if Taiwan takes sides against us?"

"Chairman Fu, your assessment is correct."

"How did this happen? Did the United States outright lie to us?"

"Well, the value they announced was $4.5 billion, but that is clearly not correct."

"So they lied to the whole world?"

"It would appear so. But I honestly don't know, Chairman Fu. Our attaché will find out the truth."

"Please confirm this information as soon as possible and revise the emergency contingency plans in the South China Sea and Taiwan Strait accordingly. Prepare to give a detailed report at the meeting of the Central Military Commission in two weeks. The U.S. is having a hard time economically, so I'm sure they need the sale to go through. But this is desperate, even for them! And it will cause unexpected consequences. Or… Do you think they may have something up their sleeve?"

Chapter 14 The Crisis In The Making

Somewhere in Cuba

José Fernandez carefully tucked a hospital blanket under his brother Juan's shoulder. In the background, the doctors and nurses were discussing Juan's medical report and the life monitor was pulsing with a soft *beep*.

At the movement, Juan weakly turned his head and slowly opened his eyes. He caught sight of the photo on the bedside table featuring him in his former uniform shaking hands with Russian General Secretary Leonid Khrushchev. The photo was taken about four decades ago, when Juan was still a colonel in the Cuban army.

Juan reached for the picture and José and moved it closer, whispering with a low and forceful voice, "Remember we won the Bay of Pigs. We were victorious over the Americans!"

Juan's eyes sparkled as he fixed his gaze upon the picture of Khrushchev.

José felt a tear slide down his cheeks as he took Juan's hand, which held the picture tightly. "We secured peace for Cuba for forty-four years, brother."

Juan's eyes flicked to him. "It was the Cuban people who won," he insisted hoarsely.

* * * *

The image of Khrushchev blurred as the memory of that day swept over Juan…

"Chairman Khrushchev, we are not afraid of these American bullies or a nuclear threat," Juan asserted. "As a matter of fact, let us build the launch pad right here in Cuba. That way the reach of your missiles will extend to all of the United States, covering anywhere between Seattle to New York."

"Juan," Khrushchev cautioned, "that would irritate the Americans and could easily cause a nuclear war."

"No, *they* are causing the nuclear war. Look what they have done in Turkey and Italy already. The missiles there would destroy your potential for a second strike. They are the ones changing the status quo. All we need to do is build it first, then we can bargain for them to switch gears."

Khrushchev frowned. "Comrade Hernandez, do you think I rose through the ranks to become the General Secretary of the Soviet just because I know how to bang shoes on a conference desk? We are dealing with a situation where any miscalculation or wrong signal could lead to the complete destruction of mankind."

"Comrade Khrushchev, we lost one hundred seventy-eight Cuban lives in the invasion of the Bay of Pigs. We captured fifteen hundreds of the enemy, and that is a great humiliation for the American imperialists. They will not stop there. They know our dear comrades in the great Soviet Union will be helping us, so their strategy is to attack Cuba. We have to match tactics with tactics. Otherwise they will gain the upper hand, and once they do they will always have it. All I need is three months, Comrade Khrushchev. This summer, with your engineers and my people, we will build the missile launch pad."

"Comrade Hernandez, it is not just some high ranking Soviet officials standing behind you, it's the entire people of the Soviet willing to give their all to secure long term peace in Cuba."

* * * *

Juan drifted back to the present and his gaze fell onto another photo on the nightstand. In it, his former fiancée Amelia looked back at him sweetly. It was also taken forty years ago, when she was in her twenties. Those were their halcyon days.

He closed his eyes. How much he had loved her. Despite her intended betrayal…

"Amelia, did the Americans send you here to kill me?" Tucked in their bed, Juan held her in his arms. "I know I owe you a lot." He bit his lip. "But my compassion and love for my country is greater than my love for you. I know you hate me because you love me more. I don't have any way to make it up to you here in this life, but if it makes you feel any better, you can get even by pulling this trigger. Go ahead and do it. At least it will make the Americans happy." He opened the nightstand drawer, took out a pistol, and handed to her, "Here. It's fully loaded."

She took the pistol and pointed it at him. "It's true. I do hate you, Juan," she said. "You destroyed my life. When they asked me to do it, I truly thought I hated you enough to kill you." A cascade of tears rolled down her cheeks.

After a long, silent moment, they looked at each other as if they had never met before.

"But I do not have the heart…to do it." She dabbed her tears and put the gun back in the drawer, then hugged him tightly. After an intense kiss, they both fell asleep embraced in each other's arms.

Juan gave a start and woke from the memory. With a brief, focused thought he whispered, "Carlos! Carlos… C-call the Chinese."

* * * *

Beijing, China

Two weeks later, Chinese Central Military Commission Conference was brought to order.

At the head of the table, Chairman Fu wore a stern face as he asked the military leaders present, "Tell me, what is going on with the U.S. arms shipment to Taiwan?"

Vice Chairman Tang said, "For those of you who do not know, we learned about this grave U.S. deception thanks to our excellent military satellite surveillance. Yesterday, the information was confirmed by our attaché in Washington D.C."

"What deception?" one of the other leaders asked.

"It's about the value of the shipment. With arms sales, the U.S. usually releases a brief stating exactly how much weaponry will be shipped and what the value is, so all countries are informed and don't get nervous. But they just released a new brief about the shipment, and the value given for the sale was ten times higher than what had previously been announced."

Chairman Fu focused on his chief military strategist. "If we end up fighting a full-blown war with the Philippines about Nansha Islands, at the same time fighting another with the Japanese over Diaoyu Tai, do we have enough coverage for Taiwan as well?"

His cheek twitching, the general lowered his head. "The math is very simple. Not enough. Not unless nuclear weapons are deployed."

"This is a serious breach of the Three Joint Communiqués agreed upon by the U.S. and China at the start of our diplomatic relationship." Chairman Fu looked down the table at his minister of foreign affairs. "You must immediately lodge a strong Chinese protest with the U.S. government." Fu groaned. "How can we make the Americans withdraw the sale of these warships and W-3 bombers?"

The minister of foreign affairs responded after a pause, "Sun Tzu tells us we should subdue the enemy without going to war. Therefore let us launch a threat against them. As long as it is credible, it should have the desired effect. When was the last time the United States was actually threatened?"

"What kind of threat do you mean, exactly?" asked Chairman Fu.

Apparently the minister had no idea what that might be. He looked stumped.

However, Vice Chairman Tang did have an idea. He cleared his throat and said, "Well, the military attaché in our embassy in Cuba recently reported that the Cuban government wishes to cooperate with us on mutual defense initiatives..."

Chapter 15 The Witness to Murder

ashington, D.C.

On the other side of the world, Mike Nolan fidgeted in bed that same night unable to sleep. He could never have imagined that he would witness an actual murder. Let alone one being committed seven thousand miles away, thanks to an unscheduled video chat.

A thousand questions swirled through his mind.

Who was the murderer? And why kill Wang Ping? Was it a hitman hired by Yan Chemical? And if so how did Yan Chemical know of Ping's tip to the U.S. Department of Commerce? The only answer he could come up with was that someone working at DOC must be in Yan Chemical's pocket.

Mike tried not to think about how his own interests—or even his life—might be affected. It was a *murder.* For the hundredth time he asked himself if he should report it to law enforcement. But why go to the trouble? The local cops would just send him on his way. And the FBI had no jurisdiction in China. Maybe the CIA would be a better option because it dealt with foreign intelligence.

But wait. Why would Yan Chemical want to get rid of Wang Ping? All the records of the antidumping proceedings may already be gone, or soon would be, because at the end of every antidumping investigation, all records under the custody of attorneys are required to be destroyed.

Besides according to the Department of Commerce regulations, Wang Ping's whistle-blowing would have been useless by now, because the duties had already been assigned.

So what other motive could someone have to want Ping dead? Because his murder was clearly a targeted hit, not some random robbery gone wrong.

Maybe Ping had been involved in some conspiracy beyond Mike's understanding.

He needed to gather his thoughts and chart out the best thing to do. He took out his iPhone and sent Heather a quick message.

Mike: Heather, I have a weird feeling about the dumping case. If something bad ever happens to me, I've saved some relevant files to a virtual server with a login and passcode. I'll give them to you tomorrow.

The next morning, he went to work as usual. In the elevator, he tried very hard to remember all the details of everything that had happened in the last few months, hoping to find a clue.

The news on the elevator's TV screen distracted him. It was showing a clip of the president giving an early White House press statement. "In August, I directed the United States Trade Representative to investigate China's laws, policies, practices, and actions and determine if any may be unreasonable or discriminatory, or if any may be harming American intellectual property rights, innovation, or technology development. During its investigation, the Office of the United States Trade Representative consulted with the appropriate advisory committees and the interagency section 301 Committee. The Trade Representative has advised me that the investigation supports the following findings. First, China has restrictions against foreign ownership, including joint venture requirements, equity limitations, and other investment restrictions, in order to require or pressure technology transfer from U.S. companies to Chinese entities."

The president listed the committee's second, third, and fourth findings.

Then he went on, "I have therefore given the following directive: The Trade Representative is to take all appropriate measures to address the official Chinese acts, policies, and practices that are unreasonable or discriminatory and burden or restrict U.S. commerce. The Trade Representative shall consider whether such action should include increased tariffs on goods from China. The Trade Representative shall publish a proposed list of products and any intended tariff increases within fifteen days of the date of this memorandum."

Mike hurried out of the elevator. The president's orders had reminded him of the accounting record Ping had mentioned during their first meeting in China. Mike went straight to the Williamson & Gray administrative proprietary office and quickly searched the shelves for the case folder on Yan Chemical. Yes! There it was. Luckily it hadn't yet been destroyed.

He pulled the accounting files out of the case folder. Some niggling instinct was telling him to make copies of all the financial and production information reported by the Yan Chemical accountants— the figures that Wang Ping had said were fraudulent. He got out his phone and swiftly took photos of the relevant files. The last one caught his attention. It was an export license application to the U.S. State Department by Swift Industries, seeking to export a host of weaponry to Taiwan, including W-3 bombers and destroyers.

Mike was puzzled and read it twice, thinking he must have misread. But no, that's what it was.

Which was very strange. Why was an application from Swift Industries in the Yan Chemical case folder? As he flipped through the pages, he heard footsteps fast approaching in the corridor. Just as the doorknob started to turn, Mike spotted a figure of $45 billion on the Swift export license application.

The door opened, and Patrick stood in front of him.

"Hi, Mike," Patrick said, his gaze flicking to the file Mike was holding.

"Hi, Patrick."

"Is that the Swift export license file?"

"Swift? No, I'm sorting out the Yan Chemical case folder to ensure all the files are destroyed."

"Ah. Very good. My secretary seems to have misplaced a file that really should belong in my safe."

"I'm sure it'll turn up. I'll be heading back to my office now," Mike said calmly. He left the room with the file under his arm. He could feel Patrick staring at him from behind. Back in his office, he quickly took photos of the export application.

His cell phone rang. It was Heather.

"What's this text about that you sent last night?"

"Can we meet for lunch at the sandwich shop on 15th and K Street to talk about it?"

"Sure. I can be there in fifteen minutes."

Luckily, Patrick's secretary had already left for lunch. So on his way out, Mike slipped the Swift file under some papers on her desk. He then headed down the street toward the sandwich shop. But not before noticing that Patrick was watching him through his office window.

When Mike got to the casual restaurant, Heather was already seated at a table waiting for him.

He slid into the seat across from her. "Heather, I need to be careful not to violate the attorney's ethical rules by saying something to you that I shouldn't."

"Oka-ay," she said uncertainly.

He handed her a note. "This is the URL, username, and password for an online server. I uploaded several documents and a copy of a...video. They may be important for a situation I find myself in. Please promise not to read the documents, and just give the access code to the appropriate authorities."

Heather had been watching him earnestly and listening attentively. "What kind of video?" she asked. "Not details, just…" She blinked, searching for what to say.

He saved her the trouble. "Last night I saw a murder with my own eyes. While I was video chatting with Wang Ping—The Sanwen Chemical accountant I met in China last year—Well, he was stabbed to death. Right there, live on my computer screen."

"What?" she gasped, covering her mouth to muffle a cry of shock.

"Ping had just told me he'd written to the Department of Commerce about Yan Chemical's accounting fraud in the dumping investigation."

"You think he was *murdered* because of that?" She looked aghast.

"I'm not sure, but if that was the reason there may be a problem."

"Like what?"

"The investigation is closed and all records will be destroyed by the time the DOC has an opportunity to question the accounting. So there is really nothing that can affect the final duty rates of Yan Chemical, even if there was fraud involved."

"True. But what about the murder? What do you plan to do about that?"

He shook his head. "Not sure. But I think I should tell someone in law enforcement."

"Mike."

"Yes?"

"I have a feeling this situation could get really dangerous. I want you to be very careful."

"I will. But I'm thinking it may be more dangerous if I *don't* do anything."

They held each other's eyes for a long moment.

"Okay," she said at length. "Who do you want to talk to first?"

* * * *

Deep inside the J. Edgar Hoover FBI building, a wall-mounted TV monitor was on in the office of Supervisory Special Agent Frank Wallace of the FBI Criminal Investigation Division. Frank glanced up from behind his desk as a CNN anchorwoman announced, "The Chinese government lodged a serious protest against the U.S. yesterday for giving false information in the press release announcing a weapons sale to Taiwan. China accused the U.S. of deliberately understating the value of twenty destroyers and W-3 bombers, which they claim are worth ten times the stated figure. The Chinese Foreign Minister summoned U.S. Ambassador Walker to meet with Chairman Fu to explain the so-called lie. This marks the lowest point in the Sino-American diplomatic relationship since the end of the Cold—"

Frank hit the off button on the remote and turned his attention to his visitor, who was slumped in his chair, looking dog tired. Frank got up and poured them both a cup of coffee.

"The CID doesn't get involved in low-level crime," he told Mike Nolan. "We deal with the bigger stuff—criminal enterprise, public corruption, financial and violent crimes, for example. With priority given to anything that poses a threat to our national security, including globalized crime. Since the murder you reported involves underlying international and financial issues, it's of interest to us. Did you actually have a recording of the murder?"

"Yes. On my laptop at home," Mike said after taking a long sip of coffee. "And probably in the cloud, since the hard drive is backed up every day."

"The story you described is obviously complex," Frank said. "We will follow up with the Chinese authorities through Interpol."

Mike said, "Sounds good. If there is anything I can do, please let me know."

"There's one thing." Frank set down his cup untouched. "Who do you think benefits from Mr. Wang's death? Someone involved in the antidumping investigation?"

"Yan Chemical," said Mike. "Mr. Wang told me he had evidence of fraudulent accounting by Yan Chemical that led to their lucrative zero antidumping rate."

"I see. What about the original petitioner, Ohio Chemical? Do they benefit?" Frank probed.

"Not really. If Mr. Wang's accusation jeopardizes Yan Chemical's zero duty status, Ohio Chemical would be thrilled. They're the ones who opened the case, wanting to have high duties levied against the competing foreign exporters."

"Which side does your firm represent?"

"Williamson & Gray represents Yan Chemical."

Frank nodded slowly. "So your firm benefits as well from Wang Ping's death."

Mike's eyebrows flickered. "Well...I suppose so."

* * * *

When their meeting concluded, Mike left the office feeling relieved. He'd done the right thing, and felt a weight lifted. He glanced back and found SSA Wallace watching him, deep in thought. Mike lifted a hand and waved goodbye, and Frank waved back robotically.

On his way home, Mike thought about the questions SSA Wallace had asked him and realized they were perfectly on target. Wallace had caught on quickly. So quickly that Mike felt a tinge of anxiety—or possibly fear—that the fed would anticipate every step, way ahead of anywhere Mike might go with his own investigation. When that thought arose, he mulled it over for a moment, but in the end he was just relieved he'd found an ally who could help him find the truth—

and perhaps keep him safe so he could fulfill his everyday duties as an attorney.

Mike opened the door to his apartment, turned on the lights, and stopped dead in his tracks.

Holy Toledo.

Nothing a single thing in the room was where it had been that morning when he left. His apartment had been totally ransacked. Which was putting it mildly. It looked as though a herd of water buffalo had charged through the living room and kitchen, bulldozing everything in sight. Plates, silverware, and all the contents of the kitchen cabinets were strewn across the kitchen floor. His computer desk was turned upside down and the drawer had been emptied on the carpet. The coffee table's glass top was smashed, with shards of glass all over the living room. The couch had been cut open, its stuffing scattered everywhere.

He couldn't believe what he was seeing.

He gingerly walked through the broken glass to look for his laptop. He lifted the desk and looked under it, finding nothing but papers. The computer was gone.

Damn. Not good. *Very* not good.

When he realized the ramifications of the stolen laptop, he dropped the table and ran to the bedroom, only to see that his briefcase was also missing. Everything else in the room had been tossed. The bathroom was the same—broken mirror, toiletries thrown everywhere.

As he was taking in the damaged bathroom, he suddenly realized he'd never checked to see if the burglar was still there. His pulse quickened.

He heard a sound coming from the living room and instinctively grabbed a pointed and very sharp six-inch piece of broken mirror after wrapping a washcloth around one end so he wouldn't be cut. He crept slowly out of the bathroom and around the corner…just in time to see a drinking glass roll off the kitchen counter.

False alarm. *Thank God.* Relief surged through him knowing the thief was not still lurking somewhere in his home…possibly carrying a lethal ice pick.

His mind slid automatically into survival mode. He couldn't stay in his apartment any longer. The mess had been created by someone who'd specifically targeted his laptop and briefcase. There were other things in the apartment worth far more than those two items, but the thief didn't take anything else. It was obvious that if the thief, or whoever had hired him, didn't find what they were looking for on the laptop or in the briefcase, they would come back—this time for *him*.

He grabbed a suitcase and threw in clothes and personal items willy-nilly. He had to get out of the apartment as soon as possible. He probably wouldn't be coming back. Oh, well. He didn't need half the stuff he owned anyway.

As he dug through the remains of his closet for his favorite shirt, he was reminded of the Rudyard Kipling line, *He travels fastest who travels alone.* It was the perfect epigraph for this stepping-off point. He would be running toward a world he knew nothing of, into one where he didn't want to go—uncharted territory.

His first step was to find a place to stay that night that was both safe and secret.

His cell phone rang as he was zipping his suitcase closed.

"Mike?" said Heather when he hesitantly answered.

"Thank goodness it's you! You called just in time."

"What's going on? Is anything wrong?"

He told her about his visit to the FBI, then coming home to find his place looking like it had been ground zero for an atom bomb test.

"My God. What are you going to do?"

"I don't know, I haven't thought that far ahead yet," he admitted.

"Let's start with now, right now. What are you going to do *right now,* after you get off the phone with me?"

"Well, I just packed my stuff. I'm going to get out of here and go… I'm not sure where. I just know that whoever did this to my apartment may soon be coming back looking for me, so I have to get out of here. Maybe I'll go to a hotel."

"Why don't you come to my place? You can sleep on the couch. It's safe, and no one will know you're here."

Mike chewed it over. Immediately after a brief emotional high, he saw the enormous possibilities and potential long term consequences of accepting such an invitation from Heather—a woman he had more than a passing interest in. As a trained lawyer, he tried to be logical in his thinking, and he also tried to keep emotions out of any judgments or opinions he might have that could affect the outcome of a court case. He was always thinking about what the facts were in relation to his client, and how those facts would eventually be used for or against the case he was working on. In this instance, he mentally slapped himself upside the head and told his logical mind to shut up. This was not a case, and Heather was a nice person whom he wanted to get to know better. She was offering him a safe harbor for the night, which he desperately needed.

After all that back and forth with himself, which in reality only took about three seconds, he told her he'd be over shortly. She texted him her address and he was out the door.

It was dark outside. From the sidewalk, he looked back up at his former abode and realized he did not really feel a thing, one way or the other, about leaving the place. He should miss the homey apartment after spending a few years there. but ultimately, it had just been a place to do homework, watch TV, and sleep. A place he'd lived in while studying to be a lawyer. He'd always known he would be moving once he signed on with a firm, it had just come a bit sooner and more suddenly than expected.

Walking to his car, he was breathing hard and his stomach felt as though it had a hundred small vampire bats flying around in it. At first he thought it was because he was being forced to flee so abruptly. But his honest mind threw that out the window and relayed the truth in no uncertain terms. He was feeling that way for one reason and one reason only.

He had started to fear for his life.

As he placed his suitcase in the trunk of his car, he couldn't stop visualizing the blood dripping from Wang Ping's mouth, or the cruel eyes of the murderer that were focused on him as if saying he would find him anywhere he went. *You can run, but you can't hide.* As those two images swirled around in his mind, a third vision joined them and made him dizzy—that of his trashed apartment, and the terror that had struck when he saw his computer was stolen.

It was all taking a major toll on his nerves.

He slammed the trunk, looked all around the parking area, and when he was sure that no one was watching him, he got in and drove to Heather's, taking a long and winding route to be certain he didn't have a tail. She lived on the outskirts of D.C. in Maryland. He pulled up and parked in front of her Victorian townhouse, which had a gray exterior with white trim around the windows. It was the only gray townhouse on the block. The adjacent homes and the ones across the tree-lined street were all different colors, ranging from green to orange to white, and every color in between.

He was almost to the top of the stairs when Heather opened the door and beamed a welcoming smile at him. "You made it."

"Thankfully," he said, wearing a bitter smile. "I really appreciate the invite."

He followed her inside and looked around. The hardwood floors balanced out the almost blinding effect of the bright white walls and ceiling. He covered his eyes jokingly, as if the sun had burst through the top of the house and was focusing all its brightness on him.

"I get that a lot," Heather said, smiling broadly. "Too much white, I know. But I'm only renting the place and can't paint it another color due to the stiff lease agreement."

"I'm just kidding," he said.

"Do you want wine or beer?"

"I'll have a beer. Thanks."

She went to the kitchen while he wandered around the room. He walked to the window and carefully parted the curtains to peek outside. He craned his neck to look left and right, then drew them tightly closed.

Heather came back carrying a beer and a white wine.

"So, what do you think?" she asked, handing him the bottle.

"This is a nice place," he said, taking a seat in the comfy easy chair she gestured to.

"No, I mean what do you think about all the stuff that's happened to you in the last few days?"

"Oh. Right. Well, it's a lot to take in. I can't believe my apartment was destroyed and my laptop stolen. That part is very scary."

"What about Mr. Wang being killed? I imagine that's scary, too?"

"Yes, and I just know it's all connected. No doubt they will come after me when they don't find what they want on my computer." He raked a hand through his hair. "You know, I really shouldn't be here. I might be putting you in danger, too."

"Don't be silly."

He got up, took a long slug of beer, and placed the bottle on the kitchen counter. "Thank you for being so concerned about me. But I think I'd better leave. It was a bad idea to come here."

She seemed taken off-guard. "No. It was a good idea! I want you to stay. I've wanted to get to know you anyway. And you'll be safe here. You don't think they followed you, do you?"

He shook his head. "I don't think so. I was careful."

"All right, then."

He gazed assessingly at her for a moment, then walked over to the window and carefully looked out again. He went to the front door and locked the two deadbolts. "Any other doors?"

"Nope. I'll get a blanket and pillow."

After they made up the couch together, he went over and gave her a sincere hug goodnight. "You're the best," he whispered.

* * * *

Heather looked up at the kitchen clock. It was 6:45 a.m. and she was making two cups of coffee and two bowls of fruit for breakfast. She placed them on the small kitchen table and set out two napkins and two sets of silverware. She walked into the living room and softly brushed Mike's arm with her fingers. When he didn't wake up right away, she gave him a slight nudge.

He jerked toward her and said in a frightened voice, "Where am I?"

She gave him serious look, thinking he might be having a mental breakdown.

He made a face and laughed. "Just kidding."

"You faker!" she said, then joined in his laughter. "I need to get to work soon. Come to the kitchen and have breakfast with me."

When he finally sat down at the kitchen table, she was almost finished with her fruit and coffee. "I have to get going to be on time to work. Stay and make yourself comfortable. In the spare room, I've set up a separate desktop for you on my computer, so you can use it and have access to the internet and whatever you need. The password is 1-2-3-4. I'll be home around six o'clock tonight. I expect the house to be cleaned, dishes done, laundry folded, and everything dusted, or there will be consequences! Do you hear me, mister?"

"Yes, ma'am," he said, saluting her with a grin.

"Just kidding," she teased. "But be careful today, and please don't do anything risky. Promise?"

He crossed his heart. "Promise."

She got up, and as she walked passed him she touched his head lovingly with her palm. At the door, she turned back to give him a wave, smiling as she closed the door. "Have a good day. Call if you need anything."

* * * *

After breakfast and a shower, Mike got his phone and pulled up the photos he'd taken of all the Yan Chemical files at the office. He needed to safeguard them somehow. He grabbed a second cup of coffee and went over to Heather's computer. He logged in on the desktop she'd created for him, bought a new cloud storage account, then uploaded all the photos to it.

That done, he went to Google and looked up Ohio Chemical. Their home page only contained what he already knew from his previous research from public disclosure documents in the antidumping case. Mike's earlier work on the case more concentrated on his client, Yan Chemical. This seemed to be the first time that he took a hard look on the petitioner of the case. Ohio Chemical was a small soda powder manufacturer in Ohio that had been acquired by a company named Wealth Pinnacle incorporated in the British Virgin Islands a couple of years ago. Information about the small company, he had already discovered, was rather sparse. Most companies, big or small, had a marketing department responsible for advertising and positioning the company well in the marketplace. They created press releases and ads, and called attention to the company by giving people something interesting about it in order to increase sales. It was all about making more money. The fact that Ohio Chemical didn't have much going on in social media was very telling. A small company always wanted to grow and make larger profits. Why wasn't Ohio Chemical interested in building their company and increasing sales? He tried to think of a logical reason. Like perhaps the company was going out of business and just didn't want to pour any more money into a sinking ship due to the foreign competition. That certainly explains why it brought the antidumping case in the first place.

Or really?

Chapter 16 The Investigation

SA Frank Wallace had over thirty years' experience in the FBI, and he had been a key part of solving hundreds of cases, from murder and kidnapping to bank robberies, white collar crime, and terrorism. He was aware that in the Bureau he was known as Bull Dog because once he got hold of something, he never let go. He didn't mind. In fact, he liked the nickname his fellow agents had honored him with early in his career and stuck with him throughout the decades and wherever he went. He enjoyed working cases that baffled other agents, investigators, and associates who had given up on solving them and were all dumbfounded when he closed the cases with an arrest or two. It gave him great satisfaction.

Frank was proud that other agents looked up to him thanks to his calming influence in life or death situations, and his dry, understated humor around the office. He always tried to see things from an out-of-the-box perspective he knew was uncommon by traditional FBI standards. His colleagues found it refreshing, and newer agents often came to him when they were stumped by a case. He gave credit where it was due, and even after being promoted up the ranks he never sought the spotlight. Working cases, he preferred to hand over the lead to younger agents to give them field experience, though he was always there to help guide them.

Frank had modeled his style of leadership after his own personal hero, Teddy Roosevelt, Jr., who'd bravely led his men onto the Normandy beaches on D-Day, 1944. Roosevelt was the only general to hit the beach in the first landing wave, and the oldest man in the invasion. He'd always remained calm, inspiring confidence in his men with the authority and love of a father. Frank had been a captain in the Marines as a younger man, serving in Panama and Desert Storm, and knew how important it was to be a steady and fair leader.

But enough was enough. In one year he was finally retiring after thirty-four years on the job. He'd been wounded once in a shootout, and won the Medal of Valor twice. He'd given the FBI his all, and it was time to hang up the badge. His colleagues had all told him they were really going to miss him. He'd miss them, too, but he was looking forward to working on his vegetable garden and going fishing. See his son more often. Maybe do a bit of travelling with his wife, whom he loved dearly but had sometimes neglected badly due to his job.

But first he had to crack this new international case that Mike Nolan had dropped in his lap.

After his meeting with Nolan yesterday, Frank had gotten right on his computer and began to work. He'd started methodically with the information that Nolan had provided—which was all he had to go on since Mike was the only source and witness to Wang Ping's murder in Beijing. According to Nolan, Wang had worked for and was fired from Yan Chemical in China, and Wang had told him he was afraid someone might try to kill him.

Which turned out to be true.

On the surface, it might appear to be an open-and-shut case of murder, but Frank knew he needed to find the motive behind it. He instinctively felt the answer lay in what, exactly, the damaging information was that Wang possessed. That was undoubtedly the key to cracking this case.

The first question to ask was, who benefitted from Wang's death?

At first glance, that was a no-brainer. Yan Chemical, the company that had fired Wang. Wang had told Nolan he possessed damaging information on Yan Chemical and threatened to use it against them if they did not hire him back. Blackmail was not unheard of as a motive for retaliation.

But to commit murder, even by hire? That path would not be embarked upon lightly. Sure, crazy people did it all the time, but Yan Chemical was an international company worth hundreds of millions of dollars, if not billions. Why would they put everything in jeopardy by killing an accountant who no longer worked there? He couldn't see a motive.

So he combed through his notes for any clues among the things Mike Nolan had told him. Eyes closed, he worked his way through their conversation. Mike was the lawyer who had defended Yan Chemical against a small American company, Ohio Chemical, a competitor who was suing Yan Chemical over antidumping regulations. He had met Wang Ping in China, where Mike had been for the verification of Yan Chemical's production and accounting.

He sat up and started googling on his computer. He found that Yan Chemical was a very successful and a highly profitable company. Next he googled Ohio Chemical. Similar to Mike, what Frank found—or rather didn't find—surprised him. It didn't make any sense that a much smaller manufacturer would be suing the giant Yan Chemical. They didn't even make the same products. Ohio Chemical mostly made detergent, with a very small production of the soda powder Yan made.

So why would they mount an expensive lawsuit against a basically non-competing company? The thought baffled him. Of all the facts so far, this made the least sense. In fact, it made *no* sense at all. He circled the words Ohio Chemical. He'd get back to this later.

He smiled to himself, already hooked on the puzzling case. This kind of thing happened to him a lot—in the beginning stages many investigations seemed to cut and dried, but as soon as he took a closer look, the case either fell apart or got stuck in the mud. As with Ohio Chemical suing Yan Chemical. There was simply no logic to it. Well, they didn't call him Bull Dog for nothing. Dead-end turns like this just made him even more tenacious. Giving up wasn't in his vocabulary.

Not that some investigations didn't get stalled at times. That was a matter of course. When that happened, he invited the power of the hunch into the investigative circle, making a list of possibilities. No idea was left out, no matter how crazy it sounded. If a hunch had any chance at all of being right, or if pursuing it could move the process forward, then he went with it.

One time a friend of his in the D.C. police department had been completely stumped investigating a series of murder-rapes. All the detectives on the case had one guy pegged as the perpetrator but couldn't prove it. They had him surveilled 24/7, and at night a cop would ride past his house on a bike in order to get a better look through his windows. No luck. They were running out of time and ideas. At a meeting, one of the detectives suggested that perhaps the killer was Jack the Ripper reincarnated. After they finished laughing, the others listened to his explanation of reincarnation—as he knew it, anyway— and to the similarities both cases shared. It was a crazy idea that came out of left field, but it compelled the investigation to pivot in a completely different direction.

Although none of the detectives believed in reincarnation, they were excited to have a new ideas in the mix. At that point they were in the doldrums, going nowhere anyway. So, they all did some research on Jack the Ripper and his modus operandi. One of them went old-school, looking up information at the local library, and suddenly he had the brilliant idea of checking to see if anyone else had checked out books on the subject. That broke the case, by giving them an entirely new slant on the perpetrator…who later turned out to be the same man they were already watching day and night.

Frank had been stalled in plenty of investigations. At first it had made him anxious, because all he could see was a brick wall that seemed impossible to break through. But over time he learned that stalls were going to happen, and all he needed was more information, more pieces to the puzzle, in order to push ahead and ultimately crack the case. All he had to do was to continue to dig and eventually he would hit paydirt.

As Frank was pondering his next step, his cell phone rang. It was Mike Nolan.

"SSA Wallace, I have some bad news. My apartment was broken into and ransacked last night."

"Okay, stay calm. Were you injured or hurt in any way?"

"No, it happened before I got home. Unfortunately my laptop and briefcase were both taken."

"I can send in a forensics team immediately. Do we have your permission to search your residence?"

"Absolutely."

"Good. Keep your cell phone on and I'll let you know the next step. Do you have somewhere else to stay?"

"Yeah, I'm crashing with a friend. I have to go in to work today, but I'll keep my cell phone handy."

After discussing a few more details, they hung up.

Frank felt sorry for Nolan, but was excited about the ramifications of this new development. Now he didn't have to worry about jurisdictional issues. Something related to the international case had happened right here in D.C. And the perp had made a big move, which would undoubtedly yield more clues as to motive. He also suspected that Nolan knew more than he was letting on, and Frank planned to dig it all out.

Quickly, he called in his team, "We have permission to search Mike Nolan's apartment, but get a search warrant anyway, and a copy of the building's surveillance video if there is one."

An email alert pinged on his computer. CID's assistant director, James Brody, wanted to see him right away. Frank put on his jacket, straightened his tie, and headed upstairs.

Sitting at his large wooden desk, Brody waved him into his office. It was twice as big as Frank's office, and had a very nice view of the Washington Monument.

"SSA Wallace, come in," said Brody. "How are you doing, Frank? You're always so busy I rarely get a chance to see my favorite special agent anymore." He got up and shook Frank's hand.

"Good to see you, Jim. I'm fine. Looking forward to retirement. How 'bout you?"

"All good. You going to the banquet on Saturday?"

"No, not this year. Pamela and I are driving over to Annapolis to see our son Kenny and his family. It's his birthday this weekend."

"He still teaching at the Naval academy?" Brody asked.

"Yep. He loves it. I don't think he enjoys anything more than teaching."

Brody sat down behind his desk again, and motioned for Frank to take a seat on the overstuffed leather couch.

"Frank, I wanted to see you because I heard that you interviewed a certain…" He looked down at a paper on his desk. "Mike Nolan."

Frank nodded. "That's right."

"Well, I got word from further up that we are to hand over everything we have on him and whatever he told you to CIA."

Frank was about to protest, but was preempted by Brody holding his hand up.

"I have no idea why or what or when, or even how, but that's the order of the day and we need to take it seriously. If I know you, and I do, I'm sure you're intent on getting to the bottom of it and finding the truth." He paused and smiled wryly. "Especially the ugly truths."

Frank plastered on his best poker face. "Unexpected. But nothing to do about it, I guess," he said calmly. "Is there a contact at Langly?"

Brody picked up a business card from his desk and handed it to Frank, who glanced at it casually before pocketing it. "Okay. I'll call him right away."

Brody stood up and met Frank's eyes. "Can't believe you'll be retiring soon. Any plans?"

Frank got the hint that the meeting was over. "Well, I've been thinking about writing a book on all the great assistant directors in the FBI. What do you think? A bestseller?"

Brody laughed and said, "I think it would make millions. Too bad about the confidentiality agreement you signed."

They shook hands again and Brody ushered him to the door, holding it open. "Thanks for dropping by, Frank. Always a pleasure seeing you. Please give Pamela my warmest regards. We'll miss you at the banquet."

"Thanks, Jim, I will. Good to see you, too."

Frank left Brody's office and trotted downstairs to his office, where fired up his computer again. He'd already made up his mind about what to do, even before he sat down on Brody's couch. He hadn't known for sure what the assistant director was going to tell him, but he'd had one of his famous hunches. He'd felt instinctively that the Nolan case would be taken away from him. Brody was obviously aware of the ransacking last night since the search of Nolan's apartment by forensics was underway and ticketed in the computer system. Frank did not even try reminding Brody that the FBI had jurisdiction. CIA was not allowed to work domestically. Their mandate was international intelligence and operations. The reason was obviously not about jurisdiction. For the Nolan case to be handed to the CIA amounted to its death sentence. It clearly meant someone high up had ordered the whole matter to be buried and never brought up again—definitely not kept open to search for the truth.

This sort of FBI-CIA maneuvering wasn't that unusual. But handing over a case to them shouldn't stand out like a sore thumb the way he felt this one did. Or maybe the Nolan investigation had been tossed over to them because the FBI brass didn't want to waste time, money, and manpower on a murder they felt had nothing to do with America's domestic security.

Admittedly, it was a strange one. Someone inadvertently witnessing a murder over the internet was something he'd never run into in his entire career.

He knew the United States had no obligation to report the incident to China, because both countries were members of Interpol, the U.S. was obligated to cooperate with Chinese authorities if they sought U.S. assistance through Interpol. The only thing that made sense was for the FBI to create a case file, terminate the investigation, and then refer the case to Interpol's U.S. National Central Bureau and wait for contact to be initiated by China. Diverting it to the CIA didn't make sense on any level. It felt like just a lame excuse to bury some morsel of information that someone didn't want getting out. If it wasn't important, why the ploy?

After all, it was an American who'd witnessed the murder and had his home ransacked, which could arguably fall within the FBI's investigative boundaries.

Maybe it was just Frank's drive for perfection, or wanting to handle one last intriguing case before retirement, but his most compelling reason for continuing the investigation boiled down to the simple fact that he'd been told to stop. The FBI was giving it to another agency to sit on, probably buried forever. It was all very suspicious. Especially because he felt certain something bigger than blackmail was behind

Wang's murder. And he also wanted to keep Mike Nolan alive, if at all possible.

Whatever the reason, the Bull Dog knew he would stay on the Nolan case, and that he would stay on it until the whole thing was solved, one way or the other. He would have to investigate it quietly, and *secretly*. He would of course give the originals of all his notes and interview information to the CIA as ordered, but he would keep copies of everything.

Just then, someone knocked on his office door.

"Come in," he called.

Assistant Director Brody poked his head in and said quietly, "I need to see you in the restroom, Frank."

Surprised, he followed Brody to the men's. Knowing the routine, they each took a spot at a urinal. This was the only place in the building safe from prying ears.

They both flushed them at the same time, and Brody quickly said, "The order came from the White House. But I want you to form a special team and pursue the case. The FBI will not be obstructed by anyone in its investigations, especially not the White House. Use top secret security measures. Tell no one else." Then he quickly tightened his belt, flushed again, and strode out of the restroom.

Chapter 17 The Layoff

After talking to SSA Wallace, Mike hurried to his office at Williamson & Gray. His secretary greeted him with a rigid smile. "Mike, Patrick stopped by and asked you to come to his office first thing."

Mike's heart gave a stutter. He had no idea what to expect. He zigzagged through the maze of offices and knocked on Patrick Steiner's door.

His boss sat behind his desk with a sullen face. After Mike was seated, he said, "Mike, you have obviously been a major asset to us for the past six months. Getting that final rate of zero percent for an important client was a real coup. However..." Patrick bit his lip.

Mike's head was spinning at the suspense, and not in a good way. Was he being fired?

His worst fear became reality when Patrick said, "I'm afraid we have to let you go."

"Is this about my performance?" Mike asked.

His boss cleared his throat. "No, it's about the firm's underlying staffing needs, which are changing."

"I understand," Mike said, although he didn't understand at all. He was devastated.

How had his life suddenly taken a one-eighty turn from rising star to just another unemployed lawyer? If it wasn't his performance—and how could it be with his good results?—he must have inadvertently touched on something pretty serious. And it could only be about the Yan Chemical case. It was the only case he'd worked on.

As he gathered his things and left the office, his mind was in chaos. But despite having just lost his job, his thoughts and worries were not about finding the money to pay for rent and his tuition loans.

They were all about how to stay alive. He had to figure out what kind of international hornet's nest he'd innocently stumbled into.

What did they think he knew that was so dangerous?

And who were they?

What was it they were so worried about that they'd started killing people?

* * * *

Mike met Heather in a sports bar over a couple of drinks in order to clear his mind.

It didn't work. They were both distracted when a map of China appeared on several of the TVs.

"Now what?" he mumbled nervously, turning to watch.

The CNN anchor reported, "The White House has approved the latest U.S. arms sale to the island democracy of Taiwan, a potential $4.5 billion deal, amid rising tensions with mainland China. According to the State Department, the sale will give Taiwan forty new M109 self-propelled howitzers along with 1,700 kits to convert projectiles into precise GPS-guided munitions. The proposed sale must go through congressional review and then through negotiations between Taiwan and the contractor, Swift Industries, before a contract can be signed. Swift Industries is also providing the U.S. Army with the latest version of the same weaponry. Taiwan's president officially thanked the U.S., saying the weapons would serve to ensure peace in the region. The sale is expected to be formalized in one month."

The anchor went on to something else, so Mike turned away again and sighed. "Whatever," he muttered morosely and took another swig of his drink. Despite only being lunchtime, today it was something stronger than beer.

"Things like this happen, Mike." Heather said sympathetically. "You're a great lawyer. You'll get another offer soon."

"Stupid job anyway. I couldn't care less."

"Easy come, easy go. It's only $160K, right?" she said, amused.

Mike rubbed his forehead, a headache already starting. "I'm telling you, I must have touched on something dangerous. I have a feeling it's either my life or someone else's life on the chopping block."

Her smile faded. "Is it that bad?"

"I think it could be," he said. "Think about it. I witness a murder online, and the very next day my house is ransacked. They must have someone here in the U.S. going after any evidence of the murder—like the video on my laptop. Which they stole in the break-in. What they don't know is, the video was copied to my cloud drive. Which they'll figure it out soon enough because the laptop is programmed to back up daily. When they do, they'll go after the copy, too. But they won't have access to my cloud storage unless they hack my username and password, which I don't think is possible."

Her brow wrinkled. "I still can't imagine what is behind all this."

"Join the club."

"I guess it's easy to imagine Yan Chemical was behind Wang Ping's murder," she said. "But why did Williamson & Gray let you go? You won the case for them. Why would they want you to leave? I think you're right. You must know too much about something."

He pushed out a breath and took another long sip. "From the start, I felt there was something strange about this antidumping case. I mean, your boss asked you to leave the note that helped me find the winning argument. And he basically gave a non-rebuttal. I felt your firm tried to lose on purpose. And when I told Patrick about the argument, he said he'd known I'd come up with something on my own. I may be overreading, but it seemed to imply that if I didn't, someone else would have helped me in some way."

"Which makes as much sense as my firm deliberately losing. Why would we, as legal counsel, ever do such a thing?

"Only if directed by the client."

"Exactly. But why would Ohio Chemical try to levy antidumping duties by mounting a lawsuit and purposefully losing it?"

"Because they benefit from losing?"

"How? Losing the case means their largest competitor will take over the U.S. market. How can Ohio Chemical benefit from *that?* Why would they do it? Only Yan Chemical benefits from this case."

"That is the million dollar question," he agreed. "Did you ever check into who owns Ohio Chemical?"

"As I recall, it's Wealth Pinnacle, an offshore company incorporated in the British Virgin Islands."

"Through an acquisition?"

"Yes, two years ago," Heather confirmed what John learned from the public records.

"And who owns Wealth Pinnacle?"

She shook her head. "There's no public record. But we can check with their registered agent in the Islands."

"Will they tell us?"

She sat back and regarded him with a mischievous. "No clue. But let's try."

They both pulled out their laptops.

"Be sure to use a VPN," he reminded her.

She nodded. "Found it. The owner is a U.S. citizen named Jacqulin Thacker."

"And who is she?"

They dove in and searched the internet for more information. Heather took on Jacqulin Thacker and Mike concentrated on Wang Ping and Yan Chemical.

After three hours of research, Heather yawned. "Okay. Jacquilin Thacker, aka Jacquilin Wilson, is a resident of New Jersey. Married to Sam Wilson." She looked over at Mike. "And you'll never guess who he is. Sam Wilson is the CEO and majority shareholder of Swift Industries."

Mike's jaw dropped. "The W-3 bomber manufacturer?"

"Yes. They're one of the largest federal arms contractors."

Mike took a moment for that to sink in. And remembered something. "Holy Toledo. Swift Industries applied for their export license through Williamson & Gray! I saw the license application myself. It was accidentally put in with the antidumping case, and I saw it when I was copying the Yan Chemical files."

Her eyes widened. "And since Swift Industries is obviously affiliated with Ohio Chemical, Williamson & Gray shouldn't be doing anything at all for Swift."

"Right. It's a clear conflict of interest."

"What does Swift have to gain by letting Yan Chemical have zero antidumping duties?"

He thought about it for a moment. "Maybe they need to trade favors with someone at Yan Chemical?"

She frowned. "But Swift Industries sells to Taiwan. How is that connected to Yan Chemical in China? The countries are not exactly friendly."

"But if there is some greater secret behind Yan Chemical that led to Wang Ping's murder than just covering up their accounting records, I may be next on their kill list."

Heather sucked in a breath. "Which means we have to figure out what that secret is and expose them."

"First I need to get my hands on the original accounting record of Yan Chemical that Wang Ping said he had. I may have to go back to China and find it myself. That is the only proof of the conspiracy."

Mike's phone rang. It was SSA Wallace.

After a quick greeting, Wallace said, "There are a few things I need clarification on regarding Wang Ping. I was wondering if we could meet today and have another chat."

"Sure, that would be fine. Should I come to your office?" Mike asked.

"No. Where are you now?"

"At a restaurant on the Maryland side."

"Anywhere close to the Lincoln Memorial?"

"Not too far."

"Meet me there in an hour. Is that good for you?"

"I'll be there," said Mike.

* * * *

Mike parked his car and started walking over the lawns to the Lincoln Memorial. He had been there many times and loved everything about the place. Walking up the elegant staircase, he saw Abraham Lincoln sitting immortalized in marble gazing toward the U.S. Capitol Building, deep in thought about safeguarding the unity of the nation. On the wall behind him was an inscription.

In this temple, as in the hearts of the people for whom he saved the Union, the memory of Abraham Lincoln is enshrined forever.

SSA Wallace stood tall and solid, a slight smile on his placid face as he waved at Mike. They shook hands and Wallace motioned him over to a nearby bench. He said somberly, "Mike, forensics found something in your apartment."

Mike hiked his brows. "What did they find? Something helpful, I hope."

"Well… It's copies of Yan Chemical's original accounting records, as well as the fraudulent accounting record, along with an email instructing Yan Chemical to use the fraudulent one to submit to the U.S. Department of Commerce."

Mike was shocked. How on earth had they gotten in his apartment? He had certainly not put them there. "What email?" he asked. "Who sent it?" Maybe that would tell him.

Wallace grimaced. "You did."

Mike froze, staring at the FBI man in disbelief. "*Me?*" He felt the blood drain from his face. "No way. I never had those papers and I did not send any such email," he said emphatically. He cursed silently. "Do I need an attorney?"

Wallace put up a hand. "No. Don't worry. We know the email is fraudulent. It did not show up on your email server. Also, the accounting records were printed on A4 Chinese paper, but the printer added a date at the bottom of the documents, and you were back in the U.S. at the time. Chinese paper is not available over here, so it must have been printed in China. I instructed them not to investigate the document any further."

Mike cursed again, his pulse in overdrive. "Someone tried to *frame* me?"

"All things considered, are you surprised?"

Mike blinked. "Beats getting murdered, I guess. What do they want from me?"

"More to the point, who are they? Yan Chemical?"

Mike took several deep breaths to calm his speeding heart. "SSA Wallace, why do you trust me?"

"Please. Call me Frank."

Mike gave him a tentative smile. "Thanks. And I'm Mike. I'm very grateful you believe me."

Wallace—Frank smiled back. "I have been with the FBI for over thirty years, and I've learned to trust my gut. Here's the deal. It's not that you seem like a good guy. You *are* a good guy. And these accounting records were found *after* the break-in. Seriously? No criminal mind, let alone anyone with half a brain, would keep such incriminating evidence at home. You are much too smart for that. And I'm pretty sure we could compare these accounting records to the real ones, and would find a big discrepancy in the dates they were created. None of it adds up."

"Anyway. I'm really glad you're on the case, Frank."

The FBI man grinned. "Yeah, about that. Full disclosure, for the first time in my career I've been taken off an investigation. Officially, I'm no longer on the case."

Mike was dumbfounded. "But… You're here. Meeting with me." When Frank's grin just widened, Mike finally caught on. "Ah. What about *un*officially?"

Frank put a finger to his lips. "Shhh. Top secret. Now. Let's go through everything again. See if we missed anything."

Mike started at the beginning and dredged his mind for any small detail. When he got to the break-in, Frank asked him what was in his stolen briefcase.

"Nothing valuable except his laptop. And that only contained a few files that shouldn't be seen by anyone outside Williamson & Grey."

"And the video," Frank said.

"Yeah. That. There's something else I need to tell you about. Something I saw right before I was fired."

"What's that?"

"A copy of an export license application I found by accident. It's technically confidential information. But you are federal law enforcement investigating a criminal issue. I guess it's okay to tell you because it relates to a possible future crime."

"Okay. I'm listening."

Mike told him about the application, and about the relationships between Ohio Chemical, Wealth Pinnacle, and Jacquilin Thacker, and her husband Tim Wilson's position at Swift Industries, and Swift Industries stake in the antidumping case.

"Interesting," said Frank. "Williamson & Grey should definitely not have handled Swift's export license application."

"True. But the more important thing is, on the news last night it was reported that the sale to Taiwan was worth $4.5 billion. But on the application—which I took a photo of, by the way— it states the value as *$45* billion."

Frank whistled. "Quite a discrepancy. Still, maybe just a typo? It's easy to put a decimal point in the wrong place."

"Maybe. But not a motive for murder."

Frank nodded slowly. "It's always the tiny, seemingly unrelated details that catch my attention." He jotted down a few notes about the Yan Chemical and Swift Industries connection. And the $45 billion price tag on the export license application. He handed Mike the notepad and said, "Write down where you're staying."

Mike gave him Heather's address in Maryland. "I'll be here for the time being. I'm still worried they might come back for me. I can't get the image of Wang's murder out of my head."

"That could take a while. Law enforcement and first responders all go through that when they first confronted with murder victims, car crashes, and other tragedies."

"I wish I could offer you protection for both you and Heather, but unfortunately the FBI can't provide it at this time."

"Why not?" asked Mike.

"Remember I said I was called off the case? Because the case doesn't exist anymore, we can't get funds for anything connected to it."

"You never said why you were taken off."

Frank pursed his lips. "This has to be confidential, just between you and me. Agreed?"

"Absolutely. The vault is sealed."

"It wasn't just me. The whole case was taken away from the FBI and given to CIA.

"So, what are we doing here, then?"

"On my boss's orders, I still have a special team secretly working on it," Frank said with a smile.

"I am totally confused."

"Well, I'm going to retire in a few months, so I was going to spend the rest of my time doing paperwork. But then you walked in and told me about Wang Ping and… How to put it? I smelled something bigger than what you or I initially saw. This case breathes intrigue, conspiracy, and collusion. Careful planning is written all over it. It's the case I've been waiting for my entire career. So, I'm all over it like white on rice. I'll work with you as much as I can without me getting fired or you getting hurt. Deal?"

"I'm in. But what about the killer and the guys who broke into my place? What if they come after me? Is Heather in danger? Should I go someplace else?"

Frank considered. "Do you have a gun?"

"No."

"Have you ever shot a pistol?"

"No."

"Okay never mind. It would take too long for you to legally get one."

"Couldn't you give me a gun and teach me how to shoot?"

Frank shook his head. "Too risky. Look, if something's going to happen, it's going to happen soon. I'd guess within weeks. Maybe days. I have vacation time coming to me, so I will put in for two weeks. Maybe three. That way I can be watching you as much as possible. You may not see me, but I will always let you know if I'm not going to be around so you can take greater precautions."

"Don't you have a family?" Mike asked, overwhelmed by Frank's generosity.

"I do. My kids are grown and out of the house, but I'll admit my wife won't be too happy with this arrangement. But she's gone through it all before. Well, what do you say?"

"Like I said, I'm all in. What can I do to help?"

"Even though the documents and email are fake, it's still considered incriminating evidence and the FBI has it. So you need to find the exculpating evidence, the real documents. I'd wager you won't be truly safe until you can get hold of them and hand it all in to us."

"In that case, I need to go China and talk with Wang Ping's wife. He might have given her his information on Yan Chemical, or she might know where he hid it. This might be a good time to go see her and hopefully get whatever secrets he had on Yan Chemical."

Frank regarded Mike, silently thinking, his facial expression giving nothing away. After a long moment, he finally cleared his throat and said, "Not a bad idea. The sooner you leave, the better. I will keep an eye on Heather, so don't worry about her. How long do you think it'll take you to see Wang Ping's wife and get the information?"

"A day there, a day back, and one or two days to find her and talk her into giving me whatever info she has. Probably four or five days max."

"Okay, that's fine. I'll take the next week off and watch over Heather. When she's at work I'll look into Swift Industries and the $45 billion sale to Taiwan."

Everything decided, they walked together to their cars. "I'll catch a flight tomorrow morning," Mike said when they reached his. "Ping gave me his wife's phone number and said she speaks English well enough to understand me. And I speak Chinese. Communicating won't be a problem. I just hope she cooperates."

* * * *

The next morning Mike boarded a Chinese Airlines flight at 6:00 a.m.

It was going to be a short trip. Just get the documents and leave. He prayed Ping's wife would help him. He'd been unwillingly ensnared in some serious international intrigue, and he needed those documents to get down to its very core and expose the fraud in order to clear himself.

And to stay alive.

Chapter 18 Tim Nolan's Airstrike

unming, China, December, 1941

Two weeks after the Japanese attack on Pearl Harbor, the painted shark's teeth nosecones of a dozen Tomahawk IIBs lifted high into the dense clouds above the city of Kunming in southern China. Their mission was to engage ten unescorted Japanese Kawasaki Ki-48 "Lily" light bombers thirty miles away. The Japanese had also been bombing Chinese cities, and often the Chinese Air Force had not been able to mount any air defense. Both residential and military targets had been bombed, and civilian casualties were on the rise.

In the cockpit of one of the American Tomahawks, Flying Tiger Tim Nolan smoothed his already neat mustache, then carefully patted the blood chit issued to his American Volunteer Group Flying Tigers in the chest pocket of his flight suit to make sure it was secure. A good thing to have, just in case, but he prayed he'd never have to use it.

Tong Fang's voice crackled through the radio, "Nolan, watch your right flank." Fang was coming up on his left, Chuck on his right.

During training, General Chenault had repeatedly warned the pilots that the American way of dog-fighting wouldn't work against the Japanese. To win against their highly skilled pilots, you had to quickly ascend then make a speedy dive and shoot to kill.

"Got him," Tim radioed back. There was a Lily bomber on his right flank that had a forward position in the formation. "I'll count to three, then we climb, dive, and blast. Ready?"

"Yep!"

"One, two, three!"

The three Tomahawks climbed fifteen hundred feet before nosediving onto the Japanese bomber. In unison, Tim and Chuck unleashed fifty rounds of ammunition against the Lily. Its right wing starting to smoke, then dipped and tumbled, roaring out of formation and falling to earth, out of sight.

"Ha ha! Isn't that a $500 bonus?" said Chuck gleefully.

"Oh, yeah," Tim said. He didn't relish killing, but after Pearl Harbor, he figured the enemy deserved what they got.

"Tim, your nine o'clock!" Fang called out.

"On it!" Tim immediately made a ninety-degree turn and came face-to-face with another Japanese bomber.

"Chuck! I'll outflank it from the right," Tim turned his aircraft and took aim. But the light bomber was moving very fast, flying an S pattern and spiraling up at the same time.

"Damn. That's a freaking good flying machine," Tim muttered. And great flying, too.

Firing a continuous five rounds, Tim saw the bomber sustain a few minor injuries before it did an abrupt one-eighty. Then it made a long curve in the sky, as if trying to exit the battlefield.

"You think this is a party?" Tim grabbed his control stick and pursued the bomber. He had a bit of an altitude advantage, so he waited for the Lily to slow down so he could make another diving attack. And waited. But a fleeing bomber carrying no heavy ordinance was swift and nimble. Soon it had been forty-five minutes since he'd started the pursuit.

He picked up the radio to ask for orders, but all he got was static. He'd lost contact with central command. Fine. He decided to keep pursuing. He'd hate for the bastard to get away.

Ten minutes later, he sped up to close in. He fired another five rounds, and this time he finally hit the enemy's gas tank. "Take that, asshole!"

With a big, roaring explosion, the bomber crashed to the ground.

Tim glanced at his gas gauge. Damn. Not much fuel left. He dropped altitude to save gas. Another twenty minutes and he should be near Chongqing.

Twenty-five minutes later, he realized he'd made a slight mistake. He'd flown south instead of west. "Damn it!" This was not good. Crash landing in enemy territory was the worst thing that could happen to a pilot.

But it looked inevitable. He was quickly running out of gas, the Tomahawk flying only two hundred feet above ground. All too soon he was skimming the dense forest treetops.

"Shit, shit, shit." He rolled his body into a defensive ball, protecting his head as best he could as the plane slashed and spun through the trees, at last coming to a teetering halt deep in the Chinese woods.

Miraculously, it was not followed by an explosion. At least not before Tim blacked out.

* * * *

Awakening from the crash, Tim found that the fighter's engine was somehow still running. In the distance he heard dogs barking. Moments later, uniformed men surrounded the plane and one of them climbed up to the cockpit. To Tim's relief, the man's uniform was neither Japanese nor Nationalist. In great pain, he slowly reached for the blood chit in his pocket. but a sharp twitch in his arm made him lose consciousness again.

* * * *

Tim opened his eyes and glanced carefully around. His right arm had been bandaged with white gauze.

A man in an officer's uniform smiled at him. "How are you? My name is Tang. I am with the Eighth Route Army, serving under the Chinese Communist Party's leadership. Here, drink this chicken soup. It will help you feel better."

Tim gratefully took a sip of soup. "It tastes great. Thank you for rescuing me."

Tang nodded. "Thank you for joining the Chinese fighting against the Japanese. We in the Eighth Route Army are guerilla fighters, attacking Japanese bunkers and destroying their bridges. How did you crash this far from Kunming? I read in the *Centre Daily* that only one out of the ten Japanese planes escaped after bombing of Kunming."

Tim smiled. "I think I shot down that tenth one." He grimaced. "I guess I chased it a bit too far."

"What great news! You are a worthy hero!"

"Your English is very good," Tim said, taking another sip of soup.

"Thank you. You should rest now."

Tang and his men took care of Tim for three days. On the third day, Tang said, "My battalion needs to withdraw into the mountains for the next couple of months. But we managed to move your airplane to a good hideout. You still need more rest, so I asked Mr. Chang's family to take care of you. Once your arm is completely healed, we will come to pick you up and get you back to Kunming."

Chang's family had lived in this village their whole lives, so he and his wife carefully planned where to put Tim in the event of a Japanese raid. Tim could soon understand their hand gestures so well, he usually knew exactly what they meant. Soon, while sitting around the small table on the *kang*, a traditional Chinese heated platform used for most family activities, Chang and his wife began teaching Tim Chinese.

They knew Tim was very impressed by the fermented eggs they

made using the eggs from their own chickens, so they started with that word.

"Song... Hua... Dan?" tried Tim.

"Song Hua Dan!" Chang's wife clapped and laughed.

Suddenly, Chang's twelve-year-old, Chang Yun, ran into the room crying and yelling, "Ma and Pa, they are coming!"

Chang quickly rose up from the kang and rushed Tim over to the stove, where there was a big iron pot the size of a table. He rolled the big pot aside with both hands, then shifted a basket filled with clay. Underneath was an opening that led to an underground cellar with a movable brick door, which Tang's team had built as a hideout. Tim grabbed his gear and weapon, and quickly slipped through hole, crawled toward the door and moved a brick slightly so he could see out.

The sound of engines was drawing near. Tim watched Japanese soldiers swarm into the front yard of Chang's house. In one corner they set up a machine gun, pointing it at the front of the house. Other soldiers used bayonets to herd the villagers into the yard. They pounded on the front door, then with the cries of the children and Chang's wife, it was kicked open.

Tim silently checked his pistol, which was fully loaded, then peeked out again.

Two Japanese soldiers were kicking Chang into the yard. His arms were bound behind his back.

A Chinese translator in a Japanese uniform spoke to Chang. "Brother Chang, this Imperial Army officer says if you tell us where the American pilot is, they will give you five hundred silver dollars as a reward."

"Oh, this one speaks Chinese." Chang squinted at the translator. "Are you truly Chinese? Tell your Japanese masters they should treat me better if they want to know where the American pilot is."

The translator relayed his words to the Japanese captain, who gave a short command and the soldiers released Chang's bonds.

"Brother Chang, these Japanese are too rude," said the translator. "You know, I am just doing a job to feed my family. Tell them what they want to know so they go away and look for the American."

Chang sneered, then relaxed his arms, glanced up at the sky, and said loudly, "Are you looking for Americans? They are in America! Why are you looking in China?"

All the villagers laughed.

The Japanese captain approached, smiled, and spoke to Chang. The translator then relayed his message. "The imperial officer says we all want the common goal of the Greater East Asia Co-Prosperity Sphere. Our common enemy is the white people, the Anglo-Saxons. They would rule over Asians like you and me if we Japanese were not fighting against them. Do you really think the American pilots are fighting for you? They are here to make money, for they are paid three times more than back in their own country. They don't care about your lives. If the Americans do care about you Chinese, and we Japanese really are that bad, why isn't your American pilot showing up right now to save everybody?"

After the translator finished, the Japanese captain stepped forward and withdrew a pack of cigarettes from his pocket. He plucked out a cigarette, put it into Chang's fingers, and lit it with a lighter.

The villagers stood for a moment in dead silence.

Chang took a closer look at the cigarette, put it between his lips, inhaled deeply, and exhaled a long wisp of smoke as he again looked up at the sky.

It was late afternoon. Out of the far west in the direction of the sunset, the sun was heavily shrouded by layers of dense blood-red clouds. The space around the small village did not seem to be filled with air, but with a transparent and oozing atmosphere of saturnine terror.

"This Japanese person seems to have gone to school and likes to talk about reasons," said Chang. "Let me say this. The Chang family has lived here for as long as our name has existed. I don't know about Beiping or Shanghai, and I don't care who your emperor is today, but you Japanese have disturbed my villagers, robbed my people, and set our houses on fire. Is this your idea of common prosperity? The Americans don't set up machine guns in my yard and point them at me. Ha! The Americans help to shoot down your bombers. Bombers that kill hundreds of Chinese! You think I don't know how to count, you bastard?"

The Japanese captain roared in anger, and two soldiers bound Chang again. This time they hung him up in an old locust tree. A Japanese soldier grasped the machine gun tightly, and with a click, he set it in position, ready to start firing.

Chang's veins grew swollen due to the tight ropes binding his body.

The translator said, "The Imperial Army officer says he will count to three. If you or any villager can tell us where the American is, he will spare your life."

Tim's forefinger caressed the trigger of the pistol as he targeted soldier behind the machine gun through the opening.

The translator yelled, "One! Two!"

Using all his strength, Chang yelled in Chinese, "The life of the American pilot is worth five hundred Japanese soldiers! Even if he were here, it would not be worth any amount of money to tell you! My fellow villagers, if you give the Japanese wrong information, you will not have a good ending! Five hundred Japanese soldiers! Ha ha, it is so worth it!" Chang stretched all the fingers of left hand and his right fist to gesture behind his back.

Seeing this, Tim put down his pistol. It was Chang's signal that Tim should not save him.

"Hey, you tell those Japanese," Chang said to the translator, "they shouldn't think that since they have machine guns they will get away with murder. The American attack planes will be looking for them!"

The machine gun opened fire and the villagers all cried out in anguish as Chang was hit with machine gun bullets until the artillery stopped and he was hanging still below the locust tree in the glow of sunset. The entire yard fell silent except for a cicada in the locust tree, which started chirping a long, mournful song.

Tim clenched his hands, and his tears mingled with his sweat as he bit his lip hard.

After an hour, he crept carefully out of his hiding place and was appalled by what he saw. The entire village had been massacred, their bodies strewn randomly around the yard. The breeze was coppery with blood, the smell of death wafting through the locust tree leaves.

He cut the ropes and solemnly laid Chang's body on the ground. He found a spade and started digging a burial ground for his friends. In a shaking voice he said, "You saved my life with yours, and I will take this to heart."

Chang's face was bloodied and Tim couldn't see anything to wipe it with. From his pocket he took out the piece of cloth and carefully cleaned Chang's face. It was pale but wore a smile.

The cloth that was soaked with blood was his blood chit. Tim read aloud softly, "This foreigner has come to China to help in the war effort. Soldiers and civilians, one and all, have a duty to rescue and protect him." In deep sorrow, he quickly buried Chang under the shade of the locust tree.

After burying Chang, he wandered the village, covered in blood and in shock. It was late October and the winds were chilly, and his body shook uncontrollably. Much to his sorrow, he found Chang's wife and their son covered in blood as well. But he didn't have the strength to bury more people. He couldn't believe what had just happened. He needed to think clearly about what to do next.

He walked slowly back to Chang's house. He noticed a tall basket on its side in the backyard. When he got closer, the lid popped off and out came Chang's daughter, Chang Yun. She looked around, her eyes wide and filled with tears, but no fear.

Tim pointed to where the Japanese had left. "They—" He wiggled his fingers to mimic a person running away.

"Follow me," the little girl said in Chinese. One of the few phrases Tim knew. She wiped her tears and walked into the house. Grabbing a piece of fabric, she starting filling it with food from the kitchen. She then took Tim's hand and led him away from the village.

Tim and Chang Yun walked for the entire night.

In the morning they came to a village. She led Tim to a family, and he showed them his blood chit. The family looked at one another in astonishment, then quickly invited him in.

A day later, one of the villagers came back with a Chinese soldier by the name of Captain Shude Liu. He spoke with Tim and learned what had happened, then contacted the Flying Tigers over the radio.

The following morning, Captain Liu brought Tim and Chang Yun to an open field south of the village. Pointing to the field, he spoke in Chinese using hand gestures.

Tim understood that he was saying the open field was a makeshift landing strip, but it was too slippery to land today after the heavy rain. Tim heard the name Tong Fang as the captain mimicked things dropping from the sky. Tim smiled and nodded. He didn't need a translator for that.

Chang Yun said, "He will come back."

Tim looked eagerly at the sky. He couldn't wait to hear the welcome sound of a P-40. Sure enough, in ten minutes, a P-40 appeared high above. He recognized Tong Fang's call number. Fang lowered the airplane and dropped a small package. Tim ran to pick it up. It was a bag of taros, antibiotics, liquor, and some cash. He waved to his friend with a grin.

Fang circled the plane, then came back around at much lower altitude, as if about to land.

Tim waved him off with both hands. But Fang seemed determined. He managed a perfect landing before screeching to a stop, tons of mud splattered on the plane.

"Damn! That was a close call, you idiot!" Tim called as he laughed and shouted and beelined it over to Fang. "You could have crashed sliding in that mud!"

"You're the idiot!" Fang called back, laughing as he hopped out of the plane. "You're the one who crashed way out here in the middle of nowhere!"

Tim and Fang hugged tightly. "Let's get out you back home," Fang said and climbed back into the pilot seat.

After waving his thanks to Captain Liu, Tim slid into the back seat and buckled in. Fang beckoned Chang Yun to sit on his lap in the cockpit.

The P-40 slid and wobbled down the runway, but finally lifted off, soaring into the air and heading for Chongqing.

Back at the Flying Tigers' base camp in Chongqing/Kunming, Tim went to report to General Chennault, who sent him straight to the infirmary to get checked out.

Chang Yun was taken to stay at an orphanage in the city.

The first thing the next day, General Chennault held a meeting. "Strategically, we need to step up our fighting," he said sternly. "We need to put an end to the Japanese inroads."

Fang nodded solemnly, rapt with attention, along with the other pilots, including Tim.

"Our mission is to secure the Burma Road, the only supply line for Chongqing, the wartime capital of China. Japanese planes are striking the supply line regularly. We need to be more aggressive. For our next fight with the Japanese, our squadron has been assigned to protect the Burma Road. We need to defend our supply route. So, let's go in and take out as many of their fighters as we can."

Tim Nolan was eager to fly again. "Will I be going?"

"You're not fully healed. You can't go out yet," said Chennault.

"My arm is basically healed," Tim Nolan pleaded. "I just need to finish these antibiotics."

General Chennault looked into Tim's eyes for a moment. "All right, then. To Burma you shall go."

Right before he left, Tim paid a visit to the orphanage in Chongqing to say goodbye to Chang Yun.

She was very excited to see him, and cried. "I am very happy here, very happy. But I am even happier to see you."

Tim stuffed one of his blood chits into her hand. He looked into her eyes. "Xiexie," he said. *Thank you.*

Chang Yun looked at the blood chit with her father's blood on it, nodded, folded it neatly, and carefully put it away.

* * * *

In the many coming air battles protecting the Burma Road, Tim always imagined he was facing the same troupe of Japanese soldiers that had massacred the village of Chang's family. Each time he steadied himself in the air, when he saw a flash out of the corner of his eye he would dash toward it. He'd aim his gun at the flash and never hesitated to pull the trigger. He didn't care if he wasted ammunition, there was only one thing on his mind—revenge. Many times, the enemy planes dove out of his sight and crashed to the ground in a plume of smoke.

He downed plane after plane without any emotions. After a time, he stopped counting his kills. He tried to remember the number...

probably fifteen? An experienced airman was usually lucky if he downed one plane in a battle, but fifteen was truly unbelievable. God was definitely his copilot. Always, deep down, he wanted just one more kill so he could feel at ease. *Yes, sixteen, that is the number.*

That day he was in the air again trying to position himself high and lock onto his target. He emptied one round of ammunition. Targeted, then another round, and another. He felt he was not a soldier but a mechanic running a flying machine that fired at other airborne monstrosities. He was a bit annoyed by this thought. After downing fifteen planes, there was no longer much heroism in operating this flying dragon.

He pulled the trigger again, but this time no round came out. He looked at the gauge. *Empty.* All of a sudden the enemy pilot gained altitude, looking like he was going to leave the engagement.

Tim immediately took control and quickly sped up. The sun glared into his eyes, nearly blinding him. He had a vision of Chang's body hanging from the locust tree, the same sun shining melting beams upon his face.

Tim pulled sharply at the controls, urging the plane forward as much as the engine would allow. He aimed straight at the enemy plane and closed his eyes as the two collided. His right wing slashed the left wing of the enemy fighter in half, his own plane sustaining heavy damage. The enemy plane fell like a rock, exploding on the ground with the pilot still inside.

As Tim's plane spiraled toward the earth, he opened the cockpit window and ejected, then deployed his parachute and floated through the sky. All he could see below were blurry fields of grain.

He landed hard, and a sudden surge of pain shot through his body. He had pushed himself to the limit during the air battle and the impact of the crash had taken its toll. He bounced and fell to his knees, the pain almost unbearable. With great effort, he rose to his feet, gritting his teeth against the pain. He took a step forward, then another, his pace slow and unsteady.

The walk to base turned into an eternity in hell, but he pushed on and on, determined to reach his comrades and receive the medical attention he knew he desperately needed. He took in the broad plains of Burma stretching out before him, dotted with plumes of smoke and the burned, crumpled carcasses of downed planes. The sounds of battle echoed in the distance, a constant reminder of being at war. The smells of death and destruction filled his nostrils, the acrid scent of smoke and burning fuel mixed with the metallic stench of blood and twisted metal.

Chang's death had finally been avenged, and despite the physical agony, Tim was grateful to be alive. He knew that his bravery and skill in the air had saved countless Chinese lives, and that was something he could hold onto.

He straightened his back and continued on, his gaze fixed on the horizon, his heart filled with a determination to fight the next battle. And trudged on toward the airbase.

* * * *

Qingdao, China

Mr. Tong could swear there were more and more Japanese wearing kimonos in the streets of Qingdao. And more and more Japanese businesses had returned to the city, or had just started up. Their numbers were overwhelming. In 1939 alone, the Japanese had opened around fifty manufacturing factories and incorporated nearly three hundred companies and stores. No wonder the Chinese business community was shrinking in size. Tong could not sit still anymore.

"Are all Chinese not only going to be under Japanese military rule, but also must work for them?" he complained to himself one day.

He could not bear that thought. So he started working on another idea. Baking soda and alkaline were used every day in every family, for cleaning, cooking, and many other purposes. The alkaline used in China was imported, and local Chinese manufacturers did not have any automated machinery for production. Everything was manual. With his knowledge of the chemicals used to dye fabrics, Tong decided he would open a chemical factory making baking soda or alkaline using modern machinery and technology.

This turned out to be extremely difficult under Japanese rule. Many people were facing economic hardship and hesitated to invest in such uncertain times. Nevertheless, after hundreds of fruitless meetings, Tong had gained the support of eighteen Chinese investors.

In 1940, after many months of meetings and paperwork, he finally had everything in place to start production. Qingdao Yannian Chemical Plant was established at No. 36, Deng Zhou Road. He thought back to the gala for the opening of his needle factory. This time there would be no festivities or big newspaper splashes. Even so, the business was soon doing very well. Even without the publicity, he was nonetheless gratified that he could hire many Chinese workers. He knew he was doing great things for China.

Chapter 19 The War Was Finally Over

It was mid-August 1945, and Tong was taking a walk during his lunch break. He was no longer the fit young man he had used to be so he wanted to exercise as much as he could to stay healthy. The humidity that day was unbearable, somewhat unusual for the seaside town. The streets were almost empty. No one wanted to go outside in this heat. There weren't even any birds out—they must have all been napping under the eaves—but the cicadas were deafening. The only people Tong saw were a few seniors dozing in the shade, their fingers wrapped around paper fans. The Japanese flag hung limply like a round Chinese medicine patch in the distance.

As Tong walked, he thought about his businesses—mostly the chemical factory that he and his fellow Chinese businessmen owned. He thought of Mr. Yin again. If Yin had stayed here, how joyful it would have been for him to share in Tong's agony and his joy. He hoped that one day Yin would suddenly be back from wherever he was now, so they could join forces again.

As Tong walked, he heard a clamor and raised voices inside a shop. He thought nothing of it as he walked by. But as he passed by another shop, he heard more shouting. Curious, he stopped and listened, straining to hear over the roaring cicadas. Then he heard the words he had been longing to hear for the past eight years.

"The Japanese have surrendered! The Japanese have surrendered!"

A man ran past him screaming with elation, his face red from both heat and happiness. Soon, more and more people came running out of the buildings onto the street. Everyone was celebrating together, throwing their arms around each other and waving in the air, dancing and jumping for joy.

"Did the Japanese really surrender?" he asked an elderly man on the side.

The man looked at him with tears in his eyes. "Yes, they did, my boy. Yes, they did."

Tong could scarcely believe it. But he had witnessed the end of The Great War and the Japanese leaving their town in 1922, so why not this time too? He turned and hurried back to his office. He had work to do!

"The Japanese surrendered!" he murmured gleefully as he walked swiftly, glad that he was not too old to see the end of these dark times.

* * * *

With the end of the war and the Nationalist government back in power, Tong quickly regained full control of his companies, including JiLu Needle Factory. He wasted no time ramping up production again to make up for lost profits during the Japanese occupation.

A few days after the surrender was announced, someone knocked on his office door at JiLu.

"Come in," he called, and the door opened slowly.

Mr. Yin stood there looking calm and with a big smile.

Tong lit up at the sight of Yin, but he didn't move for a moment to make sure the sight of his friend was real.

"Brother Yin!" Tong broke the spell and held his arms out wide, a huge grin curving his lips.

"Brother! You're alive!" cried Yin.

"Damn right, I am!" said Tong. "Come in! Come in! How are you doing, Mr. Yin? What have you been up to all this time during the war?"

After more hugs they sat down, and Yin said, "Well, I traveled to many different places outside of Japanese control. Shanghai, Hong Kong, Chongqing, Chengdu. I've been all over the East. My businesses have all been fairly successful. But they couldn't compare to the JiLu Needle Factory that I established together with my brother."

"I am happy to hear that, Brother Yin. I always knew you would do great things. But I'm glad you're back."

"It is very good to be back in Qingdao. Now, tell me, what have you been doing? How are the businesses? Did they survive?"

Tong smiled. "Yes, they survived."

"Wonderful!" said Yin. "I am truly happy to see that business was going well for you. I heard the Japanese took control of many Chinese companies."

"Yes, that's what they tried to do," said Tong.

Yin's eyes widened. "They tried to take the companies from you, the most successful businessman in Shandong?"

"They did." Tong smiled to himself. He explained how he had managed to get around them taking total control of the needle factory. "They did end up buying my other two businesses, so I moved my most skilled workers from to JiLu Needle Factory, where their high wages cut into profits. I sent all the less skilled workers to the other two factories, where production slowed considerably. The shareholders got most of the profits of JiLu, and the Japanese barely got any. They did not have enough good workers, I heard."

Mr. Yin looked at him and his belly started to shake as he burst into laughter. "You!"

"I know, I know. This how JiLu is still ours."

"You've always been a clever one!"

Tong and Yin continued catching up, then Tong brought up an idea he had. "Do you ever think about teaching the next generation about what we do?"

"It's funny you ask," said Yin, "I've been thinking about that lately. I have accumulated much experience, and I would like to share my knowledge."

"Yes, exactly," said Tong. He glanced at the clock. "Gosh, the workday is almost over. I should say something to our workers about the victory. But we should discuss this idea later."

Tong went downstairs, followed by Yin.

"Hello, everyone!" Tong yelled above the noise. "Stop the machines. Can I have your attention please?"

The clamor in the factory slowly died down, and all the workers crowded around.

Tong took in the sight of them. These workers had been with him through everything, standing by him as he shuffled them around to ensure the Japanese didn't get any profits or technologies. He had known all of them for many years, and each face told a story he was so proud of. He could never have achieved his success without them.

"My fellow citizens, many of you are from Changyi, my hometown, and I have known you for many years. You are all like my own brothers."

The workers gazed back at him expectantly.

"I feel so happy today. Happier than when the Germans withdrew in 1918, happier than the first time the Japanese withdrew, happier than when Mr. Sun Wen visited this factory. We have been working together for almost fifteen years now! I have always known that China could not be defeated. How could we?"

Tong's eyes filled with the emotion he felt. He swallowed his tears and continued speaking.

"We eat the grain we grow and wear the cloth we weave. As long as we can eat, use, and live in the things we make ourselves, we will never, ever be slaves without nationhood."

The workers burst into applause and shouted their admiration. Many of them were crying. Tong looked down at their faces with such pride. He was also proud of himself for leading them through the tough times and for being able to provide them with safety and income, even when the Japanese were in control. He was still moved by how much they trusted him.

* * * *

Soon after the Japanese left China, the conflict between the Nationalist authorities and the Communists started up again. The Communists soon had control over the rural areas, but they wanted the urban areas, too. The Land Reform Movement started in the countryside, where peasants humiliated and even killed the landowners. Hundreds of thousands of landowners were executed—some said millions— throughout the country.

At first the Nationalist forces seemed more organized, but the Communist forces grew in number. Everyone who had been allocated a piece of land during the Land Reform wanted to help the Communists fight. Even some former Nationalists were joining the Communist army. First the Communists won the northeast, then BeiPing, and soon Qingdao.

Tong heard that his hometown of Changyi had been greatly affected by the Land Reform. His old neighbors were shaming and killing landlords in so-called struggle sessions. Some of them even went on to fight for the People's Liberation Army. Then war officially broke out between the Communists and Nationalists. Soldiers' limbs and other body parts were seen hanging from trees in neighboring cities. These images were horrible, and wouldn't leave Tong's mind for a long time.

One day Tong and Yin had a discussion about the situation.

"Are you going to flee again?" asked Tong.

"Flee? What do you think? Mr. Tong, these are the Communists. They take away all your property!"

"Yes, but—"

"Do you know what they did in the countryside? The peasants rounded up the farm owners and killed them. They lost all their land, their possessions, and finally their lives!"

"So now all the poor families own the land they grow their crops on? I don't think it's such a bad idea. I would not have to come to Qingdao if I'd had that opportunity back in Changyi."

Yin scowled. "This is not a joke, Brother Tong."

Tong knew he might be out of line, but he was bitter to see his business partner talk about leaving again. Bitter in more ways than one. All he had ever known was Changyi and Qingdao. He didn't have the ability to move around the world like Yin did. Yin was multilingual, easily able to adapt to new cultures and environments. Tong didn't speak any other language, and he didn't know how to do anything except stay in a familiar place with his familiar people. It had been like that in the past, and it was still like that now.

"So you're going to make me run all these factories while you scurry away like a coward, yet again?" Tong could not withhold his anger. "Our companies need you! What about our plans? The schools? The Communists are not German or Japanese, they are Chinese. And we are Chinese, too!"

"They may be Chinese like us, but they are just as dangerous as the Germans and Japanese!" Yin roared back.

Tong sighed. "I see we have a great difference of opinion."

"That seems true." Yin's tone carried half stubbornness and half apology.

"This is our native country. What exactly are you running from?" Tong pursued. It's different than running away from the Japanese."

Yin looked baffled and uncertain.

What was Yin thinking? What if he wasn't safe wherever he ended up? Who knew where the Communists would go next. Tong could not understand why Yin was running away from other Chinese just because they called themselves communists. Tong and Yin were, after all, business owners. Don't people in a Communist society use needles and wear clothes? The Communists were Chinese. They spoke Chinese and acted like Chinese people. Surely, they could be reasoned with.

"Brother Tong, oppression! That is what I am running away from. It does not matter if it is the Japanese or the Chinese who oppress us."

"Well, Brother Yin." Tong held out an envelope to Yin, looking deeply into his eyes. "I know you've thought this through. Here is a bank check drawn on Citibank for the value of the shares you have in our businesses. Take it and take good care of yourself and your family."

"Thank you, Mr. Tong." Yin rummaged through his pockets. "Here, I bought this for you."

He handed Tong a two-inch piece of jade carved in the shape of a dragon. "I also had one made for myself," he said, showing his piece to Tong. "Hopefully this jade will protect us both, wherever we are."

Tong was touched. "I don't know what to say," he said. "Thank you."

"I truly hope fate brings us together again," said Yin.

Mr. Tong nodded. "As do I."

But the way things seemed to be heading, he didn't think it would ever happen.

Chapter 20 The Days After Liberation

By 1949, the Communist troops had established control over most of China. Everybody was excited to see what the future of China would look like. The youth were especially excited, holding street demonstrations, discussing the new government, and touting the ideas of Mao Zedong, the new leader.

Mr. Tong was happy to see the Chinese in control again. After all the violence of the past foreign occupations of Qingdao, it was nice to have some stability. He felt the new leadership would help China become the great country it was always meant to be. In addition, he was reassured because the government said that private ownership would be kept intact for at least ten years. Communist grassroot organizers were assigned to his factory, and Mr. Tang, an earlier Eighth Route Army officer, became the party secretary of Yannian Chemical.

But just a few years later in 1953, the government began pushing for a fully socialist society, and Tong started to worry about his safety. As a businessman, he was considered part of the bourgeoisie. Since he owned several factories and was in charge of all the workers who manufactured his products, he was not only a bourgeoisie, but a *major* bourgeoisie. But he told himself that whatever happened to his businesses, surely it couldn't be as bad as what the Japanese did.

At least that was what he thought.

Sure enough, the government soon announced that business owners were encouraged to volunteer for joint public-private ownership of their companies. Tong wasn't exactly sure what that meant, or what was going to happen, but he knew he had no choice but to go along with it.

* * * *

Soon Tong was invited to attend an important meeting at his Yannian Chemical factory. He didn't think it was optional.

Secretary Tang started by giving a speech outlining the procedure the party was taking to move toward socialism. "Comrades," he began. "In light of the party policy and the economic objectives for our country, we are gathered here today to draw up a socialist transformational mobilization plan. As you may have heard, our new government, under the great leadership of Chairman Mao, is implementing some fundamental changes to bring about a great socialist society. Large businesses will be transferred to be under government control, medium businesses will become public-private joint ventures, and small companies will be bought by the government." He looked at Tong. "JiLu will undergo public-private ownership."

"This sounds familiar," muttered Accountant Liu, who was sitting next to Tong. "The Japanese had a similar line when they took control of your companies."

Tong shushed him. "Don't say that. Mind your mouth."

Secretary Tang said, "And I am proud to announce that this business, Yannian Chemical Factory, will also become a public-private joint venture."

The crowd burst into applause. Obviously there was much support for the new government scheme.

"And now," said Secretary Tang, "we will bestow an honor on Mr. Tong as a representative of the bourgeoisie capitalists."

Surprised, Tong nervously went up to the podium.

But Secretary Tang simply pinned a paper flower to his lapel. "I look forward to our collaboration." He shook Tong's hand.

Tong was not looking forward to it so much.

After the ceremony, he and Accountant Liu discussed the developments.

"Mr. Tong, a few years ago, they limited the amount of profit taken by business owners to twenty percent. Now there will not be any profits. Doesn't it worry you that this is just like when the Japanese were here?"

"Yes, but what can we do about it?"

Accountant Liu held up a brochure. "According to this document, *Provisions of the State Council on Several Major Issues Regarding Asset Clearance and Estimation when Private Enterprises Implement Public-Private Partnerships,* factories must pay a fixed interest rate of five percent to private equity shareholders for ten years. We also have to evaluate the business based on the numbers provided by the industrial valuation committee."

Tong grimace. "Yes. And who knows what they will come up with those numbers."

"It's outrageous," Accountant Liu declared. "For ten years, that will only amount to fifty percent of the value of the company. And after that, the business will totally belong to the government. This will lead to the state controlling all means of production!"

"Hush, hush. Listen, it doesn't matter whose factory it is, right? We are all Chinese. I will still be the general manager, appointed by the government instead of the board of directors."

"Because the government is now the board of directors," said Liu with a scowl.

"Exactly! We are all employees. We are all…comrades."

Accountant Liu shook his head, and Tong shuddered.

* * * *

More changes were happening every day to create the socialist society the government was aiming for. In 1955, Yannian Chemical Plant was merged into the Guangyi Chemical Industry Plant.

In 1958, the government wanted to ramp up production as much as possible to compete with Western industrial nations such as England and the United States. Propaganda posters were put up everywhere telling workers to increase output and instructing farmers to use modern farming methods to grow more crops.

Tong heard the government was collecting all the iron it could from the Chinese people and melting it down to make tools and machines.

"The Great Leap Forward is here!" Mr. Tang said enthusiastically to Tong one day in a management meeting in the Guangyi Chemical Industry Plant. "We must increase our production to advance China's economy."

"So I've heard," said Tong. "I already have our machines running at double speed, as fast as they can go."

Secretary Tang wasn't impressed. "Double speed?" He looked at the machines that were whirring away. "This is double speed?"

"Well, yes," said Tong nervously. "This is as fast as they can go."

"Hmm."

"What is it?"

"Well," said Secretary Tang, "The machines at the weaving factory go much faster than this."

"Yes." Tong laughed. "That's because it's fabric. You see, here the chemicals can corrode the machines and shorten their lifespans. You don't have that problem with weaving machines because there are no chemicals involved."

Secretary Tang was not convinced. "I want these machines going double this speed so we can have the present output doubled."

"Doubled?" Tong was incredulous. "Sir, there's no way the output can be doubled. The machines simply cannot take it. They already have only around five years left, even at this speed, with the corrosion. It's a simple chemical formula."

Secretary Tang leaned closer to Tong, looking angry. "It sounds like you are against the Great Leap Forward movement."

"I never said that!" Tong protested.

Secretary Tang smiled, and Tong's stomach churned. He was disgusted by the man's stupid ideas and his evil smile.

"You are the production expert." Secretary Tang said. "You do want Chinese industry to grow and make our society better for everyone, right?"

"Of course." Tong realized that these machines were no longer his, therefore any problems with the machines were also no longer his. May as well just go along with the fool.

"Then let's make these machines run twice as fast!" said Secretary Tang.

Tong collected himself, looked directly into the other man's eyes, and smiled back. "Of course. Whatever you think is best."

Tong watched with narrowed eyes as Secretary Tang turned and walked away. He let out a breath of relief that the odious man was gone.

He would definitely have to watch out for the pretentious Secretary Tang.

* * * *

The Great Leap Forward ended up being a horrible failure. GuangYi Chemical's equipment failed by 1959. Production had to stop completely.

And the era that would later be known as the Great Famine began.

It first started in the countryside. With all the focus on iron and steel production, the farmers were forced to abandon their crops, which led to mass starvation in the rural areas. In tears, people butchered their dogs, and ate dirt and chewed bark just to fill their bellies. There were reports of cannibalism in some areas. The famine then spread to the city.

Even though Tong was very well-to-do, even he could not escape the horrors of the famine. The city of Qingdao was filled with moans of hunger and pain. Tong was walking to work one day carrying a bundle of steamed buns for lunch. A man came out of nowhere, snatched the bundle out of his hands, tore it open, and stuffed the buns into his mouth as he swiftly ran away. Tong was so shocked he couldn't move, and just watched the man's back as he ran willy-nilly through the streets.

* * * *

Secretary Tang had returned to the military and was promoted to head of the provincial military authorities. His son, Tang Jisheng, worked in the Division of Security in one of Tong's factories.

One day, Secretary Tang came into the factory looking for Mr. Tong.

"How is your family doing in this famine?" he asked.

Tong was not fooled by his fake sympathy. "We're getting by the best we can." The truth was, even Tong was struggling.

"I'm glad to hear that," Secretary Tang said. "My family is going through very hard times. The army had to scale down because of the famine, and my wife and I don't have enough to eat."

It wasn't anything Tong hadn't heard of before. "I'm sorry, Secretary Tang. If there's anything I can do to help, please let me know."

"There is, actually." Secretary Tang became more excited. "With you, I don't need to beat around the bush. I was wondering if I could borrow some money to help us get by."

Tong hiked his eyebrows. "How much?"

"We need ten thousand *yuan* per month for six months."

Tong's jaw dropped. Ten thousand *per month*? He couldn't believe his ears. "I'm sorry, Secretary Tang, times are hard for everyone. Our companies are struggling because we're low on workers." He added pointedly, "And the machines in the chemical factory gave out."

Secretary Tang smiled. "I know you were a great industrialist, I heard you even sold some companies to the Japanese."

Tong was utterly confused. "I was forced to. What does that have to do with anything?"

Secretary Tang stepped closer. "We cross-examined Zhao Qi shortly after we liberated Qingdao. Did you know he was thrown into prison? Well, he's not there anymore, but he told us several stories about you before he was released."

Tong clamped his jaw. Was this still about the ten thousand *yuan*? Tong had been in business long enough that he was familiar with people bluffing. "I don't understand what you're talking about."

"An industrialist like you is never without plenty of money. Keep in mind the old days when you sold your factories to the Japanese." Secretary Tang left no doubt he was threatening Tong. "I will need the money in two weeks."

* * * *

The next month, several policemen confronted Mr. Tong in his office.

"Hey, hey, hey!" shouted Tong as the policemen started to drag him away. "What did I do?"

"You are being tried for treason," they said.

Tong was aghast. "Treason?"

One of the policemen chuckled. "Have fun defending this in court.

You are under arrest."

The trial wasn't as much of a trial as it was a public humiliation. Tong sat there staring blankly ahead as the crowd yelled all sorts of terrible things at him.

"Comrade Tong, you colluded with the Japanese during the war by expressing willingness to participate in the so-called Security and Maintenance Committee, right?"

Tong slowly raised his head and said, "I was never a member of the Security and Maintenance Committee. I refused Mayor Zhao Qi's invitation to join. But I had to work with Zhao Qi to coordinate factory issues."

"What coordination? Didn't you financially support the Japanese invasion of China?"

Tong had no idea what they were talking about. "No! Have you charged me with treason because I betrayed the Chinese government by colluding with the Japanese?"

"Yes!"

"When was that?" Tong demanded.

"Before 1945 when the Japanese surrendered."

"What was the government in China at that time?"

"It was the Republic of China of course. What are you trying to say?"

"If I turned against that government by committing treason, shouldn't I be prosecuted by that government? And even if I did commit treason, didn't our new government overthrow that old government? You say I was committing treason, but wasn't *everyone* committing treason?"

Harangues came from every direction.

"Your remark is beyond counterrevolutionary!"

"You good-for-nothing traitor!"

"Bourgeoisie scum!"

"You anti-Communist!"

"You must confess!"

Tong closed his eyes, and suddenly remembered what Zhao Qi said. *A hero does not take a direct hit that he can avoid.* Probably good advice.

"Okay, I confess, I confess!" Tong shouted. "I paid the Japanese good prices for the dyeing and weaving machines as far back as in 1928. Those were the best machines in the world back then. I suppose they must have used the money to launch war against China."

He didn't even flinch as he was convicted as a national traitor. He was sentenced to two years in prison and fined ten thousand yuan per month for six months.

That night when he was alone, he thought of his life up until that point. He thought of opening up his factories and transforming Chinese manufacturing. He thought of the recognition he had received. He thought of his workers, his business partners, and the schools he was planning to open in his hometown. He thought of his son, Tong Fang, and the way they had worked together to help the Chinese army while under Japanese rule. He thought about Fang as a young boy, so bold and outspoken, and how he had matured into a successful pilot who had fought with the Flying Tigers. He also thought of his friend, Mr. Yin, fidgeting with the jade dragon in his pocket, and wondered where he would be now if he had gone with Yin.

Tong had done it all during the many tumultuous years that Qingdao was under foreign rule. And here he was, now being put in prison by his own people.

* * * *

Qingdao, China, 1964

Tong didn't come out of prison the same person he was when he'd gone in. All the horrors of the past few decades and his time in prison had caught up to him.

His memory had blurred and was no longer clear. He would be standing on the street in 1964 but he thought he was back in his office as the Japanese seized his companies. He wandered through the streets silently and did not greet people who knew him and beckoned to him. The only parts of the city he went to that still made him happy were the DengZhou Road and GuanTao Road, where he had built his companies as a young man. At home he would burst into tears and wail at the thought of Brother Yin. He would stay up late at night thinking about what could have been or might have happened. His doctor thought loss of sleep could be making him delirious, so he prescribed sleeping medication.

Thus Tong found a way to escape by sleeping. When he was asleep, he saw only the good memories play out in his dreams. He dreamed of equipment, factories, and of course Mr. Yin.

* * * *

British Hong Kong, 1968

At that time, Mr. Yin was in Hong Kong working on his fifth company. He had been elected chairman of the Hong Kong Business Council. He was thriving and making many new business connections. He also thought about Mr. Tong every now and then, wondering if he had survived the famine and the Communist takeover. But he knew how resilient Mr. Tong was, and was sure he was doing great things with his life.

One day, as Yin was getting up from his desk in Hong Kong, his jade dragon fell out of his pocket. When Yin went to pick it up, he was surprised to find it had shattered. He gasped and gingerly picked up the pieces from the ground.

He was perplexed. "I thought jade was never supposed to break."

As he put the broken pieces onto his bookshelf, he wondered once again how Mr. Tong was doing.

* * * *

Qingdao, China, 1968

The recent years had been too much for Mr. Tong to handle. He'd had enough of being resilient. He was tired of starting new businesses only to have them taken over by whatever government ruled the country at the time. He felt he had no more purpose as an entrepreneur. He wished the good times would come back and stay forever.

One day, he gazed out at the scene outside his window before going to bed. Out there on the street, you could catch the bus and ride to Deng Zhou Road where he had started his Shuang Sheng Wei Dyeing Fabric Company fifty years ago, and built his Liu Fu Weaving Factory thirty years ago. From Deng Zhou Road you could ride the bus to Guantao Road Qiyan Mansion where he had later co-founded Qingdao Commodity Exchange, probably one of the first in China, forty years ago. You could continue on the bus to Lijun Road where he had co-founded JiLu Needle thirty years ago, and then travel on to Cang Kou District where he had founded Yannian Chemical Factory twenty years ago.

He became immersed in his thoughts of the past, as always, then finally went to bed.

But this time he did not wake up the next morning.

On the bedside table beside his bottle of sleeping pills lay the jade dragon that Mr. Yin had given him before the revolution, its red tassels hanging over the edge.

Chapter 21 Yannian's Later Years

Qingdao, China, 1978

The ten years after the passing of Mr. Tong were a time of great political turmoil and upheaval in China. The seaside city of Qingdao was not spared. The Cultural Revolution engulfed every organization, factory, school, and village. Any representatives of the bourgeoisie were publicly denounced and humiliated, all according to the whims of the various political movements at the time.

Accountant Liu was the oldest person remaining with Yannian Chemical Factory, which had changed its name to Guangyi Chemical Factory. As the man in charge of the company accounts, he was summoned to a few of these sessions where he was subjected to abject criticism. For a long time Guangyi Chemical Factory had been running at a loss so workers' wages had to be subsidized by the government. He felt it was unfair, because he had warned management long ago of the problems. But what could he do?

In 1978, it was announced at the Third Plenary Session of the Eleventh Central Committee of the Chinese Communist Party that the government would be pursuing an open door policy in order to increase economic growth. The new Chinese government was trying to rebuild the economy and society after the Cultural Revolution and the death of Chairman Mao.

In 1982, Tang Jisheng became the director of Guangyi Chemical

Factory. The production still ran at a loss and the business still received subsidies from the government to survive, as most of the state-owned enterprises did in China at that time.

Three years later, Director Tang Jisheng spoke to the workers at the general meeting of Guangyi Chemical Factory. "Today we will study the directive, *Preliminary Regulations on Further Expanding Independent Management of State Owned Industrial Enterprises*, issued by the state council in May last year. The directive points out that since the Third Plenary Session of the Twelfth Party Congress, the main goal of this economic reform is to improve the financial performance of state-run medium-to-large enterprises. We must encourage the management responsibility system, the leasing system, the capital management responsibility system, and even the stock sharing system. But do so under the condition that ownership and management remain separate."

A few workers yawned and stretched their legs.

* * * *

In 1989, Director Tang Jisheng assumed the role of manager of the Guangyi Chemical Factory , and was responsible for its financial profit or loss. The company was still running at a loss.

Director Tang again presided at the Guangyi employee meeting. "Let us warmly welcome Mr. Wu from the Municipal Economic Reform Committee to present the latest news from the party leadership."

Mr. Wu nodded as he took center stage. "In order to deepen the reform and help open China to trading with the outside world, we need to decentralize management powers. Among various measures, the State Council is actively promoting lifting pricing controls and adopting a market-oriented pricing system."

Two factory workers were whispering to each other during the speech.

"When are they going to finish this boring meeting?"

"It has already been two hours!"

"I need to leave early and talk with a friend about getting a washing machine ordered through his connections."

"Do it quickly, the yuan will devalue soon and become toilet paper."

Throughout the country, department stores were flooded with people bringing their hard-earned cash to buy color TVs, washing machines, and other household products. People used their meager life savings of thousands of yuan in exchange for a few domestically made shoddy electronic consumer goods.

****

Years later before the new century started, Director Tang could be found wooing bureaucrats in banquets and social gatherings held in private ballrooms. Guangyi Chemical Factory was on the brink of bankruptcy, and people were saying the government would probably not be able to provide further financial assistance.

Director Tang smiled behind the workers' conference podium. "We warmly welcome Mr. Xu from the Provincial Reform Working Unit to address us, and we all applaud!"

Wearing a fancy suit and tie, Mr. Xu stepped up to the podium. "In 1998, as many as six hundred state-owned enterprises went bankrupt in China. Recently, a spokesperson for the finance ministry claimed that eighty-one percent of the top state-owned enterprises reported false assets and profits. I am sure Guangyi Chemical was not one of them."

"Yes, yes, we were one of the other twenty-nine percent," Director Tang chimed in, still smiling.

Some workers laughed. They knew better.

Mr. Xu continued, "In the Third Plenary Session of the Fifteenth Party's Congress, it was stressed that a basic economic system should be established where private ownership coexists with the public ownership. What does this mean? It means that we need to adopt a capitalist system in our state-owned economy. We will be working actively with the current management of Guangyi to deepen the reform of the corporate structures."

Later, officials from various organizations, including banks, came to the factory and held a meeting in Director Tang soundproof glass conference room above the factory floor. The workers looked on from below as government officials congratulated Director Tang, who posed for a photo as he signed several documents. The name of Guangyi Chemical Factory, formerly Yannian Chemical Factory, was officially changed to Yan Chemical Industry Plant.

The same two workers as before looked at each other.

"Does anything change for us?" said one of them.

"Nope, he just owns it now instead of the government. It's business as usual for us."

"Except maybe a pay raise when the boss gets rich?"

The other workers burst into laughter. "You wish!"

"What's changed for you?" the foreman barked at them. "Here's what. You'll only get paid as long as you keep these products going out the door! If you don't like it, you can be fired or you can quit. Or even go to America! Now get back to work!"

The workers turned sullenly back to their machines. One of them said, "My English is not good. I guess I'll have to wait for the Americans to invade."

"You're such a reactionary!" The foreman muttered from behind him.

"What year is it now?" The disgruntled worker asked.

Above them, Director Tang was silently smiling as he chatted with the officials and signed the loan and privatization documents that would make the company his. By borrowing money from the state bank with the assets of Guangyi as the collateral, with a few strokes of a pen, Director Tang Jisheng became the majority shareholder, owning eighty percent of the shares of the seventy-year-old factory.

✳ ✳ ✳ ✳

Qingdao, China, 2005

One day in 2005, Accountant Liu was walking through the streets of Qingdao wearing a dark suit. His few gray hairs were slicked back and his balding head shone in the sun. He came to a crosswalk and hovered, waiting for the traffic to clear. The cars didn't stop for him, so he had to make his way across the street and hope the cars and trucks would see him and stop.

Accountant Liu's face was etched with the wisdom and sophistication of a life long-lived, but still with the same old sparkle in his eyes he'd had when he was young. Deep wrinkles marked the corners of his eyes and mouth, testaments to the countless smiles and frowns he had worn over the years. Despite his body always aching, his posture was still upright and regal, reflecting the pride he'd taken in his work in the past, and now in his old age. The faint lines of his spectacles adorned the bridge of his nose, hinting at his scholarly nature. His face was a warm and noble tapestry woven from the threads of many years.

He had been retired for thirty years now. A lot had changed since he had been Yannian Chemical's accountant. The buildings in Qingdao were so tall they disappeared up into the smog. All around Liu were bright flashing lights, speakers blaring announcements and music, and colorful advertisements, all screaming for his attention. The crowds were larger than ever, with young people brushing carelessly past

207

him. Eight lanes of traffic whizzed past him as he tried to collect his thoughts.

Though he found it difficult to see where he was going, he finally managed to find Chongqing Road in order to do what no father should ever have to do—send his own son to the crematory. Only forty-five, his son had been an office worker, but the stress of his job had been too much and he'd died of a heart attack. Accountant Liu was shocked by this terrible news, but unfortunately, it was not unheard of. Many young workers in their twenties, thirties, and forties were dropping dead from the stress of their jobs.

After the funeral, Accountant Liu walked through the graves, thinking about his son. He saw one of the cemetery workers and stopped to thank him for the service. "Thank you for helping me send off my son."

"Of course. I'm sorry for your loss. No parent deserves to bury their child."

Accountant Liu nodded. Something about this man's voice was familiar. "Hey, do I know you from somewhere? Did you used to work in a factory in Qingdao?"

The man tilted his head. "Yes, I did."

"In the Yannian Chemical Plant?"

"Yes! It's called the Yan Chemical Industry Plant now."

"You're Wang Yun!"

"That's right! I was a manager there. It's funny, many of the processes we used to produce chemicals are similar to cremation."

"Ah, I see."

"You were Mr. Tong's accountant, right?"

Liu smiled wistfully. "You still remember."

"He's buried around here somewhere, too."

"Yes. That was many years ago. So many years..."

Accountant Liu had been here some forty years ago mourning Mr.

Tong's passing, and had a vague recollection of where he was buried. From memory, he wandered through the lines of graves, reading the names on the tombstones.

"It was right around here. I remember he was buried along the road uphill," he murmured to himself.

This time his memory didn't fail him.

"Ah, Mr. Tong, here you are. Finally, I have found you."

Accountant Liu stood before the tombstone, and the old memories started to revive, dragging him back some sixty years. He was silent for a minute, then slowly said, "You treated me well. Mr. Tong. And now I am ninety-two years old."

The wind whipped up a little and became bitter cold as he stood on the hilly tomb site in respectful silence, paying tribute in his heart and wiping the dirt off Mr. Tong's tombstone.

"You were such a smart man," he told his long-dead friend. "It's a shame you're not around anymore. You know, despite all the smart things you did, you did not leave China. If you had, I would have left with you. And that would have spared me all the tortures of the Cultural Revolution."

Mournful, Liu started to weep. He inhaled deeply of the cold air, then exhaled, closing his eyes to let the tears flow down his face.

"In fact, now that I think about it, you were the smartest one. You did not suffer through the Cultural Revolution, and you were buried in your hometown." Liu chuckled. "Where was your business partner, Mr. Yin, buried? I heard he died in 1984 in Hong Kong. It's good to be buried in your hometown. This is the sacred land of Qi and Lu where Confucius used to live and teach." Qi and Lu was another name for Shangdong province.

Accountant Liu looked up at the sky. The sun was high, pouring warmth that radiated through the gusty winds.

"Without you, we Chinese would not know how to machine dye

fabric, and would have had to use needles made in Japan." He looked down at Mr. Tong's tombstone. "Director Tang is now the owner of the chemical factory you founded. All the machines are much more advanced these days. The economy is developing so much. It really is. The foreign investors, they've all come back—the Germans, the Japanese, the Americans. Young people are working harder these days."

Liu shook his head, suddenly reminded of his son, and wept some more.

"There are many economic laws now. But shouldn't there be also health laws? My son died of a heart attack at just forty-five. Ah, Mr. Tong, he had his whole life in front of him. Isn't this just another Great Leap Forward, with people working to death instead of starving to death?"

He wiped the tears from his cheeks and glanced around at the other tombstones nearby. He noticed the tombstone of Chen Jiefu, the cotton factory owner, then he saw the grave of Zhang Zongjie, the machine tool factory owner.

"Look, all the old timers are here." He chuckled humorlessly, new tears swelling in his eyes. "Leave a place for me and I will be here soon to accompany you all. I will do the accounting for you." He gave a laugh, which echoed around the valley below the hilly graveyard.

"We will all return to the earth…"

Accountant Liu stumbled away from graves and left the cemetery.

The sun was setting over the city of Qingdao, casting a warm glow over the bustling streets. The salty sea air mixed with the scent of spicy street food wafting from the vendor carts. Children laughed and ran along the promenade, chasing each other down to the shore. The sounds of the city echoed in the streets as merchants called out their wares and boats honked their horns, the soft lapping of the waves in the background. The tall skyscrapers stood tall against the sky, reflecting the orange and red hues of the setting sun.

As the day came to a close, the crowds began to thin and the city lights twinkled to life. Shopkeepers closed up their stalls and locked their doors, making their way home to their families. On the pier, a lone fisherman cast his line into the sea, hoping to catch a good dinner. The peace and stillness of the night settled over the city, as if in tribute to the recollections of Accountant Liu today.

Chapter 22 Mike's Second China Trip

"Sir, sir, wake up, wake up," a soft voice said, making Mike sit up quickly and look around. "Your blanket fell to the floor."

Mike pulled down his sleep mask. It was the gentleman sitting next to him. "Oh. Thank you." His dream switched to reality, accompanied by the low hum of the plane engine.

Mike turned on his cell phone, linked up with the airline's wifi, and messaged Song Mei, the pretty Yan Chemical accountant he'd become friends with last time he was in China.

Mike: *Hey, Mei, how is everything?*

Mei: *Mike? Are you in the U.S.?*

Mike: *No. I am on my way to China. In the airplane right now.*

Mei: *Are you coming for business?*

Mike: *Yes, for business.*

Mei: *I know you are coming. You need to be careful.*

Mike: *What do you mean? How did you know?*

Mei: *Call my cell phone after you land.*

She knew already? Which meant Tang must also know he was on his way to China. Mei was the closest contact point he had to Tang. He'd hoped Mei could help him get to the documents that Wang mentioned.

As soon as he landed in Beijing, Mike went straight to the inexpensive hotel he'd booked near WangFujing Street.

The hotel had a bigger lobby than he expected. The lady at the front desk exchanged a few words with him and gave him his room key. The room was adequate, but the AC was not working and felt warm and stuffy. After he lodged a complaint with the receptionist, he thought over what he should do first. He decided to call Wang Ping's wife, Liu. They arranged to meet at a café close to a nearby branch of the Bank of China.

He greeted Liu in Chinese, and they sat down at a table and ordered tea. Liu was a woman in her late forties, and today she looked rather haggard and wan.

After the waitress left, Liu pulled a small zip drive out of her purse. "I just retrieved this from Ping's Bank of China deposit box," she said in Chinese, her voice shaking slightly. "It is what my husband told me to give to you in the event—" Her words halted and tears filled her eyes.

"Are your two daughters still in the U.S.?" Mike asked, sticking to Chinese.

"Yes." She dabbed her eyes. "I haven't told them about their father yet. I think Iowa is the best place for them. My only thoughts are for their safety. Their father was murdered so cruelly, and I am such a weak woman. I am begging you to take care of my two daughters in America if you can."

"Please don't worry," Mike said sympathetically. "Wang may have offended someone here in China, but I'm sure they are safe over there. Honestly, I am not entirely sure what this terrible situation is all about. But I promise to do the best I can for them when I return."

After an awkward few minutes drinking tea with Liu to be polite, Mike returned to the hotel. The hotel phone rang.

"Mike, it's me, Mei."

"Hi! I was just about to call you," he said. "Where are you?"

"Downstairs."

"How did you know I was in this hotel?" he asked in surprise.

"I'll explain. Can I come up?"

"Of course."

Despite his very fond memories of their recent time together, Mike couldn't exactly recall what Mei looked like. He opened the door, and recognized her immediately. How could he ever forget such a beautiful woman? She stood there, a pale but graceful lady in an overcoat, her purse over her shoulder. She wasn't smiling.

She stepped into the room and hurriedly said, "Mr. Tang has asked me to call you. He has been tracking your whereabouts and knows you are here."

"How?" Mike asked. Not that he was overly surprised.

"Mr. Tang has access to your airport entry information as well as your hotel registration, because both are reported to the Entry and Exit Registration. I'm not sure if I was followed coming here. But I'm sure you are."

Which meant Tang already knew that Mike had met with Wang Ping's wife.

He motioned for her to take a seat at a small table in the corner and he sat in the chair opposite. "What does Tang want you to do with me?"

"He wants me to tell you to give up what you are doing and leave China without taking anything with you. Otherwise... I think he will probably do the worst."

Mike nodded grimly. "I knew the danger I'd be in when I decided to come here."

Mei bit her lip. "Aren't you worried?"

"I'll be careful," Mike said, more calm on the outside than he felt inside.

Mei leaned close to him and said, "Please. I don't want you to get hurt. Hand me the package from Wang Ping and I will take it back to

Tang to keep you safe."

Mike couldn't figure out Mei's purpose here. Did she truly care and want to save him, or was this visit merely to threaten him into turning over the zip drive to Tang?

"Mei, I'm sure your intentions are good, but I don't think it would be to my advantage if I give up the package. What if I am falsely accused of being connected to Wang Ping's murder and end up in some Chinese prison, or worse?"

"There are worse things than prison." She looked him straight in the eye. "I'm afraid for you, Mike. These powerful men can do anything they want."

Mike was silent for a long moment. He was moved by Mei's words and the genuine care in her expression. But could he trust her?

"If you don't turn in the package to Mr. Tang, you will be in great danger." To his surprise, a tear trickled down her cheek. "I wish…"

He reached across the table for her hand. "What do you wish, Mei?"

"I wish God had gifted me with plentiful wealth. If He had, I would make it as difficult for you to leave me…as it is now for me to leave you." She looked down at their joined hands, a blush blooming across her face.

"Mei, I…" Tender feelings he didn't know he had for her bubbled to the surface. "I wish that, too. I wish I could stay in China longer and get to know you. Perhaps one day, when all this is over…"

She let out a quiet sob. "I need tell you something terrible. Mr. Tang ordered me to poison you if you don't give me the package. Please run away! I can cover for you."

Mike was speechless.

Just then Mei's phone pinged with a message. She picked it up and looked at the screen, then silently showed it to Mike.

Mr. Tang: *Mei, did you get the package?*

Mei: *No, I don't think he is willing.*

After a moment, the phone pinged again.

Mr. Tang: *Ask him to meet with me in his hotel room. I'll be there shortly.*

She looked up at Mike. "What should I tell him?"

"I don't think you have any option."

She took a shuddering breath and typed.

Mei: *Okay.*

* * * *

Mike pretended to be unaware and unconcerned when he opened the door for Tang and invited him in and to take a seat at the small table.

Tang sat next to Mei and Mike sat across from them.

Tang said jovially, "Mike, it is good to see you again. It has been quite some time since we became friends."

"I've enjoyed working with you and Yan Chemical," Mike said, and caught a glimpse of a black handgun hidden under Tang's suit coat. Mike's pulse surged in alarm. Not good. Did Tang plan to shoot him? What happened to the poison idea?

Tang's expression turned more serious. "I need you to do me a favor, Mike. I have been informed that you are in possession of an important piece of information about my company. Since you are our attorney, you are aware of your duty of loyalty. So I hope you will consider returning to me the information you were given."

"Mr. Tang, I appreciate your concern," Mike said, fighting to keep his voice and his heartbeat even and calm. "But I'm sorry, this matter is outside the scope of our attorney-client relationship. In fact, I no longer work for Williamson & Gray."

Which, by his expression, Tang already knew.

"I understand. No one is forcing you to do anything. Let's sit and talk about this. Perhaps I can offer you a job here in China." Tang turned to Mei. "Could you please make us some coffee?"

"Of course."

She went to the sideboard where there was a kettle and coffee fixings. As she brewed the coffee, Mike and Tang talked casually about the weather and the various places in China that Mike had visited. All the time his pulse raced. Would she poison him? Or...?

Surreptitiously from the corner of his eye, he watched as Mei turned her back to him and emptied a small amount of white power into one of the cups. She poured the coffee and brought him and Tang each a cup at the table.

Mike swallowed heavily. *This was it.* One way or another, it would be over.

Tang watched him swallow the coffee.

The last thing Mike saw was the cruel, satisfied expression on Tang's face as Mike's muscles turned to jelly and everything went black.

* * * *

Tang Jisheng, the honored CEO of Yan Chemical walked closer to the troublemaker Mike Nolan's body and felt for his pulse. Thankfully, there was none. He patted down body for any papers or other things he might be carrying. Again, he found nothing, other than a wallet that was empty except for a U.S. driver's license and some money.

He turned to Song Mei and said angrily, "He must have hidden it. Wait here until my men come to search the room. When they're finished they will pick him up and throw him into the river. These Americans always think they are heroes in Hollywood movies." He made a call on his cell phone. "It's done. Come immediately and search the hotel room thoroughly." He hung up.

"Why is it so important to get this information you are looking for? What is it?" Song Mei asked him.

"It's the genuine and correct accounting record of Yan Chemical. It is what Wang Ping was blackmailing us with. If Mike Nolan were to expose this information, we would lose the entire U.S. market."

Song Mei's eyes grew wide. "I understand. I will keep watch here until your people come to search and get rid of the body. But it is only five o'clock and still bright sunshine outside. If they try to move him now, people will see them and report it. Have them come later tonight, after eight o'clock when it's good and dark out."

Tang regarded her closely, searching for any sign of betrayal. She looked upset but still humble and respectful. "Very well," said, and stalked to the door. "That is why I did not use the gun. Call me immediately if there is trouble."

* * * *

At 8:00 p.m., Tang returned to Mike Nolan's hotel room with several men. And found the room silent and empty.

Rage surged through his veins. The bitch had betrayed him after all!

He furiously punched in her cell number. To his shock, when the answering message played, what he heard was his own voice incriminating himself to Mei, which she must have recorded right after Nolan's death. He stood frozen in panic.

Seeing him, one of his men immediately called the Public Security Bureau. "I'm calling from the president of Yan Chemical's office. We urgently need you to issue an exit-blocking order immediately to all train, bus stations, and airports. The American Mike Nolan is wanted for committing industrial espionage against China. He is traveling with a Chinese woman, Song Mei. They must both be stopped."

"It is too late," Tang muttered. It had been three hours. He should have known Song Mei would help him. The two had become close the last time Nolan was in China.

But where could she go? She didn't have a U.S. visa. He clamped his

218

jaw. He could find her anywhere in China. If when did, she would pay dearly.

Chapter 23 Saipan

he Beijing Airport, China, two hours earlier
On a plane taxiing down the runway at the international airport outside of Beijing, Mike and Mei reached for each other's hands. Their destination was Saipan.

"How are you feeling?" Mei asked him.

"Still a little unsteady, but I'm good. Thanks to you, Mei. I owe you my life."

Mei blushed sweetly. He loved it when she blushed. He found he loved a lot of things about Song Mei.

"I could never kill you, Mike. I… I was so worried I wouldn't be able to inject the antidote quickly enough."

He rubbed the spot where she had inserted the needle that had saved his life. It was sore, but he didn't care. "I'm just glad you came up with this plan. I can't believe you could find the antidote so quickly."

"Mr. Tang always keeps it in his office, just in case." She scowled. "He sometimes uses that poison to…solve his problems."

Mike mumbled a curse. "I hope he rots in jail."

The plane wobbled a bit as it was taking off.

Mike gave her hand a squeeze. "Soon we'll both be safe."

"But I don't have a U.S. visa," Mei said nervously.

"Even though Saipan is a U.S. commonwealth, you don't need one. Chinese passport holders are visa-exempt in Saipan."

"Really, how do you know?"

"I am a lawyer," he said with a grin.

She smiled back. "I am very happy to be with a lawyer. How long can I stay in Saipan?"

"Up to three months as a visa waiver applicant. After that, I will figure out somewhere for you to stay permanently."

* * * *

Mike and Mei landed at Saipan smoothly and Mei got her visa, good for three months. Saipan's coastal waters were crystal clear and the day was humid and sunny.

They were staying at a modest seaside hotel, and one night after dinner they took a walk to a local monument called the Japanese suicide cliff. The flat and green plateau contrasted sharply with the vast void below the sharp edge of the cliff. The landscape was hauntingly symbolic, representing the duality of peace and war, life and death, meaning and meaninglessness.

As they gazed over the cliff, Mike said, "It was here in the caves along these cliffs where the wives and children of Japanese soldiers had hidden themselves at the end of the war." He sighed, feeling sad over the tragic story he'd heard. "When Japan lost, they all jumped over the cliff and committed suicide."

"Mei gasped softly. Why would they do that?"

"They thought their fates would be very dismal after being captured by American soldiers. Instead, they chose their own fates."

"Why did they think that way?" she asked as they started walking along the clifftop path.

"I guess because of the Japanese wartime propaganda against the

Americans. And maybe they believed that was the way their own soldiers would treat the enemy."

"Crazy nationalist sentiment." Mei sighed, stooping over to pick up an antique-looking bottle from some shrubs beside the path. She tipped her head. "Could that kind of war ever happen again?"

"It could happen at any time, given the right circumstances." Mike took the bottle and peered inside with one eye, then continued their stroll.

"Why can't human beings ever learn from their past?"

He took a big stride forward and threw the bottle far into the ocean. "The only thing we learn from history is that we learn nothing from history."

She smiled. "Karl Marx?"

"Close—Hegel."

She moved closer to him, joined her arm with his, and leaned against him while they walked along the cliff. It felt so good to have her body touching his, warm and comforting, and at the same time a little thrilling. He hadn't felt this way about a woman in a long time. Maybe never.

The sea breeze soothed their skin as they returned to the hotel and reluctantly headed for their rooms At Mei's door, Mike gave her a long, tight hug and lightly kissed the top of her head. "Good night. Sleep well."

She looked up into his eyes and smiled. "Good night."

In his room, Mike climbed into bed and tried to sleep. But his mind whirled with thoughts of everything had happened in the last few days.

Mei had saved his life. He would never have imagined that she could be so strong and confident. His feelings toward her had grown deeper each day.

He thought of Heather back in D.C., and admitted his feelings for her were very different. Heather was a graceful, knowledgeable, down-to-earth, and reliable lady. He really liked her. A lot. But his feelings didn't go any further than that.

Mei was beautiful, mysterious, tender yet powerful, and ready to save him at whatever cost.

And he realized he was quickly falling head over heels for her.

* * * *

The squeal of car tires in the parking lot and the flashing blue lights of police vehicles woke Mike up. He yanked up the window blinds and saw a handful of officers wearing FBI vests jump out of the cars and run toward the hotel entrance.

He hurriedly dialed Mei's number and said urgently, "Stay right there. I'm on my way."

He pulled on his clothes and rushed to her room.

"Mei, the FBI is here. I have a feeling they came for you. I need to find out who sent them before we trust them. Go quickly to the suicide cliff and stay there until I call you." He opened the window that looked out over the back of the building, but from the third floor it would be much too dangerous for her to climb down the downspouts. He looked around and hid her in the closet behind all the clothes. He left the door open a tiny crack so she could watch what was happening through the opening.

There was a knock on the door. Mike opened it.

"Mr. Mike Nolan?" asked the FBI special agent after a brief moment of surprise.

Interesting that the fed knew his name. "What can I do for you?" Mike asked firmly, shifting into lawyer mode.

"Where is Ms. Song Mei?" the FBI agent demanded.

"Who's asking?" Mike responded.

"I am asking the questions! Where is she? You checked into the hotel with her."

"I don't know where she is. I believe FBI special agents are required to identify themselves when they knock at a door," Mike said pointedly. "Or maybe you're just impersonating an agent?"

The fed's eyes narrowed and he flipped out is FBI credentials. Mike examined them closely. They seemed authentic. He handed them back after memorizing the man's name. "Very well. May I know why you're looking for Ms. Song? I am her attorney."

The man's nostrils flared. "She is on Interpol's wanted list. We figured she's hiding out here in Saipan."

Right. More likely they'd gotten a convenient anonymous tip from Beijing.

"I can try to locate her. But I'll need to make a phone call."

The fed nodded grudgingly "Make it snappy."

Mike started to close the door on him, but the man put his boot against it. "Leave the door open," he ordered.

"Fine." Mike walked past the closet tossing her a quick win, and went out on the balcony for a better signal. He dialed SSA Wallace's number.

"Frank," said Mike. "I didn't expect we would be having more problems with your team here in Saipan than we did in China."

Frank gave a huff. "Tang must have gotten Mei put on the Interpol wanted list on suspicion of stealing state secrets, and Interpol got the FBI involved. I'll call the Saipan field office right now and explain that Mei is a key witness in an important case here in the States, and our jurisdiction prevails. Just remember, don't take her to any U.S. federal agency offices, so as to avoid any bureaucratic red tape. "When will you be coming back to D.C.?"

"Not sure yet. I'll let you know."

Two minutes later, the phone of the fed standing at the door rang loudly.

* * * *

Mike sat on the hotel balcony in the shade of a huge overhanging tree, gazing out at the ocean, lost in deep thought. Seeing couples chasing each other and frolicking on the beach, he naturally thought of Mei, and his mind wandered back to the unusual conversation they'd had at the nightclub the first night they met. The part about love.

He'd called love a transient emotion that made a person vulnerable. But she'd said no, people benefit from true love, spiritually, and materially.

But what is true love, really?

Wasn't the care one person gave to another during extremely unfortunate times evidence of true love? He felt it must be. If that was the case, wouldn't true love always shine through at the worst times of disaster, loss of health, or imminent death?

Surely, he was a lucky man, having experienced most of those things in the past few weeks and survived…with Mei's help. Did that mean she truly loved him?

But didn't true love also mean that another person's fortunes were also your own?

He thought about how Mei was not able to seek political asylum yet, not until the Interpol charges were cleared up, and that could take time. And her visa waiver here in Saipan would expire in two and a half months.

From a distance he saw Mei walking toward him from the beach, smiling. She was wearing a white shirt and jeans, and her long black hair was in a tangle, blowing in dark drifts around her slender body.

"I brought a gift for you from the sea." Her eyes sparkling, she presented him with a large pink shell. "It's a conch."

"Thank you, Mei. It's beautiful." He admired it for a long moment, touched by her thoughtful gift. Overwhelmed with certainty, he put it on the table and took her hands in his. "I have a question for you."

Her eyes filled with curiosity. "What?"

"Will you marry me?"

Her mouth dropped open and she stared wide-eyed at him, not saying anything. Slowly, she said, "You don't have to do that, Mike. Not just to give me a visa."

He shook his head. "I'll admit that's part of it. But I promise, that's not the only reason, or even the biggest reason. I think we could be happy together, Mei. I really do."

Her eyes were warm and tender when they met his. "I feel the same way, Mike. But…it's an important decision. May I have time to think?"

Mike nodded. "Of course." They hugged each other and he gave her a tender kiss. "Take all the time you need."

As he held her, his chest pressed against something hard. "I've always meant to ask about your necklace," he said so things wouldn't get awkward because of his sudden proposal. "You always wear it. How long have you had it?"

She looked down at metal pendulum with an enamel porcelain design and a delicate engraving and reached up to touch it lovingly. "For as long as I can remember. My mother gave it to me. She told me it was my grandmother's."

"It looks like a locket. Is there a photo of her in it?"

"I don't know. It feels sealed, and there seems to be no way of opening it."

"Well, it's very beautiful," he said, kissed her again softly, and they said goodnight.

Chapter 24 The Souring Relationship

ashington, D.C.
Two months later, Mike and Mei became boyfriend and girlfriend and went to Washington, D.C.

The first thing he wanted to do was to visit Heather and introduce her to Mei. He had texted Heather as soon as he started having feelings for Mei, and let her know about his new relationship. He'd wanted to be fair and honest with Heather, but he hoped she hadn't been hurt.

"Heather, this is Song Mei, the woman who saved my life in China. She's also my girlfriend."

Heather looked at Song Mei, who was holding onto his arm affectionately. Heather hesitated for a moment, then a broad smile flashed across her face. She stuck out her hand. "Hi, I'm Heather, Mike's friend from law school."

"Nice to meet you," Mei said, shaking her hand with a smile.

"We're staying at a hotel in Foggy Bottom," Mike said, "and we probably won't go out too often."

"I understand," said Heather. "I'll bring you over the clothes you left here." She paused. "Is everything all right? SSA Wallace has been checking in on me but he won't say much…"

"I'll call you after I talk with Frank. Don't worry, it should all be cleared up soon."

* * * *

Later that day, Mike agreed to meet with SSA Wallace at a quiet Chinese restaurant in Adams Morgan. It was mid-afternoon so there were very few people at the scatter of tables.

When Mike arrived, the TV over the bar was tuned to the Chinese Central Television station. A vehement statement from the Chinese Foreign Ministry's spokesperson against American aggression was being broadcast live.

"Since the founding of the People's Republic of China in 1949, there have been twists and turns in the bilateral relationship between the U.S. and China. The Three Joint Communiqués laid down the foundations of our diplomatic relationship. It was built on an understanding that mutual benefits would enable the two countries to have a sustained friendly relationship. However, that understanding has been greatly challenged in the last month as the United States Congress approved an unprecedentedly large arms sale worth tens of billions of dollars to Taiwan. The sale includes destroyers and W-3 bombers, threatening regional stability in the Pacific. China considers this an act of aggression. Taiwan is part of China and Beijing is the only legitimate government representing China. China has been a key promoter of world peace, but we cannot stand by while such acts of aggression are carried out in gross violation of international law. To condone acts that jeopardize regional peace goes against the basic principles of the U.N. Charters which the international community has long abided by. We will work with our allies in Africa, Europe, and Latin America to forge a strong barrier to resolutely deter such acts of U.S. aggression."

Mike watched with concern. The wording of the announcement was much stronger than China's usual diplomatic statements.

Frank walked in and shook hands with Mike. Apparently he had been watching the report too. He said, "Everywhere I checked it was $4.5 billion, not $45 billion. But now the Chinese are adamantly claiming the weapons are worth that much, and the claim may not be baseless. Based on the export license application you found, it's possible the official U.S. number was wrong to begin with."

"Which would be a diplomatic disaster," said Mike.

Frank agreed and went on, "The license application is the only document I've seen where the number is the same as the Chinese are claiming. Even the congressional notice report I reviewed contained the lower value."

"Here." Mike pulled a manila folder from his briefcase containing printouts of the documents on the thumb drive Wang Ping's wife had given him. "This is the information from Wang Ping showing both the original and fraudulent files, as well as the original accounting ledger of the company." Then he gave Frank a folder with printouts of the photos he'd taken of the Yan Chemical files at Williamson & Grey before he was fired. "Not sure if these contain anything important, but I'd like you to have them just in case. Do me a favor and don't look at them unless you really have to. Client confidentiality, and all."

"Thank you. I won't peek," said Frank. "Are you and Mei somewhere safe?"

"Hope so." Mike gave him the name of the hotel where they were staying.

"Move here instead." Frank handed him a slip of paper. "I'm back on the case, and Mei is a key witness in the investigation. It's a safe house in Fort Washington with surveillance around the property to protect you."

Mike glanced down at the address with a wash of relief. "Okay. Sounds good."

"The next step is for the FBI to investigate your statements. We'll get a warrant to search Williamson & Gray for any complicity or wrongdoing in connection with Yan Chemical."

The waitress came over. "What can I get for you?" she asked.

They ordered and the waitress jotted down the orders. She turned away and started to collect dishes and cash from the table in the next aisle. "Oh, darn" Mike heard her say, then she called over to the hostess, "Hey, Sharon, someone left a bag behind."

"Maybe they went to the restroom?" the hostess answered.

Mike turned back to the TV when the waitress walked back to the kitchen with the dishes.

Frank was already watching it closely with a frown.

The CNN reporters were talking about missiles in Cuba. "Today the Pentagon released satellite images of new missile launchers being built in Cuba."

Enlarged images flashed on the screen of missile launchers with large Chinese characters plainly painted on them that Mike easily read as saying Made in China.

The anchorman continued, "The antidumping duties levied by the United States can only deter consumer products shipped to the U.S., not Cuba. It appears China has now added missile launch pads to the list of products made in China for export. Missiles carried by these launchers could easily target any city in North America, posing a huge threat to the security of the United States."

A spokesman for the White House appeared on screen. "We strongly oppose the Chinese government helping to build and maintain missiles of any kind in any part of the Western Hemisphere. The United States will take resolute action to secure America from any and all threats. We will use any means necessary to prevent any shipment of missiles, particularly those capable of carrying nuclear warheads, into this region from anywhere, I emphasize *from anywhere* in the world."

The waitress returned with their orders and then walked past the table she'd cleared earlier. "He hasn't come back," she called to the hostess and pointed at the bag across the aisle.

Mike frowned, but Frank paid no attention to the waitress. He turned away from the TV report and said, "I'm just glad it's still only rhetoric and posturing." He dug into his meal. "Anyway, I did some research and found the export license application you found was filed under the Direct Commercial Sales program, which requires an application for license at the Department of State. All such sales need congressional notice from the president for any potential sales. The congressional report has the right number, too, unless the president's report is also a lie."

Mike couldn't get his mind off that abandoned bag. In the movies, it was always a—

"Frank!" he shouted, jumping up from his chair.

Frank looked startled. "What?"

"Someone left a bag at that table. I think it may be—"

Frank turned and focused on the bag on the other table. He suddenly stood up and shouted, "Bomb! Everyone out! Go!" He grabbed the waitress and sprinted for the door herding out everyone else he could gather along the way.

Mike was behind him urging stragglers to hurry.

Seconds after they were out the door, a huge explosion boomed, shattering all the street-facing windows of the restaurant, billowing smoke, and pushing everyone to the ground from the impact.

* * * *

Half an hour later, the handful of restaurant patrons had been seen to by EMTs, and were being interviewed by the D.C police. Mike and Frank were the last to be checked over by the EMTs. Neither of them was wounded, except some minor scratches and temporary loss of hearing.

"Someone must have been following one of us," Frank said quietly to Mike. "Go grab Mei at the hotel and go straight to that Fort Washington address. Stay there until I personally tell you otherwise. There should be plenty of food and supplies already stocked, and a car in the garage that you can use. Take the SIM cards out of any cell phone you have. Here, use this one instead." He handed Mike a burner phone. "My number's on speed dial."

"Okay. I'll get us out of the hotel right away," Mike replied. "You need to be careful, too. What's our next step?"

"As I said, with these documents you brought back from China, we should easily get a search warrant for Williamson & Grey. A search there may reveal more clues to the possible relationship between the antidumping case and the arms sale to Taiwan."

"Okay," Mike said, still a bit dazed. "Keep me informed."

"I will," Frank said, and went over to speak to the police officer in charge.

Mike sat there for another minute trying to absorb the shock. This had really brought home the danger he and Mei were in, and the importance of staying safe. He thought of Heather, too, and called her.

"There's been a change in plans," he told her when she answered.

"Has something happened?"

"Someone just bombed the restaurant I was in with SSA Wallace. I'm sure it was meant to kill us. We are moving from the hotel to be safe. You should take precautions, too."

"Oh, my God."

"Can you bring my clothes to the 7-11 in Fort Washington? I will meet you there." He deliberately didn't tell her the address of the safe house.

"Okay. Stay safe," said Heather.

Mike returned to the hotel and quickly checked out with Mei. She had jet lag and looked tired. They flagged down a taxi and were on the way to the safe house.

Mei frowned at the scratches on his arm. "You're hurt. What happened?"

Mike told her, "A bomb in the restaurant where I met with Frank. Someone was trying to kill us. It was close." He blew out a long breath.

Mei looked horrified and reached for him. "Oh, Mike! I saw the explosion on TV. I never thought— I should have gone with you to help keep a watch."

"No. I'm glad you didn't come. It was quite an explosion. If the waitress hadn't noticed a bag that was abandoned close to our table, it could have turned out badly… Frank arranged a safe house for us. We'll be okay there."

The taxi let them off in front of a large colonial-style house. Mike unlocked the front door and cautiously entered the house, turning on all the lights as he went. Thankfully, no one was lurking in the shadows.

* * * *

The next day, Mike got out the car from the garage and he and Mei drove to the 711 to meet Heather. After Heather gave him his suitcase and a hug, she said she had to get back to work, and left.

He and Mei decided buy some breakfast. As they were eating their sandwiches, he got a weird sensation, like someone was watching them. He looked around and saw a man approaching them from the back of the store. Mike could see a bulge under his jacket.

He quickly pulled Mei from her seat and gave her a push toward the front door. "Run to the car! Quick!" he ordered.

He hurried after her, clicking the remote to unlock the doors. The man fired a shot just as Mei opened the passenger door. She fell to the seat.

In a panic, Mike started the engine with a roar as the assailant fired a second shot.

Mike peeled out of the parking lot and drove several blocks before pulling into a hidden alley. "Mei? Mei?" He gathered her in his arms. "Mei, say something. Please stay with me!"

Mei lay there breathing hard and blinking rapidly. "Mike, I… Mike, I think I'm fine."

"Thank God!"

He looked over her body, searching for blood. Thankfully there was none. But on her chest, her pendant had been cracked and caved in. "Oh, my God," said Mike in amazement. "The bullet ricocheted off your pendant!"

She glanced down and her face fell when she saw the precious memento of her mother. "Oh, no. You must be right. It's all smashed," she said shakily, her eyes filling with tears. "But… What's this?" She reached for the pendant. "There's something inside."

"Careful! It might be hot," he said, and pulled a couple of tissues from a packet on the console. He gingerly opened the pendant with it.

With two fingers, Mei delicately pulled a piece of fabric out of the locket.

"What is it?" she asked in wonder.

He looked closer at the piece of fabric. It was torn in places, but the printing on it was as vibrant as the day it was printed. The background was stained, by what looked like…blood. He could scarcely believe what he was seeing. "This is what your grandmother kept in the locket?" he asked in a hushed voice.

Mei glanced up at him. "I guess it must be. Why?"

He didn't answer, just helped her to sit up and started the car again. "Let's get back to the safe house. I'll take a circuitous route, to be sure we're not being followed."

When they got back to the safe house, opened the suitcase Heather had brought him and took out one of the few things he'd saved from his ransacked apartment. The photo of his grandfather posing before his Flying Tiger Tomahawk. He opened the back cover of the picture frame and carefully took out a piece of folded cloth from behind the back cover.

"You know that piece of cloth in your grandmother's locket?" he said, giving Mei a look and feeling an emotion he'd never felt before.

"Yes?" she asked, looking puzzled by his expression.

"I have one just like it." A shiver went up his spine as he put the two blood chits side by side and showed them to her. He studied them closely, then gazed at her. "I was right. They are both blood chits used by the American Flying Tiger pilots fighting in China during World War II. The woven codes in the corner are identical."

* * * *

Outside the offices of Williamson & Gray, five black vans and two police cruisers pulled up. A dozen FBI agents and a handful of D.C. cops poured out of the vehicles and into the building. The startled receptionist threw up her hands. "Please don't shoot!"

SSA Frank Wallace refrained from rolling his eyes. Barely. "FBI Criminal Investigation Division. We have a warrant to search the offices of Williamson & Gray. Please step away from the desk, ma'am. Special Agent will accompany you outside."

He gave the signal and his team began unplugging her computer and packing her papers into boxes. One by one, they repeated this process with all the other Williamson & Gray employees.

Frank signaled to a couple of his men and they followed him to Patrick Steiner's office.

He knocked firmly on the door. "FBI. We have a warrant. Open up." No answer.

He jiggled the doorknob. "It's locked. Get the key from the receptionist."

An agent came back with the key and, weapon drawn, Frank pushed open the door.

"Shit."

Patrick Steiner was dead, his face down on the desk in a pool of puke.

* * * *

Two days later, Frank dropped by the safe house. Mike knew about the raid on the law offices and was eager to hear what the FBI had found.

"Did you find anything?" he asked Frank as soon as they sat down at the kitchen table.

Frank nodded. "We did, yes. But..."

"What is it? Why do you look disappointed?"

"Patrick Steiner is dead. We found him in his office. Poisoned. Somebody must have tipped him off, because it happened only fifteen minutes before we got there. There was nothing we could do."

Mike cursed. "Well, were there any incriminating documents at least?"

"We found no specific evidence of forgery in Yan Chemical's proprietary information or in its submissions to DOC. The original record with Williamson & Gray had been destroyed according to regulations. We did obtain a copy of their original submission with the Department of Commerce, and we found an overall reduction of costs by exactly twenty-five percent for all inputs. That is evidence of some kind of fraud. But we found no proof that either Williamson & Gray or Yan Chemical did it."

"Uh..." Mike was about to mention the folder he'd given Frank that he'd asked him not to look at. The one with all those files…

But before he could say anything, Frank went on. "The strange thing is that Patrick Steiner apparently committed suicide. Why would he do that? He must have known there was no real evidence to incriminate him. He must have been scared about something else. Scared enough to kill himself."

"Wow, that's…" Mike didn't know what to say. He had once liked the guy…right up until he'd fired Mike, showing that he and his law firm were corrupt. "What about the forty-five billion worth of weaponry to Taiwan?" he asked instead of commenting on Patrick's unfortunate death.

"We've skimmed through all the records and found none that said $45 billion. Everything we saw stated it was $4.5 billion. I also tracked down the U.S. Customs officer handling the export declaration, but he didn't have anything on paper. We need to find out exactly the number and types of weaponry that was actually exported. That should tell us which figure is correct."

"Right."

Mike thought back to the class on Export Control he'd taken at Georgetown. "Do you happen to know who monitors Direct Commercial Sales?" he asked Frank.

"I can't say I do."

"It's the same person who's in charge of the Blue Lantern program in the Political-Military office of the U.S. State Department."

"The Blue Lantern program? That sounds vaguely familiar."

"It's an end-use monitoring system that monitors all foreign exports of weapons so they don't fall into an enemy country's hands. Our embassy in Taipei should have those records for Taiwan since they do all the checks and inspections."

Frank nodded slowly. "Great idea. Right now my hands are tied to within the borders of the United States, but yours aren't. And all things considered, you are probably safer out of the country. We need original documents as evidence and electronically transmitted ones can be intercepted or falsified. You speak Chinese and know this thing in and out, so I think tracking down those records in Taiwan is a perfect assignment for you. Don't worry about Mei, I'll have more agents assigned to keep her secure." He rose. "Meanwhile, I'll find someone you can talk to in Taiwan."

* * * *

The next day, Frank gave Mike some fake FBI IDs and called the American Institute in Taiwan so that Mike could go to Taipei to do an actual investigation.

Chapter 25 The Taipei Trip

n Route to Taipei, Taiwan

Mike was always amazed at how fast those in the government could make things happen when they wanted to. Just the next day, after a brief stopover in San Francisco he was on a thirteen-hour flight headed to Taipei.

Flying over the Pacific Ocean, his ears were still ringing with Frank's last instructions.

"I've gotten you temporary FBI credentials and airline tickets in the name of Andy Elliot so hopefully you are not flagged by the Taiwanese. Otherwise you won't get out of the country. When you get there, talk to Kenneth Parker. He's worked for State in the Foreign Service for ten years as a monitor for Blue Lantern. He's currently assigned to the American Institute of Taiwan."

"Right. Our de facto embassy in Taiwan," Mike said, familiar with the sticky diplomatic situation in that country.

Frank continued, "If there is any shipment discrepancy, the evidence will be with him."

"Good. Glad you found the right contact."

Frank winked at him. "We have a new FBI gadget you'll need." He handed Mike a pair of glasses. "These are wifi-connected glasses with a built-in audio distorter. They look like regular specs but the lenses are also a camera and the frames are able to make phone calls like normal earbuds. Turn on the distorter and it will scramble any nearby listening device so they can't understand your actual words."

Mike had lifted the glasses and tried them on. "Wow. That's amazing." He'd felt like James Bond getting goodies from Q before one of his missions.

Returning to the moment, he looked out the window as the plane was about to land in Taiwan. He could see the skyscraper of Taipei 101, the World Financial Center, lit up in the dusk outside. Designed in a pagoda style, it was covered in little cells of teal, yellow, and red light. Impressive to say the least.

After making it through customs and checking into his hotel, he opened his small duffel bag. He'd only brought a few things with him since he would only be there a day or two at most. He took out the souped-up glasses and put them on. And figured he may as well test them out. He turned them on and called Mei.

"Hi, Mike. Did you get there okay?"

"Yep. I'm at the hotel."

"Good. How's the connection?"

He knew she was asking about the glasses. "You're coming through loud and clear."

After a short conversation talking about what was on the news in US in the last 24 hours, he said, "Okay, I'll call you tonight. I have to get to my meeting now."

* * * *

Mike had arranged to meet with Kenneth Parker for breakfast at the hotel. After chatting over bagels and fruit about their careers and Taiwan, Mike started asking his real questions. "Have you seen any major imports of weapons into Taiwan recently?"

Kenneth took a sip of his coffee and waved a hand. "I oversee so many weapons imports, it's hard to tell them apart."

Mike chuckled. "Did anything stand out to you?"

Kenneth looked at his watch. "Well, Mike, you sound like a fine young man and I wish you all the best in your career." He stood up and stuck out his hand.

Mike was taken aback. Hadn't Frank briefed him on what was at stake?

"Sir," said Mike, rising and shaking his hand, "I think something is brewing between the U.S. and China. Have you seen anything in the imports here that could be an issue?"

With a grim look, Kenneth picked up his briefcase. "It was nice meeting you."

"Let me walk you to your car," Mike said.

"I'm fine, thank you," Kenneth said, and started to walk away.

Mike didn't give up so easily. He followed him out of the hotel and to the porte cochère where his chauffeur was waiting.

"Sir," Mike repeated, looking around. "I think I accidentally saw some documents no one was supposed to see. I believe some of the reports about weapon exports to Taiwan were falsified." Mike looked desperately at the officer. "People are dying, and my life is in danger."

Kenneth suddenly pulled Mike into the car and closed the door. He said, "Listen carefully. All the tracking uses a ten-digit code but the last batch used a six-digit code. Since they don't track the regular number of digits, there is no way to tell if it is $45 billion instead of $4.5 billion. But the smaller digit could mean the tracking was only for that group. The report could be for just one W-3 bomber and one destroyer. Here are pictures of the delivered destroyers and W-3 bombers and their specifications." He shoved a folder into Mike's hands.

Mike grasped it tightly. These papers could well save his life.

Kenneth said, "If anyone asks, you didn't get these from me. But if the authorities ever investigate, I have done my duty and cooperated with the FBI."

Mike put the folder under his jacket and went back up to his hotel room. He wanted to call Frank but was worried about doing it in the room despite his precautions. He put on the special glasses and went out to find a place where their conversation couldn't be listened to. Like maybe a public park.

As he walked through the streets, he looked around to make sure no one was following him. At a crosswalk, he noticed a Western man in a polo shirt standing behind him. The man was on his phone, but didn't appear to be texting or talking. When it was time to cross, his tail didn't step into the road immediately but waited a while, seemingly engrossed in his phone. But he kept following Mike, staying well back.

Mike saw a park and headed over to it. There was a group of middle-aged women doing exercises together, accompanied by blaring music from a speaker. He sat near the speaker so his tail couldn't hear his conversation. He fired up the glasses and dialed Frank's number.

"Did you find anything?" asked Frank.

"Yes, I got some very important information. Kenneth Parker gave me the import records and it looks like the weapon shipments were split up into individual batches."

"So they wouldn't have to report to Congress."

His tail wandered closer to Mike. Mike tried to casually keep him in his line of vision and turned on the camera in the glasses.

"Right," affirmed Mike. "Because Congress would have blocked any weapon export of this size."

"You have the records with you?" asked Wallace.

The man made his way behind Mike, so he was out of his field of vision.

"Yes" He still had the folder under his jacket.

"Hold onto them. They will be very important for the investigation."

Mike stood up suddenly. "Frank, I'm being followed. I've got the camera in the glasses turned on. Will you get the pictures?"

Before Frank could answer, Mike felt a movement behind him, so he took off running. He glanced behind him and saw his tail chasing after, holding something behind his back.

Mike looked up and saw he was right next to the Taiwan 101 hotel. There was an advertisement for skydiving off the top of the building, so he tore through the hotel lobby and went right for the elevators. One was closing, but he slipped inside just in time.

The elevator lurched upward, speeding past floors, stopping only every ten or so. He knew the tail must have grabbed another elevator. What if their elevators stopped on the same floor at the same time? When his elevator stopped on the ninety-eighth floor, he stuck his head out to check. The doors to the elevator next to him were closed, so he hurried out and ran down the hall to the stairwell and headed up.

Suddenly he heard the door behind him slam open. His heart jumped. He sprinted up to the last level and ran through the doors.

Oh no. The room Mike had entered had rows and rows of white folding chairs. The aisle between them was covered in pink rose petals leading up to an arch of white and gold balloons. A crowd of people was looking out the window at the balcony.

On the balcony, a bride and groom were being strapped into parachute harnesses. As the crowd cheered the bride shrieked, "I can't do it, I can't do it!" She wiggled out of the harness and burst into tears.

"C'mon, honey, it was your idea!"

Everyone around them yelled. "Go, go, go!"

His tail burst into the room holding a gun.

Mike didn't hesitate. "Thank you, gramps," he muttered, and shoved through the crowd, climbed into the parachute harness, and leaped off the balcony. The gasps of the crowd faded as he fell rapidly through the sky.

He pulled the ripcord on his parachute and floated toward the ground.

He looked around at the bright blue sky and fluffy white clouds. The buildings looked so tiny compared to Taipei 101. Beyond the skyline of Taipei, he could see green mountains, and beyond them, the blue sea.

He felt the most freedom in his life while falling through the air. Skydiving with his grandfather had been the highlight of his childhood. Gramps must have felt the same way flying his plane, this sense of unbridled freedom, with no need to rely on anyone or anything, even for a brief moment. And when he no longer flew planes, skydiving gave him the same feeling.

Mike managed to land in a park without breaking his leg, and quickly took off the harness.

No way was he going back to the hotel. He headed for the nearest street and hailed a taxi to the airport.

Chapter 26 The Evidence

He spent his early years building this giant company from a small federal contractor to the conglomerate it was in the defense industry today. The business could not be better with sales skyrocketing to new highs every month and stock prices quadrupling in a six-month period. There were rumors in the local media about him serving a possible cabinet position in the next term of the presidency, but he did not bother to comment. He was going to meet Frank from the FBI this afternoon; it was not the first time he talked with the law enforcement. Over the years, the lawsuits with the vendors, employees, and even the federal government inundated this company as it gradually extended into the military industrial complex. It was just a matter of negotiation and settlement. But this time, it just seemed a bit different. He felt a bit uneasy, and was unduly perplexed by the feds' visit. In fact, he was quite frustrated. He looked disheveled and pale.

Sam Wilson stepped outside his office and snapped at his secretary, "You need to work on my speech to the local business community. I need these reports photocopied immediately."

Joyce, the secretary replied, "I will ask Janice Yang to do it after her daily nap."

Sam Wilson turned his head back and frowned. "What!"

"It has been like this since she joined," Said Joyce. "You know she was brought in by the VP of Development, who secured some business with China's Yangtze Bank."

"Wake her up, damn it! I need it now!" He shook his head, slamming the office door behind him. "Doesn't this bitch know what's on the line?" He sighed and picked up the phone. "Hey, honey, dump three million worth of Swift Industries' stocks. And delete all my personal emails, their backups, and archives when it comes to any communications with China."

SSA Frank Wallace and two of his team walked casually into the offices of Swift Industries. Waiting around the corner were five black vans and two police cruisers.

Frank identified himself to the receptionist. "We need to speak to Sam Wilson."

Frank had done his research. Wilson was the largest shareholder of Swift Industries, with the reputation of an extremely successful business executive. From a small federal contractor to the conglomerate it now was and from a businessman to a possible cabinet position in the next term of the presidency, Wilson seemed to Frank to have all the markings of one more corrupt asshole worming his way into the government.

The receptionist led Frank and his team to a nearby conference room, and a moment later Sam Wilson entered. "How can I help you SSA Wallace?"

Wilson was in his 60s with a sharp and cunning demeanor, and a face that reflected his years of experience in the business world. Despite the stress of running a major public company, his expression as he took a seat across from Frank remained composed and controlled, betraying his ability to handle any situation with ease. Even being interviewed by the FBI.

"Mr. Wilson," Frank said, "what can you tell us about Swift Industries' involvement in the antidumping case against the Chinese chemical products."

"Oh, that is simple. Swift Industries is looking to diversify its product portfolios, and we decided to enter the chemical supply market. But in the product line, heavy foreign competition existed, mainly from China. Therefore, we used one of our subsidiaries to bring an antidumping proceeding against the foreign exporters." Wilson tilted his head. "Is there something wrong with that?"

"Not a thing," replied Frank, not fooled for a second. "How did it go?"

"As far as I know, the case was a great success, except for one foreign competitor. But I'm sure you're aware of all that. It's all public information."

"Yes. Mr. Wilson, according to our sources, there was a very large amount of weaponry exported to Taiwan from Swift Industries. Was it all licensed?"

Wilson cleared his throat. "Oh, that is an entirely different subject. Yes, we obtained all the required licenses from the Department of State."

"And what was the total value of your exports?"

"I think it was approximately five billion this year."

"Thank you, Mr. Wilson. But I'm afraid we need to conduct a thorough investigation into this matter." He handed Wilson an official document. "This is a search warrant issued by the D.C. Circuit Court to search the premises."

If Wilson was surprised, he didn't show it. He stood and gave a slight bow, a smug smile on his lips. "Feel free, SSA Wallace."

* * * *

A few days later, Mike and Mei heard a knock at the safe house door.

Their FBI babysitter grabbed his handgun and looked through the peephole. "It's SSA Wallace," he told Mike and opened the door.

"Come in, Frank," Mike said, glad to see him and hear any news.

Mei came in and said, "Come to the kitchen. I'll make some coffee."

When they were all settled around the kitchen table Frank said, "I have some important information about the case. We've found some new evidence."

"Finally. That's great!" Mike said.

"We were able to get into Sam Wilson's private email account," Frank said. "It was very difficult for OTD to hack into, so we figured he must be hiding something."

"What did you find?" asked Mike.

"We found an email thread between Sam Wilson and Mr. Tang Jisheng, CEO of Yan Chemical. They were coordinating the Taiwan shipment. The email instructed Tang to time the shipment of weapons to Taiwan only after Yan Chemical's won their zero percent antidumping duty."

Mike nodded. "Which would mean an immediate lifting of Yan Chemical's antidumping duty cash deposit rate at the U.S. ports of entries," he said. " Sounds like Tang was making sure that his business interests were covered before he could return some favor Wilson was asking for."

"But what could be the favor?" wondered Frank. "And how would Sam Wilson's weapons export to Taiwan be something that Mr. Tang, a Chinese CEO, could influence?"

Mike pondered for a moment, then suddenly it came to him in a flash. "Oh, my God!"

"What?"

"When did the sale of weapons to Taiwan occur?"

"The president announced the arms sale in April last year. The congressional approval happened in May, for $4.5 billion. The shipment was to be completed in three months."

"Exactly. And when did the Chinese government oppose the arms sale?"

"In December of last year." Frank's brows shot up. "I see where you are going with this. The Chinese waited an entire six months to oppose the sale. When they objected, the delivery was already over."

"Tang's father is the Vice Chairman of the Chinese Military Commission," Mike said. "He must have suppressed the information to the Chinese authorities until it was too late."

Frank's eyes brightened. "Sam Wilson was obviously engaged in an illegal act of violating the Foreign Corrupt Practice Act of bribing Tang Jisheng and his father, a high Chinese government official, with zero antidumping duties."

Mike slapped his forehead. "No wonder I was tipped off to the winning argument by the opposing counsel. They intentionally lost the case, using the zero antidumping duty rate as a bribe Yan Chemical. A rate which would allow them to monopolize the American market."

Frank grimaced. "My God, that sounds more than plausible. But it will be very hard to prove the actual bribe. The authority to issue the antidumping order is the U.S. Department of Commerce, not Sam Wilson. Still, the intent seems very clear from the email. I think there may be just enough to indict Sam Wilson."

Mike lowered his head to think. "As I recall, the Foreign Corrupt Practice Act has five elements: making a payment, a foreign official, corrupt intent, purpose of influencing the official act in violation of his lawful duty, and obtaining business. Sam Wilson did obtain business, even though it was from a party different that the bribed party. Would he obtain the same business if he did not bribe? No, because the Chinese authorities would have vehemently objected to the publicly announced arms sale before the congressional notice, and the U.S. Congress would likely not have proceeded with authorization of a sale of this magnitude."

"Okay, that's at least four out of five..."

Mike wrinkled his brow. "One thing I don't understand is..."

"What?"

"How could Sam Wilson get away with congressional oversight? Wasn't the president supposed to issue notice and secure congressional approval of an arms sale? With all the federal agencies involved—the DOC, U.S. Customs, the State Department..."

"Well, the deal got congressional approval but at a far less value," Frank noted.

"Exactly. The export license application at Williamson & Grey was for the true number but it was never submitted. But even if Sam Wilson lied in that license application, all the other agencies were still watching every step of the sale."

Frank looked thoughtful. "You're right. So are you saying there could be even greater power behind this?" He peered over at Mike. "Is Sam Wilson just a scapegoat?"

* * * *

Assistant Director James Brody had been the head of the FBI Criminal Investigation Division since its inception. Before that he'd been the U.S. Attorney at the Department of Justice for some twenty years. Overall, he had served under three presidencies. Jim knew if a behavior was right or wrong, lawful or unlawful. For him, the law was always by the book. Sure, there were a few gray areas, but illegal was illegal once the Rubicon was crossed.

Like his best SSA, Frank Wallace, Jim would soon be retiring, but today, he was on his way to the West Wing of the White House to brief the president on the latest developments at the CID. Among his files was the memo that SSA Wallace had prepared on the excessive shipment to Taiwan without congressional approval. Jim was undecided if he should present it to the president. The presentation of such documents might be viewed as a political threat to the president. The FBI was in charge of enforcing federal criminal laws and investigating criminal activities—including that *of* the president. Still, if the FBI could not investigate the president, Jim believed the United States would cease to be a democracy.

He was ushered into the Oval Office and the president reached out to shake his hand with a huge smile. "Hey, Jim. Sit down please." He sneezed. "Ugh. Too much pollen in D.C. compared to where I come from. Ha ha. What can you do?"

"Well, Claritin works for me." Also smiling, sat in the visitor's chair in front of the president's desk.

After presenting the president the weekly update on key issues facing the CID, Jim cleared his throat. "Mr. President, one of my best SSAs has discovered something I need to brief you on." He pulled out a memo and offered it.

"What's this?" The president leaned forward, took the memo, and read through it quickly. He sat back in his chair. "Oh, it's about that arms sale to Taiwan." He pushed the memo back to Jim.

"Yes, sir. And I think—"

"Jim, do you have any plans for tonight?" the president interrupted. "Why don't you come over for dinner? I got a bottle of 1929 Bodegas Toro Albala as a gift from the Spanish president last time he was here."

Jim tilted his head. The president never interrupted. And dinner? What the heck?

"Come on," the president cajoled with a grin. "There isn't any issue with the wine, is there?"

"As long as it's worth less than $350." Jim said, deciding just to go with the abrupt topic change.

"Ha! You are such a stickler, Jim. Well, it was only worth $349.99 last time I checked."

"Okay, then I gladly accept. Thank you for the invitation, Mr. President."

He'd think about what it all implied later.

****

The dinner was in the president's private quarters at the White House. It was just Jim and the president, since the First Lady was out of town. The waitstaff brought in the steaming plates and dishes, then were dismissed.

"Well," the president said between mouthfuls of filet mignon, "now that we're finally alone, I can reveal the true purpose of this dinner."

"And what might that be?" Jim had anticipated it must be something the president wanted to discuss in private.

The president finished chewing. "I'm sure by now you've heard of an investigation into some exports of weapons to Taiwan."

"Yes. One of my teams is involved in that case."

"Good. I'm glad we have our top investigators working on such a critical case."

Jim bristled. Blatant flattery was never a good sign.

The president continued, "I believe your team should concentrate on matters that are more important right now." He watched for Jim's response.

He simply stared blankly at the president.

The president tried to act casual. "Well, as you know, when it comes to foreign affairs, I have broad authority. I need to take measures to protect Taiwan, the only democracy in Asia. Therefore, some of these international issues, you know," —he hesitated and looked up at the ceiling as if the correct words were written there—"well, they may have their own, er, characteristics that should not be impeded or hampered by certain domestic issues."

Which meant what, exactly?

"What kind of measures did you take?" Jim finally said evenly, acting as if he hadn't been part of the case for the past few months.

"Well, I, uh, I had to export some weapons to Taiwan so they could defend themselves from a possible invasion from mainland China."

A horrible suspicion began tiptoeing through Jim's spidey senses. "I see."

"Well, uh, you know. Our humongous trade deficit is already such a critical international issue. China is undervaluing their currency and now they are mounting pressures on our good ally, Taiwan." The president sighed. "We've got to do what we've got to do."

"I get it. The FBI doesn't have a problem with any of that, if things are done legally."

"Look, Jim. You and I…" He lost his words again. "Hell, would you like to be my running mate next term?"

Jim's jaw dropped. He was stunned by the out-of-the-blue offer. He had always toyed with the idea of getting into politics, but by now he was getting too old to start that long road. Jumping right into the vice presidency, that would be a great end to his career. "I don't know what to say, Mr. President."

"Look, Jim. This Taiwan thing is an international issue. Foreign affairs are totally within my power." He looked directly into Jim's eyes. "There's a lot of tension between China and Taiwan, and I just want our friends to be able to defend themselves in case anything should happen. The United States cannot afford to lose an ally in Asia."

"I see," said James, finally. "I totally understand."

* * * *

Unfortunately, Jim did understand.

He went home, stepped into his office, opened his laptop and started to jot down notes about his conversation with the president. Jim kept a record of all his top-level meetings.

When this was done, he called Frank Wallace.

"It's ten o'clock, Jim," Frank said with a tentative laugh. "What's up? It must be something important."

"Sorry. I know it's late."

"I take it you're not calling to catch up. What's going on?"

Jim told Frank about his dinner with the president. "He asked me to set aside the investigation since it falls under international affairs. But there's obviously a clear domestic procedure that was sidetracked."

"He thinks he is above the law?" muttered Frank.

"Apparently so. I'm about to prove him wrong."

"What can I do to help?" Frank asked.

"Dig deeper into the president and his international affairs. I smell a rat."

* * * *

The next morning, the front page of a small New England tabloid carried an alarming headline.

U.S. Sold Foreign Weapons to Taiwan Without Congressional Approval.

As expected, Jim got an early morning call from the president.

"I thought your people would act with more prudence, especially with an ongoing investigation!" the president yelled. "The FBI is trying to discredit this administration and interfere with my handling of international affairs."

"I'm sorry, sir, if that's truly what you think."

"Jim, I know you are about to retire, but right now you are still working for me. Be careful of our enemies and tread cautiously." Then the president actually hung up him.

* * * *

Sam Wilson had been formally indicted on FCPA charges by the Department of Justice, and the law firm of Meyers & Meyers represented Wilson and his company. Mike was watching the trial, which was being broadcast live on TV.

A DOJ attorney was examining Wilson. "Mr. Wilson, did you instruct employees to set up the U.S. company, Ohio Chemical, as a petitioner in the antidumping case against the Chinese soda powder industry?"

"No," Wilson answered, "it was a corporate decision to enter into this product line. I felt it was more productive just to purchase an existing company."

"Mr. Wilson, did your company apply for an export license to supply weapons to Taiwan?"

Wilson's attorney called, "Objection! Irrelevant to the charges."

"Sustained." The judge said calmly.

"What was the value stated on the export license?"

"Objection! Irrelevant again."

"Sustained."

"What was the value of the weapons you exported to Taiwan?"

"It was $4.5 billion."

"How long have you been doing business with Williamson & Gray?"

"Over twenty years."

"Since you have been doing business with Williamson & Gray for so long, why did you not also hire them for your antidumping lawsuit against Yan Chemical, but instead hired a different law firm, Baker & Lynch."

"Objection, ambiguous."

"Overruled."

"Because Williamson & Gray was already representing Yan Chemical, the opposition, in the same litigation," answered Wilson.

"How much was Swift Industries paid?"

"As I said, $4.5 billion."

"Can you explain to the court why Ohio Chemical's parent company, Wealth Pinnacle in the British Virgin Islands, was paid $45 billion for the weapons sold to Taiwan, while paying Swift Industries payments totaling $40 billion?"

"My wife was the main shareholder of Wealth Pinnacle. Swift Industries hired her company to help the export control process by providing consulting services. The foreign importer directly paid the consulting fee to them."

"Over $5 billion? What kind of consulting would that be?"

"Obj—"

"Withdrawn. You hired Baker & Lynch to bring the antidumping litigation against Yan Chemical. But did you instruct Williamson & Gray, a firm you have retained for Swift Industries to represent Yan Chemical so you could maneuver the antidumping proceeding to give Yan Chemical a zero antidumping duty rate, to fulfill a different purpose altogether?"

"Objection! Speculation."

"Overruled. You may answer."

"No comment."

"Why, Mr. Wilson, did you conspire with Mr. Tang, CEO of a Chinese company, to delay the shipment of W-3 bombers to Taiwan until after the preliminary results of the antidumping duty rate was published, when legally Yan Chemical was entitled to a zero cash deposit rate at U.S. Customs upon entry of their exported products?"

"Objection!"

"No comment."

"Were you trying to time your business to be completed only after your foreign collaborator's interests are secured? Why were you doing this?"

"Objection!"

"No comment."

"No more questions," announced the DOJ attorney.

Sam Wilson's counsel stood to question him on the stand. "Mr. Wilson, did you make the decision to grant zero antidumping duties to your foreign competitor?"

"Of course not."

"Was it the Department of Commerce who gave the foreign manufacturer the zero antidumping duty rate?"

"Objection! Leading."

"Overruled."

"I'll rephrase. Who ordered the zero antidumping duty rate?"

"The U.S. Department of Commerce."

"To your knowledge, did someone deliberately set up a scheme to give a foreign competitor a zero duty rate in exchange for non-interference by China in the arms sales to Taiwan?"

Wilson paused before calmly responding, "Yes."

Everyone present was surprised.

In the cross-examination, the U.S. attorney asked, "Mr. Wilson, who was the someone you just mentioned who set up the scheme?"

"It is a lawyer by the name of Mike Nolan. And by the way, my wife does not own Wealth Pinnacle anymore," Sam Wilson said. "It was transferred to the same lawyer who worked on the opposite side of my case."

"And the name of this person?"

"Also Mike Nolan."

"And when did Mike Nolan acquire the BVI company?"

"After Yan Chemical got the zero rate."

"Do you have any evidence of that?"

"Yes."

Sam Wilson's lawyer passed a manila folder to the judge. "Here is a record of the interests of the company being transferred to Mr. Nolan's account."

"Nolan secured the zero rate antidumping duties for Yan Chemical and was their defense attorney," Wilson informed the court. "He is also the true owner of Ohio Chemical, since he bought the parent company, Wealth Pinnacle, from my wife for $3 million so he could continue to bring antidumping duty reviews against other Chinese producers in the future, thereby perpetuating Yan Chemical's monopoly of the U.S. market. My wife has copies of the transferred stock certificates and payment records. The $3 million was wired to Wealth Pinnacle before the stock certificates were transferred. For some reason, Nolan sent $100,000 more by mistake, and we had to wire back the $100,000."

In his closing statement, Wilson's attorney said, "First, where is the evidence? Is it just because Baker & Lynch did not respond as hard as they could have? What is hard enough? It is all speculation! Assuming all these crazy allegations are all true, what does it mean? Does it mean that Sam Wilson violated the FCPA? What is the evidence? Just an email exchange with Mr. Tang? Did you ever receive spam emails from yourself, with your own name on it? Mr. Wilson has obviously been framed. The fact of the matter is, some other individual was behind the scenes, manipulating this antidumping case to their advantage."

* * * *

His head was still spinning from the accusations made against him in court and on national TV, as Mike watched a news report that followed.

"The first court session was held today in Washington, D.C. in the case of Sam Wilson, the man accused of violating the Foreign Corrupt Practice Act. This is a messy cobweb of possible violations of the

FCPA in a complex antidumping case between a U.S. manufacturer and a Chinese exporter. Some have even speculated that the United States president may be involved because earlier today, the president introduced a bill to rescind the FCPA, which would make it legal to bribe a foreign official. This is just days after the FBI received intelligence that $45 billion worth of weapons were exported to Taiwan without adequate congressional notice. On top of that, it was reported that Chinese missiles have been found in Cuba. Our U.S. politics correspondent is here to talk us through the case."

"Well, I believe the president may be involved," said the correspondent.

"In what way?" asked the anchorman.

"There is no official record that weaponry of that value was exported to Taiwan, and there is no federal power that can suppress this number other than the president."

"How does he benefit?"

"That's the issue we don't know."

"If he is involved, will he still have the power to pardon Wilson if he's convicted?"

"He will," the correspondent said.

"Do you really believe Sam and the president could be involved in what seems to be contributing to a worsening relationship between these the U.S. and China?"

"Absolutely. The court trial today revealed a possible connection with another individual, Mike Nolan, who is alleged to have purchased Sam Wilson's company. Nolan used to work for the law firm representing the Chinese company Yan Chemical on the opposite side of Wilson's antidumping case. Nolan has not appeared at the proceedings."

"Well, that sounds highly suspicious. Anyway, with the presidential reelection drawing near, it remains to be seen what political and legal drama is yet to unfold."

Mike anxiously watched the news with Mei.

"Mei, I think I'm screwed. They framed me legally, and will no doubt finish me physically.

"But you're innocent."

"Innocent men are convicted every day. And the other way around. Congress may repeal FCPA, the law that would convict Sam Wilson. And even if he's convicted, the president will no doubt pardon him."

Mei said, "Evil always looks like a giant at first."

Mike was surprised as she said it with such force.

"What if the president is impeached for breaking the law?" she asked.

"They said *I* was the one who set up the whole scheme and bought Ohio Chemical. The money returned must have been that damn bonus from Patrick Steiner. But where did the $3 million come from? Maybe a side payment from the Taiwan authorities buying the weaponry. There is no way I can be associated with any of those accounts. But it's confusing enough to divert attention from the real issues."

"The FBI knows you're in danger," said Mei. "They're protecting you."

"Technically, they're protecting you, not me," he said. "I should call Frank."

Mike pulled out his cell phone to call, but it was already buzzing with a call from the man himself. "Hey, Frank."

"Mike, I saw what happened. How are you doing?"

"Not good."

"Yeah, I guess not. Someone is definitely playing hard ball."

"I have a question. Why didn't the president go through a normal congressional notice and approval process for the arms sale?"

"I don't know, but probably because if he did, he wouldn't get the approval."

"True. Congress has always been friendly on arms sales to Taiwan.

But sales of such an enormous magnitude that can tip the balance of the Taiwan strait, Congress would think differently."

"But it still begs the question, what does the president get out of this by going out of his way to do it, just to defend Taiwan and make money for Swift Industries?"

Chapter 27 The Impeachment

The news about contested arms sales blew up in the media. The U.S. Congress decided to hold a public hearing on the arms scandal and asked FBI Assistant Director James Brody to testify.

Mike wanted to go to the hearings in person, but Mei objected. "It's too dangerous! Do you remember why we have to stay in this safe house? What if they recognize you?"

"But I have to see what happens. Who knows what they could be saying about me." He sighed.

****

The U.S. House Committee on Oversight and Reform held the hearing on the Taiwan arms sale issue. James Brody sat quietly in the main witness chair at the front of the audience. Several members of the press sat behind the him. A few were holding cameras and chitchatting, and a tall blond lady was taking notes alone on her laptop in the back of the room.

Senator Brown entered the room, took his seat at the center of the dais, and opened the hearing with his deep and stern voice, "There have been rumors about the current administration's failure to notify and obtain approval from the U.S. Congress on this latest arms sale to

Taiwan. The Chinese government has vehemently opposed such sales. The U.S. Congress has always consistently worked with the president in making sure arms sales to our allies are processed smoothly and in legal manners."

After the opening remarks, Senator Brown looked down at the witness chair.

"I'd like to welcome our first witness, a longtime friend of this committee, FBI Assistant Director James Brody. Mr. Brody, has the FBI identified reliable evidence that U.S. weapons exceeding the stated value of the sale have been sold to Taiwan without a license or congressional notice or approval?"

Jim maintained his serious and calm demeanor. "No, the FBI has not identified any reliable evidence to that effect."

"Has the president been cooperative with the FBI?"

"The president has been cooperative, yes."

"Has the president made any effort to impede your investigation?"

"No, he has not. He has been totally cooperative throughout this whole process." Jim brushed back his hair. "He's actually made my job very easy."

"Well, that's all we need from you. Thank you, Assistant Director Brody. I'd like to call our next witness," said Senator Brown.

The tall blond rose and quietly left the hall.

"The next witness is—" Senator Brown looked down at a beep from his cell phone. "Hold on, what is this?"

At the same time, every person in the large room received a set of files related to the Taiwan arms sales. Someone had airdropped the documents to everyone's phones.

The blonde hurried out of the Capitol building and issued a sigh of relief, then took a taxi to Mike and Mei's safe house. After entering, she took off the blond wig and blouse.

"Aw. I kind of did not recognize you," Mei said to Mike with a laugh.

Mike had used the disguise to set the record straight. *He* was *not* a crook.

Mei handed him a cup of tea and he drank it gratefully, then lay down for a much-needed nap. After getting up later, he and Mei watched the late news.

"Today the United States Congress experienced one of the most unprecedented events in its history. A stockpile of crucial evidence was airdropped to everyone in a congressional hearing investigating possible unlawful behavior of the administration. Based on that evidence, House majority leader Nancy Eigenheim has called for an immediate vote of impeachment for the president. The general election is just one month from today. No one can predict what will happen," the anchorman said.

"Mike, did they just say they would impeach the president?" Mei asked.

"No use, the president's party is the majority in the U.S. Senate. Impeachment requires two-thirds of the vote of the Senate."

They sat quietly watching, but Mike was quickly searching his memory for a certain name. What was the name of that political science professor that his old boss at the non-profit had mentioned? Didn't he jot it down somewhere? He cranked up the laptop and searched through the contact list in his Outlook.

Bingo! *Bob Durr!*

Mike dialed Bob Durr's number. "Hi, Professor Durr. My name is Mike Nolan."

"Do you have any idea what time it is, Mike Nolan?"

"I apologize for calling you so late. I'm a close friend of Neil Kreschmar who was in the same class with you at the University of Chicago. He gave me your number."

"Oh, Neil. My God, it figures. He was the one who bothered me constantly chanting the two hundred digits of pi when he was getting ready for our final exam. Of course, what can I do for you?"

"Professor Durr, this is very important. Please, tell me…"

"Go on."

"Will the president be reelected according to your model? Neil boasts that you have never missed one."

"Holy cow, I already signed up for exclusivity with CNN about this one!"

"I swear I won't tell a soul. Please, you must help me. I'll owe you big."

"How big?"

"I will get Neil to apologize to you for all the chanting."

"Something I could never beg, borrow, or steal. Okay. Mike, you're on. My model says…yes, he will."

"Oh, no!"

"Why?"

"Why the yes? I thought right now the country is very much against him."

"Well, admittedly it's a very, very close call. But he's going to take Butler County in Kansas, thereby winning that entire swing state, and then the entire United States will follow."

Mike felt the veins around his temple pulse. "Professor Durr, are you saying that the voters in Butler County, Kansas, will decide who the next president is?"

"For this election, yes, that is what I am saying."

"You are truly a lifesaver. I will make darn sure Neil apologizes to you. Good night, Professor"

Mike searched the internet, and wasting no time, he hastily called Frank Wallace. The line was busy, so he left a message to call him back asap.

The TV anchorman interrupted programming with a special report. "The White House is giving a surprise special address by the president of the United States."

The President came on the screen and said, "My fellow Americans. In light of the recent international development, I would like to let the American public know that this administration is trying its best to secure our borders and deter any potential act of aggression. Recently, the People's Republic of China has been trying to transport weapons of mass destruction to Cuba, where launch pads have already been built with the capability of launching nuclear warheads anywhere in the Western Hemisphere. These nuclear weapons are en route to Cuba in international waters, and are under our close surveillance as I speak. We have repeatedly made our position clear with respect to these shipments. These nuclear warheads, or any facilities for launching nuclear warheads, will be our immediate targets for attack, using both conventional and nuclear weapons, in the event that they cross the longitude 168 degrees west into the Western Hemisphere. The Monroe Doctrine still holds today."

Just then, Frank called him back.

"It is Butler County, Kansas!"

Frank chuckled. "Okay. What about Butler County, Mike?"

"That is where Swift Industries builds the W-3 bombers. That is where the president promised to restore employment in order to win local votes. He knew that Swift Industries would help him significantly improve the local employment rate. He ordered and organized this entire plan so the local constituents would credit him with saving their jobs and vote for him in the next election."

Frank made no response.

Mike forged ahead. "Because saving these local jobs could get him reelected, he let the DOC issue a zero dumping rate to a foreign producer and leave the domestic market wide open without fair remedy. I am sure it is his people behind all the attempts to pursue me. It couldn't be anyone else. If he is reelected, his accomplice Sam

Wilson will be pardoned, FCPA will be repealed, and who knows what he is going to do with his foreign friends. My life is at stake. If he didn't do it, he wouldn't have ordered Brody to stop pursuing the case."

"Mike, that's the most likely version I agree. But…"

"The evidence!" Mike cried out. "Frank, there is an old Chinese saying: Those who steal a hook are punished by death, and those who steal the country become kings. Once the country is stolen, it is stolen. And these people will get away with murder!"

"Calm down, Mike. You are an attorney, and you know that just because he can benefit from a crime doesn't mean he committed the crime. And the good news is Congress is going to vote on the president's impeachment next week," argued Frank. "They should be able to get enough evidence to prove he was involved. Maybe something will happen then."

* * * *

A week later, the news broke that the Senate vote was basically split down party lines. Because his party held the majority in the Senate, the president would not be impeached or removed from office.

Mike was leaning on his bed and looking at the photo of his grandfather with his Flying Tiger. Tim Nolan was vibrant and ready to ride the fighter plane to pursue the enemy. Did his grandfather look scared? Worried? Hell no! Gramps knew the Japanese fighters were much nimbler, but there were always ways to deal with that. And any adversity.

There *were* always ways.

His grandfather could do it then, and Mike could do it now.

* * * *

Mike drove to 3505 International Place, the Chinese Embassy in Washington D.C. He took out his cell phone and dialed the embassy's phone number. "My name is Mike Nolan, an attorney in the District of Columbia. I need to talk to the Chinese ambassador immediately to inform him of something that needs his attention."

"The embassy has closed for the day."

"This is urgent. I must talk to an embassy official."

"Mr. Nolan, I'm afraid—"

"I am the attorney who worked on the antidumping case against Chinese exporters."

There was a pause. "Hold on, Mr. Nolan. Let me call someone."

There was a two-minute silence before the voice resumed. "Mr. Nolan, you may come to the embassy right now. The ministerial consular, Mr. Zhou, can meet with you."

Mike entered the embassy and was escorted by an officer to a conference room.

"Mr. Nolan, what can we do for you?" Mr. Zhou greeted him after being introduced.

"Mr. Zhou, I recently witnessed a murder that took place in China, while chatting with the victim over the internet. A few days later my apartment was ransacked, and I was subsequently assaulted at gunpoint both in China and the U.S. I feel it is my duty to inform the Chinese authorities about it. I hope this information is taken seriously, even though it comes from a private citizen, not the FBI. But I have reported the incident to them and am working directly with them as well."

"Mr. Nolan, do you have any evidence of this murder? Such as a recording, perhaps?"

"Yes. I have a recording of the incident, plus a file with evidence of all the other assaults."

"Could you please wait here? I believe the ambassador would like to see you."

Mike waited for half an hour before Mr. Zhou returned and led him into a bigger office with the Chinese flag displayed in one corner.

The ambassador sat behind a dark brown desk. "It is a pleasure to meet you, Mr. Nolan." They shook hands and the ambassador continued. "Mr. Zhou briefed me about your story. Thank you for reaching out to us. I can assure you of one thing. No great country can be taken hostage by people with special interests aligned against its citizens. We will report these events to the highest authorities. Please continue to work with your law enforcement. I appreciate the assistance you have given us to help resolve this matter."

For once, Mike smiled at his turn of fortune.

Chapter 28 The Election Result

One month later

"The current president really needed to win Kansas to secure reelection," announced the TV anchorman. "Today Congress tallied the president's final counts of electoral college votes. It can finally be announced that the current president…was defeated."

Sipping a cup of morning coffee in his pajamas with the day's newspaper, Mike looked up at the TV. "Great news!"

Mei came over to him and he smiled and hugged her.

After breakfast, Mei sorted the mail that had just arrived. She opened a letter from an overseas mailing company, and found a paid invoice of $100,000 for 100,000 mailers. Attached to the letter was a sample mailer. She opened the mailer and glanced at it, then handed it to Mike. "Is this yours?"

Mike took the sample mailer from Mei. It looked like an official letter addressed to voters in Butler County, Kansas.

Dear Butler County Voter,

There is ample evidence that the incumbent president bribed foreign officers to secure the business that increased the employment in Butler County recently. As citizens, you are advised to exercise your best judgement to cast your vote. Abraham Lincoln said the following:

On the question of liberty, as a principle, we are not what we have been. When we were the political slaves of King George, and wanted to be free, we called the maxim that "all men are created equal" a self-evident truth; but now when we have grown fat, and have lost all dread of being slaves ourselves, we have become so greedy to be masters that we call the same maxim "a self-evident lie."

Today, America needs you to vote for principle, not for who you think benefited you.

Sincerely,

The Whistleblower

Mike turned on the gas burner and burned both the invoice and the mailer. Mei did not ask any more questions.

There was a knock at the door. Only SSA Wallace would knock in that particular pattern. Mike opened it, and Frank walked in carrying a bag of freshly-baked pastries and wearing a big smile.

Mei took the food from Frank and went to the kitchen to prepare lunch. Mike and Frank joined her and sat down at the table.

"The final verdict will be reached next week for Sam Wilson," Frank said. "Now with the Foreign Corrupt Practice Act intact, it looks like he will be convicted and sentenced to five years, and Swift Industries will be fined—talking about billions of dollars here. The president may face the same charges after the new president takes office. My team discovered a secret memo from the White House to the Department of Commerce ordering them to issue a zero antidumping duty order to Yan Chemical."

"That's amazing!" cheered Mike. "And I understand the Chinese turned its shipment of warheads around when it was already halfway to Cuba. The U.S. will retrieve a significant number of the weapons that were sent to Taiwan, since they were illegal."

"And guess what? The Chinese authorities took into custody the Vice Chairman of the Chinese Military Commission, Tang Shengli, the father of your Mr. Tang of Yan Chemical," Frank informed him. "I heard they arrested him in the middle of a suicide attempt and will charge him with treason."

"Jesus."

"The Chinese government also issued a statement about wanting to work with the U.S. to rebuild their diplomatic relationship."

"They did? That's incredible!"

"Yes. I hope the U.S. will follow through with it," said Frank.

On the TV, the president was giving his concession speech. "My fellow Americans, it has been my pleasure serving as your president. I have certainly learned a lot about this country these past four years. I feel so honored to have been given this chance, and I thank you all for that. I congratulate the good man who will take over from me, and I say this to him: Lead with the values of this great nation, and you will do no wrong. It is the American people who have won."

Mike turned off the TV. "Time for some authentic Chinese food and pastries for dessert. Mei has cooked some real delicacies."

All three raised their glasses and toasted. "To a successful mission."

After dinner, Frank reached for his fortune cookie. "Mine says: If lawmakers do not abide by the laws they make, no one will."

Mike gave an ironic laugh and opened his. "The rise or fall of nations is the duty of common men."

Mei said with a grin, "Hey, I know how to say your fortune in Chinese. *Guo Jia Xing Wang, Pi Fu You Ze.*"

"Amen."

All three raised their glasses and drank to the bottom.

A pure white dove flew onto the patio railing. Mike walked out and offered it some birdseed. The dove stepping back and forth, then approached him fearlessly to take the offered food.

Frank looked this way, "Mike, it seems that you are having fun with the bird."

"The bird?" Mike paused a bit and murmured slowly and mysteriously, "Oh, yes, the bird."

Chapter 29 The Finale

Q*ingdao, China*

After his father was charged with treason, Mr. Tang Jisheng, CEO of Yan Chemical, worried every day. Not about his father, but about his company and his own destiny. One day, a working group dispatched from the Chinese Central Disciplines Review Committee in Beijing arrived at his office door at his Qingdao office.

Mr. Wang, the head of the working group, told him, "Comrade Tang, we are here to carefully review the financial, operational, and legal records of Yan Chemical. We need to start without delay, and hope you will cooperate. We understand your company is a private enterprise, but as long as you have employees who are Chinese Communist Party members, this action is within our jurisdiction. Are you a Communist Party member?"

Mr. Tang wiped the sweat from his forehead. "Yes, of course. Comrade Wang, after my father was detained, I have had a hard time concentrating on my work. I will fully cooperate. Please let me know what you need. The assets built over the years by Yan Chemical belong to the State, and I would like to turn over my equity shares to the government."

"Comrade Tang, as a longtime Party member and one in the first batch of entrepreneurs after the privatization in the '90s, you do not have to create additional plots or intrigues for us. We know what you are up to, Comrade Tang. What did you do to the assets of Yan Chemical during the last five months? Have you transferred any tangible assets to yourself from Yan Chemical?"

Mr. Tang faltered. "I will need to ask the accountants. There may be some dividend distribution to shareholders…including some offshore trusts."

"All ill-gotten dividends must be returned immediately to the company!"

"Comrade Wang, I will fully cooperate, but I have to remind you that I am still the lawful owner of eighty percent of outstanding shares of this company. According to the property rights law of the People's Republic of China passed by the People's Congress in 1999, I have the absolute legal right to receive distributions."

"Absolute legal right?" Wang sneered. "Comrade Tang, you are currently under formal review for your past economic and other activities, and we will let you know about your absolute legal rights after the review."

"Do I need to have my attorney present?"

"Do you?" Wang asked slowly.

"Oh, no… No, I don't. Not right now."

"You can have one whenever you feel the need. The Chinese government can let you privatize a company, but it can also take the company away from you and return it to the people, whenever and wherever the people want it."

Tang was filled with a sense of defeat and helplessness as he faced the intimidating Comrade Wang. The mention of a formal review for his past activities and the threat of losing his legal rights added to his already-heightened stress and worry. Tang felt as though the ground beneath him was unsteady and he was on the brink of not being able to stand on his legs. He dropped down helplessly in the couch, where for some reason he experienced an unexplainable relief.

"It did not belong to me from the beginning anyway," Tang slowly uttered without emotion.

One month later, Mr. Tang, along with Yan Chemical, was indicted for murder, bribery, conspiracy, leaking state secrets, insider trading, embezzlement, and several other charges. Tang's personal shares were appropriated and transferred back to the government through the nationalization process. The factory's zero antidumping duty rate was rescinded by the U.S. Department of Commerce, and all the company's U.S. importers were reassessed retroactively at one hundred fifty percent antidumping duties by U.S. Customs. That meant all the prior U.S. importers who had imported at a zero percent duty rate were required to pay retroactive antidumping duties.

* * * *

At the Bureau of Customs and Border Protection's national headquarters in the Ronald Reagan Building in downtown D.C. a clerk was going over the duty applications by domestic manufacturers to claim the antidumping duties collected against imports laid out by the Byrd Amendment. One application was from Ohio Chemical Corporation, for a total payment of $10.56 million.

"Wow. Sounds like a lot for one company," murmured the clerk. But it was the only U.S. manufacturer in the soda powder industry, so it made sense. "And the application came in just in time," he said to no one in particular. This could well be one of the last reimbursements made. Congress recently passed the law to rescind the Byrd Amendment. The new president was expected to sign it.

* * * *

The industrial complex of Yan Chemical in Qingdao, China seemed awfully quiet these days as the new government-appointed leadership was trying to figure out ways to fight the high U.S. antidumping duties. The employees were all crestfallen and worried about their futures, and some had already started applying for other jobs.

On a humid and dark evening, moonlight poured down over the open field at Yan Chemical's entrance. It was so quiet only crickets could be heard above the distant dull thunder that spoke of an impending storm. A white dove nestled in the high branches of a locust tree, watching over the entrance. Its feathers were ruffled by the gentle breeze, and its eyes were focused and alert, taking in the scene before it. In the stillness of the night, the dove appeared at peace, its white feathers contrasting against the dark foliage of the tree. Its beady eyes scanned the open field as if seeing the happiness and sorrows of the last hundred years in this very location.

Inside Yan Chemical, faint, muffled voices sounded. Mr. Yin and Mr. Tong were discussing business in low voices. Gradually, they grew clearer and louder.

"The machines can be adjusted using the computer-programmed automatic controls so the output can be significantly increased."

"I agree! But the computer program must—"

"As long as it can automatically recognize—"

The dove flew up from the tree and circled above the grand entrance of the company. The front door slowly opened. The dove flapped its wings, flew into the building, and soared through the office, opening one door after another, searching for the voices.

The dove landed on the desk outside the general manager's office, looking through the big glass window into the manager's office.

Mr. Yin and Mr. Tong faced a white board on the wall.

"With this technology, the efficiency will be increased by one hundred forty percent."

"And the cost of the final products will decrease by one hundred percent. We are not afraid of any antidumping duty orders anymore."

Mr. Yin and Mr. Tong nodded to each other, and continued their discussion.

Another peal of thunder boomed.

"It looks like it is going to rain really hard," Mr. Yin said.

"It is time to go home," Mr. Tong said as they looked out the window.

The dove turned around, flapped its wings, and flew up from the desk and back outside. It flew past the slowly closing office doors, the huge number of machines, and then the computers, workstations, and cloud-computing centers. As the company's front door closed, the dove flew up into the sky. It looked down on the massive factory buildings sprawling on the ground below. The dove uttered a few long but steady cooing sounds before it soared further upward, gradually viewing the entire city sparkling with lights, mingling with the stars. It then dove to the downtown area, flying through the high-rises with their neon lights.

The time drifted into late hours. With occasional sounds of nightly frolicking and brawls here and there, the age-old city was shrouded with a deafening quietness, but underneath roiled a sensation of deep commotion. The German-styled villas with their delicate structures and designs had dominated the eastern shore area for a hundred years before giving way to modern high-rises to the east, murmuring to the waves of the Pacific, their stories forgotten by many. Far out in the ocean a vast storm was in the making. The clouds, thunder, and waves churned up murky layers of pressure that needed to be released. These layers of pressure finally all exploded, creating vast billows of current under the surface of the sea and pushing forward to engulf the shore. There was a humming sound from an old German fog detector uttering a sullen, deep, nonstop siren in the background, accompanied by waves of murmurings coming from the city. The sound of the wind, waves, humming siren, and city murmurings mingled and permeated the foggy air, as if uttered by the unredeemed souls buried in the last hundred years under the city, with their pride, dignity, humiliation, and moans of not letting go, yearning for rebirth.

The dove was fiercely flapping its wings, flying across the vast expanse of endless sea, the undulating scales of waves beneath it reflecting the moonlight.

The dove was finally returning home.

* * * *

The night was over, and dawn set in. The dove was resting on top of a reef near a small island in the Pacific. Another dove was also nearby, and around them was a swarm of hungry seagulls. The two doves looked peaceful and kept their own graceful paces. This island, more like an islet, was called the Island of Love, and it was not far from the island of Saipan. It was not part of the Mariana archipelago when becoming a part of the United States, and therefore was not U.S. territory, and not claimed by any other country.

Mike and Mei had bought the island and moved there last summer. They didn't watch any TV news coverage, read any newspapers, or listen to any talk shows. All they worried about was catching the sunset in time, perfecting their cocktail recipes, and avoiding sunburn.

Watching a sunrise from the beach, Mike held Mei's hand. "Song Mei, I want to spend the rest of my life with you."

Mei looked deeply into his eyes as the waves rolled in. "I couldn't imagine it any other way."

They kissed to the sounds of the rolling ocean.

* * * *

Mike was on a three-way call with Neil and Bob Durr. "Hey, Neil, what about the promise you made?"

"Oh, yeah!" Neils said. "Bob, it is absolutely all my fault that I annoyed you back at the University of Chicago during test prep time. I apologize. Can you forgive me? Please?" Neil was holding a $50,000 check in his hand, signed by Mike Nolan.

"Somehow, I find your apology to be less sincere than I thought," said Bob. "You know what? I actually prefer your chanting 200 digits of pi. Nevertheless, apology accepted."

The three laughed.

* * * *

On his last day working at the Federal Bureau of Investigation before his retirement, Frank was lost in reminiscence, thinking of the decades he'd worked at the Bureau and looking at all his award certificates as he put them in the box of office belongings he was packing.

Special Agent Johnson walked in with a bunch of sample mailers addressed to Kansas voters and put them on his desk. "Frank, congratulations on your retirement! My new assignment is a possible federal voting scam. Just wondering if you have any clues or if you can point me in the right direction. Someone obviously mailed them to the voters in Butler County, Kansas, on the day before election. They were sent from overseas. Strangely, it only happened in one county, but it's a possible federal election scam so we need to crack down on it."

Frank looked at the mailers. "Hmm…"

"You think it could be the Russians, or maybe the Chinese?"

"I think…" Frank rubbed his chin, glancing at the clock. The hands pointed to exactly 5:00 p.m. Frank smiled at Agent Johnson. "I think, I am now retired."

Frank grabbed his coat and the box of belongings, went to the FBI building parking lot, and started his car to drive home. As he drove away from the FBI building, a sudden smile came to him and he called Mike on his cell phone.

"Hey, Frank. What's up?"

"Hey, Mike. What's the legal status of a crime if that crime perpetrated, avoided, or defeated a much bigger crime by others?"

"I'm not sure. But if I was a suspect, I would hire a good criminal defense lawyer." Mike said calmly.

Frank furrowed his eyebrows. "So, are you still in D.C.?"

"No. Mei and I found a small island near Saipan and bought it. We moved here last month." Mike looked over the vast expanse of glittering sea beyond the beach. "I apologize for not telling you earlier."

"Bought an island? That must have cost you an arm and a leg."

"A little over $2 million."

"Also sounds like you are well beyond any U.S. jurisdictions."

Frank paused. "I don't have any evidence, but I think you must be behind that mailer to voters in Kansas."

Mike sighed. "Well, are you assigned to investigate it? I'll fly to D.C. and all I need is a criminal attorney."

"You son of a bitch. The good news is I don't have any authority. I am officially retired. Plus I don't think the mailer said anything untrue or illegal."

"Congratulations, Civilian Wallace!"

Frank smiled to himself and squinted his eyes. "But I'm just curious," he went on. "You pulled off sending the mailers that prevented W-3 bomber employees from going to cast their vote for the former president. How did you know it would work?"

"I knew because someone told me Butler County was going to be the swing county in the swing state of Kansas. Someone who's never wrong."

Frank whistled. "How much did you spend on the mailers?"

"My entire bonus on the Yan Chemical's case, $100,000."

Frank's brows furrowed deeper. "Then where did you get the money to buy the island?"

Mike paused. "Remember I was framed with the claim that I was the rightful owner of Ohio Chemical? The jury did not buy the argument, but the evidence that was cooked up was legit, other than my signature. So, I just claimed the Byrd reimbursement from U.S. Customs."

"And bought the island to stay outside U.S. jurisdiction for good. You always were very clever."

The two white doves were standing calmly on the reef as seagulls hovered and squawked above them.

"You know, Mike," Frank said as he was driving by the Department of Commerce Building, with Washington Memorial towering on the right, "when I was about to retire, I was burned out. Burned out by the system. I didn't want anything to do with it. But you inspired me, kid. You inspired me to keep fighting for the principles both I and this country cherish." He chuckled. "You have done more for this country than any of those damned politicians. Hey, enjoy the island, you deserve it. *That* is the duty this country owes you for what you have done."

"Well, thank you, Frank."

"I'll let you go. You must be busy sipping piña coladas or something. Say hi to Mei for me."

Mike laughed. "I will."

"Just one last question before I hang up. What was Heather Hanson's role in all this?"

Mike paused. "Oh, Heather. I think she was one of the president's men all along. I believe she arranged my interview with Williamson & Grey, because she knew I speak Chinese. Her leading me to the argument in the library was intentional too. She helped me uncover quite some key facts of the case. Now on hindsight I think she knew that I would get to the bottom of this anyway and just tried to earn my trust and watch what I was doing. And after I got back from China, she was the only one who knew I'd be at the 7-11 waiting for her, and must have sent the gunman to kill us."

"Mmm. I see. Well, take care, Mike."

"You too."

Mike hung up the phone. He stood on the sandy beach watching as his wife splash playfully in the shallow waters of the Pacific. The sun was setting, casting a warm orange glow over the sea, and he felt a wave of gratitude wash over him as he reflected on the last two years of his life.

Mei had been a constant source of light and love in his life, especially in the dark days when he had been falsely accused of wrongdoing. She had stood by him, helped him clear his name, and fled with him to this beautiful island in the Pacific. Now, as he watched her laughing and playing, he realized just how far they had come.

The days he spent arguing for Yan Chemical in the antidumping case seemed like a lifetime ago. So much had changed since then. He had uncovered a vast conspiracy, been framed for a crime he didn't commit, had to fight for his life, and much more. And yet, here he was, on a small island in the Pacific with the love of his life.

As he watched Mei, he was filled with a sense of peace and contentment. He knew that they had each other and that they could face any challenge that lay ahead.

As the sun disappeared below the horizon, he went to her, wrapped his arms around her, and whispered in her ear, "I love you more every day."

"I love you, too. Oh, look!" She ran ahead, bent down, and dug from the sand a big white conch. She jumped up and ran back to him, holding the large white shell in her hand. "Isn't it beautiful?"

He smiled. He loved this little paradise away from the maddening world. "Yes, it is, my love. It is really very beautiful."

The Afterword

Washington D.C.
The newly elected president signed the law rescinding the Byrd Amendment. The trend toward globalization continued.

The End

About the Author

Born in Qingdao, China, the author pursued studies in English Language and Literature and Diplomacy before earning a Master's in Political Science, an MBA, and a JD in the U.S. With over two decades of experience in international trade law and immigration law, the author offers insights into global challenges.

A published high school author, his literary influences include Wilde, London, Beckett, and Mo Yan. Residing in the U.S., the author draws inspiration from bestsellers like John Grisham, aiming to tell stories that explore individual responsibility, complex decisions, and the lasting impact of the past on our globalized world.

You can connect with me on:
🌐 http://www.amazon.com/author/zhangchen